ORANGE BOY BLUE

Julia Roddy

Published by New Generation Publishing in 2015

Copyright © Julia Roddy 2015

First Edition

www.newgeneration-publishing.com

 New Generation Publishing

'Love allows understanding to dawn, and understanding is precious. Where you are understood, you are at home. Understanding nourishes belonging.'

— *John O'Donohue, Anam Cara:*
A Book of Celtic Wisdom

To Michael and the good people of Belfast

ÉMIGRÉ

THE GREAT ESCAPE FROM BELFAST

The sky was a pale October nameless grey and it felt like it was closing in on us, reclaiming us. Will locked the car, relieved we had made it this far. We walked to the little red and green cabin door and stepped outside. The wind pulled us back and we laughed at the irony of its force, as if it was begging us to stay. Hand-in-hand; the certainty as our feet stepped forward with a conviction that something better awaited us. We didn't look at each other, we kept our heads tucked into our chins to avoid the cold, sharp attack of rain pelting at us. We climbed the steel ladder up onto the top deck and clung to the railings as we walked to the back of the boat to bid our farewell to the country that had nurtured us, through troubled times. I already felt nauseous and we hadn't moved an inch. We stood huddled together on the boat bound for Scotland and then on to London. 'A whole new world' my mother Annie had said with gritted teeth, 'it's all ahead of you Ella' said Nana, encouragingly. We were silenced by the enormity of what we were leaving behind us. I held on to the little relics in my pocket that Nana had given me before leaving. I had forgotten who the saints were, I had accepted the relics disbelievingly but I knew they were for protection and I needed them now. I kept seeing Annie fighting the tears and I wondered why it took her so long to show me she cared. All those years I questioned the icy distance as if I carried some kind of threat. Will put his forehead onto mine and held me in his warmth. 'I'll put our stuff into the cabin' he said. I stood up on the top deck watching the pier awash with activity, muscular men with wind-swept faces lifted ropes and ladders. Police and army drifted about with walkie-talkies, surveillance helicopters flew overhead, horns blew, whistles screamed, people smiled and waved goodbye. Some joked because they were beginning something new but I saw others, just like us, with bewilderment spread across their faces, people with stories to tell. Will returned with a bottle of water for me, smiling. We stood and watched as the boat pulled away into a fog. Larne disappeared so quickly we didn't have time to question any of it. Will wrapped me in his arms and I could feel his heartbeat on my back. Three hearts beat together as one. Eventually I fought the nausea and slept beside my lover. I awoke to the sound of the engines rumbling and loud horns. Will was standing over me with anticipation. I got up and we went outside to watch our arrival, a rainbow stretched across a clear blue sky. We were safe. We were free. There was no looking back and it didn't matter who was Catholic or who was Protestant.

We drove to London in my fully-packed, red Renault 4 car listening to Prefab Sprout and Santana over and over. We finally arrived into the bright lights of London at ten o' clock that night. It was so full of promise, people dressed in their finery, people with different skin colours to our opaque Irish white. There were shops and restaurants everywhere, Indian, Thai, whatever your desire, zoomed-up cars with hoods down and music blaring. Luke met us at Piccadilly station and we followed him to his home in Maida Vale. He opened the door to his flat with the same excitement I remember him having the day our parents left us to go and visit the Pope. When we stepped inside he hugged me with gusto and Will put out his hand politely and cautiously, Luke grabbed it and pulled him in for a hug too. London had made him a man and a happy one, it seemed. We still had our coats on when he brought us in to meet his girlfriend Petra, who was sitting on the edge of the sofa shyly; a beautiful-looking Indian girl dressed in a magenta pink sari stood up and bowed her head at us as if we were royalty and then she opened her mouth and spoke with a thick, English, quirky accent. She had made us a pot of hot pumpkin soup and she laughed later as she told us how Luke had bribed her into wearing a sari; we slipped into our new world without a hindrance.

Two weeks later we got up at five am on a Monday morning to start our separate journeys into work. Will had secured a job in a youth centre, a place he described as something akin to a mental institution. For me it was a maze of chaotic Tube stations, shoulder-to-shoulder with strangers. My first job was in St Teresa's Hospital, as an assistant psychologist to a group of old-hand doctors who were, mostly, set in their ways. Basically, I did the paper work and occasionally, through Cecilia, I got to do a case study when they were oversubscribed. Cecilia was a typical Londoner, with an abundance of great ideas and solid advice. At first I thought Londoners were different to the Irish, that they were self-absorbed, needier and more fragile, they didn't have the harsh cover of a war-torn society. Yet, as time passed and I got an insight into some patients' lives, I realised that they had had their own wars, family wars, ethnic wars, that left them just as scarred as and even more vulnerable than their Belfast neighbours. Will was bemused that everyone assumed he was Irish, he insisted he was British and was consistently laughed at.

We settled into a small two-bedroom flat which was on the third floor of an old Victorian house, it was a dark vacant hollow and the landlord was a fat balding Pakistani man with gold teeth who had very little English, which we reckoned was deliberate because he didn't want to converse with us regarding general maintenance. The furnishings in the flat consisted of a rickety double bed, with a mattress that stank of stale piss, a picnic table with matching picnic chairs and an old fine chest of drawers that we later discovered had woodworm. It was depressing but close to the hospital that I worked in and easy to get to when the baby decided to come. Several pots of white paint transformed the floors and walls and a few geraniums and pictures reflected us as a couple in their early thirties starting afresh. Will was fussy about where things were placed; he was a bit of a perfectionist. I had to make a conscious effort not to drop my belongings at my feet when getting dressed, he provided a chair we had salvaged from a skip for my clothes in the bedroom and put up shelves for our books and photos. A black and white picture of him and his brother Sam took prominence on the shelf facing the sofa from where we watched television. It was a reminder of why we were here. Sam was missed. We spent Saturdays trawling through markets for cheap bargains and love kept us fuelled.

I went into labour on the Tube on a Monday evening after work, I was two weeks early. I tried to assure myself that it was Braxton Hicks but I knew it was more than that. I was lost amongst strange faces. I changed stations and got my final Tube home; I phoned Will to alert him, he pretended to be calm and offered to meet me at the station. The contractions started coming every ten minutes, I was frightened. I closed my eyes and imagined Nana beside me, praying to all and sundry. Then I saw Sr. Nula, I could almost hear her, smell her, see the little convent room, I saw the midwife, his face, the door that swung closed. A sharp contraction gripped my insides and caused me to let out a yelp, no-one seem to notice; it occurred to me I could be lying on the ground giving birth and no-one would take any notice. The train stopped abruptly, the doors flew open and more commuters boarded the already overcrowded carriage. I searched for the little relics at the bottom of my bag and I held on to them. I prayed to Mary asking for calm, it worked, the pains eased. People scanned newspapers and sat with headphones on to block out the noise. I closed my eyes again. All I could see was his little face. I opened my eyes and looked across at an old lady dressed to kill in a red velvet tight dress that clung to her skinny frame; a white fur shawl covered her shoulders. She was wearing black patent stiletto heels, she must have been at least eighty and she smiled over at me and put a finger up to her heavily painted ruby red lips, she knew I was in labour. She put her fingers up to her eyes and closed them as if instructing me to do the same. I followed her instruction and I imagined I was sitting by a calm river, breathing steadily and listening to the wind, only six more stops, the train stopped gently, then moved again, only five more stops, a calmness overcame me and then a wash of warm liquid from between my legs spilled out onto the floor of the carriage, I looked over at the old lady and she was gone, a tall handsome man who was sitting next to me jumped up with a fright and walked away. I put my coat, which thankfully I had taken off, over my knees. Suddenly a blind man walked into the carriage shouting, he started to tell us his story, something about being robbed, and living homeless, he had fled his burnt-out Bosnian home, had lost his family, all of them. 'My two little girls, dead, dead'. No-one was listening, they had heard it all before and didn't believe him, and they stared into nowhere, eagerly contemplating their hard-earned warm dinners washed down with a cold, crisp, white chardonnay. I had been one of these people so many times before tonight but tonight I heard this man and I listened to his story. He approached me with an empty woollen hat and I delved into my pockets and found a five pound note and placed it in the hat. He kissed his fingers with the five pound note and touched the holy medal that hung around his neck.

I got off at my stop and walked out into the fresh air, Will was standing there: a still, white man in shining armour, with a fresh coat and blanket. He continued to pretend to remain calm but he had parked the car on a double yellow with the back wheels on the curb and started mumbling about going to a shop to buy nappies. He was excited and terrified because this was new to him and yet he knew but he couldn't say. Finally, we got to the hospital. The labour pains came every five minutes and they brought me straight into the delivery ward. It was when I saw the midwife put the new blue cotton baby-gro and vest over the radiator that I realised that this was actually happening. I did everything I was supposed to, and so did Will, we had it all planned out, a natural birth, music, candles, and a birthing ball but nothing went to plan. I had three epidural top-ups and several shots of Pethidine and still no baby, then I heard whispers of a C-section. I knew he wasn't going to survive. I knew that fear had gripped me but I couldn't let it go. I felt so alone. I just wanted Nana. The harder Will tried the more I resented him even being there. The past had come to haunt me. I sent Will off to buy coffee, and I cried as soon as he closed the door. The monitor attached to my stomach started to beep and a midwife came in. She handed me a box of tissues.

'It will be fine,' she assured me, I spoke with the doctor and you are next on the list for a C-Section, it should be no more than an hour.'

Will returned exhausted-looking, his brown hair and sallow skin looking a pale grey, I hugged him and he leaned down to my ear and whispered.

'Ella, no–one is going to take him away'

Two hours later via a C-section, a baby arrived. He had a shock of jet brown hair and wandering eyes that said 'I've been here before'. Will held his son and cradled him close to his chest.

He pulled a chair up beside me and showed me the little face and I started to cry again. He gently placed the baby in my arms and he looked up at me. 'I think we should call him Sam' I said. Will nodded yes, unable to speak.

We left the hospital the following morning. The sky was a cloak of pale nameless grey, the wind against us and our feet a little less sure as we made it to the car with our little bundle of hope.

THE GRAVEYARD: PART ONE

A RETURN TO BELFAST

WILL'S STORY

I sat down beside my wife, Ella, on the snow-white granite surround that I had chosen for my father's burial place, a plot my dear mother, Maggie, had spent many afternoons nurturing. The orange lilies were about to bloom, just in time for The Walk. My young son, Sam, was running around the neighbouring graves, stopping occasionally to read the names of the dead, and then jumping on to the next. Ella didn't like graveyards; she wanted to be cremated and scattered over the sea.

'Get down from there at once, Sam!'

Her tone was scary, but he smiled back cheekily.

'But they're dead, Mum.'

'Now!'

So he jumped off and came and sat beside her. I lifted the flute my father had given me, on my sixteenth birthday, and began to play, 'Draw me nearer' and as I did, a host of starlings rose out of a clear blue summer's sky, giving Sam the excuse to chase them. As the notes echoed, Ella unfolded her culinary delights: cheese scones, gooseberry jam and caramel squares. It was nice to be back in Belfast, even if was just the holiday weekend. It was a lot more peaceful than London; less noise, less pollution.

I loved London, especially the museums and the Indian food. The work was good and we lived in a nice two-storey terrace in Maida Vale. Ella's brother, Luke, lived just a few streets away with his girlfriend, Petra.

I missed Belfast, my mother, the trees, and the calm. On our return trips home it was difficult for us not to dwell on the past; memories haunted us. We would stay with my mother for a night and then a night with Ella's family. Mum would go all out for our arrival; planning our visit in advance. Then she would fight the tears at our departure, especially when saying goodbye to Sam. Mum and Ella got on great, which was nice. They had a quiet understanding, different to each other but respectful. Father had disapproved of Ella at first; but once Sam was born, Father came to life. He hadn't realised how much he needed someone like Sam.

'I think that boy has preacher's blood in him.' he said one day, beaming with pride.

We would smell Ella's house before we made it to the front door. Nana's freshly baked pastries, the same pastry smell that Ella was trying to master at home because Nana kept threatening to visit.

Ella's father, Jack, would sit and read stories to Sam in the dilapidated greenhouse out the back, anything from the Famous Five to the newest Harry Potter story. Sometimes Ella would join them. Sam believed everything Jack told him, including the London trolls he kept warning us about.

Ella always brought Annie fresh freesias. Sometimes they would travel into a new painting.

Belfast had changed a lot since we were kids, the bombs and empty building sites were replaced with new cosmopolitan coffee shops. The presence of British soldiers had disappeared. It felt a bit like being a tourist; I suppose that's exactly what we were now, tourists.

THE PAPAL VISIT AND GETTING
DEFLOWERED

ELLA'S STORY

BEFORE THE GREAT ESCAPE

My downfall began when I was fourteen in 1979, the year
the Pope came to Ireland. Nana lifted the fur fox-head that
hung around her neck and pointed it at me; his beady eyes
met my eye-line. She slipped her little finger into his
mouth and his jaw dropped.

'Be good Ella'

Said the fox. I shuddered. Nana smiled, delighted that
her form of twisted discipline still had the desired effect.
She attached a black lace neck-cover to the inside of her
black linen dress and ordered me to go upstairs to find her
black Clarkes shoes that still looked new despite years of
dutifully attended parish funerals.

She packed her crystal rosary beads, and Murray Mints
with the same air of excitement I was to have before going
to see my idol Bob Geldof perform with the Boom Town
Rats in Belfast's renowned Ulster Hall. I was happy for
her.

Tomorrow she would stand among thousands, and
receive his Grace Pope John Paul's blessing on Irish soil.

Annie, my mother, was less enthusiastic about the
event. She stood three heads taller than Nana in her latest
creation of mauve tweeds, rapidly filing the tips of her
nails. Her soft leather half-full travel bag sat beside Jack's
stuffed hold-all at the front door. She was the reason
mobile phones were invented.

Annie was a deeply spiritual person, an honest soul
who was sadly afflicted with narcissism. Her current trend
was Buddhism which resulted in the placement of little

Buddha statues around the house, much to Nana's distress.

Nana had secretly hoped that Annie would see the light after visiting his Holiness, and her faith might be restored a little. The chances were slim. Jack was excited that his wife was actually going to accompany him. He stood in front of the Venetian mirror adjusting his bow tie with the enthusiasm of a circus clown. He had spent most of his married life chasing after his bride. He was a devout Catholic who liked to linger after Mass to chat with the other parishioners, occasionally offering free legal advice. Everyone had time for Jack, he was seen as a pillar of the little Catholic community that sat in amongst a dominance of Protestants.

They would depart in my father's newly polished red Mercedes Benz. Stop overnight in the Dublin Gresham Hotel, then to the holy ground where his Holiness would walk with, no doubt, a later opportunity for a relic market or stall selling pieces of the carpet or ground that he'd just walked on. The shops were already selling Pope Soaps, bottles of holy wine and statues of the Papa.

Nana had talked about this day as if it were the opening of the Pearly White Gates she was attending. She explained to me that because she would be in the presence of his Divine Sanctity, it would in turn fill her with His Holy Presence making her a creature of divineness herself, which no doubt she would pass on, in her, with her, and through her and unto me.

Thankfully, my big brother Luke managed to talk our parents into trusting him to parent me for the weekend, with the promise that he would revise his school work and that I would be tucked up in bed by ten o' clock sharp. Luke and I stood at the front door of our Georgian five-bedroom house and waved bye-bye, innocently, as we watched the suckers head off into what was later described by my mother as her weekend from hell.

As soon as they were out of sight, I turned to Luke who was smiling with the excitement of a boy getting his first candyfloss. We ate pizza for tea and set about our busy schedule. I immediately went to check out the drinks cabinet because I knew where the key had been hidden but when I opened it, I saw a large note taped to a bottle of vodka *'Don't even think about it'*. The party kicked off around nine that evening after our phone call to the parents, and our check-up visit from Auntie Nora. Not really an aunt, just a busybody neighbour from down the road. The band arrived around twelve-thirty, electric guitar in tow, the vodka got watered down, and all hell broke loose, the house rocked, literally. Luke had invited around thirty friends and three times that many turned up, most of them male; a mix of hippie and punk.

I invited two friends, Robert, my Boy Scout, whom I had plans for later and Ali, my beautiful best friend from school. Ali hit it off with a friend of my brother's shortly after her arrival. Robert wasn't a punk and was feeling a little apprehensive amongst my brother's mates. He looked a little out of place in his freshly-starched white shirt and clean-shaven face. I tried to get him to relax by sitting on his lap and kissing his neck but he felt embarrassed despite the couple directly in front of us with tongues sliding down each other's throats.

I had grown up watching Elvis and Paul Newman seducing women into their boudoirs and was curious as to why Robert wasn't taking the lead as much as I had hoped; by now I should be hanging on his arm on the upstairs landing, head bent back ready to be engulfed by his manliness. But he was sitting po-faced, looking pretty in-between two punks with earrings in every morsel of their being, wearing ripped vests and jeans held together by safety pins, once used on towelling nappies. They were so out of it they were conversing in a language unbeknown to anyone but themselves.

'You need to keep this lot under control'.

Said Robert like a police officer. I smiled and met his luscious lips and slowly teased my tongue into his mouth until someone handed me a joint, which I did my best to smoke. Then I took him into the middle of our living room floor to dance. Between songs our lips met each other's and the thrill of anticipation of what lay ahead in this night of freedom was electric. Luke was surprisingly responsible, putting place mats and ash trays where they needed to be, he was also relatively sober. I wasn't. He weaned us off the Clash with Hendrix, Bowie and finally Cohen and, by five am, with the lull of '*Famous Blue Raincoat*', he encouraged the walking zombies to gather their minds and leave for bed. I took Robert by the hand up into my locked, prepared bedroom of scented white sheets and candles and walked him straight to the bed to undo his trousers; he smiled nervously. He pulled me down unto the bed. I laughed as my virgin body lay screaming for love as he lay beside me kissing my throat and mouth.

'We can do it if you want to.'

I said as I stroked his hard cock through his jeans. He stopped me.

'No Ella … I want to wait.'

'Wait … ? Wait for what?

'Until we are ready; until you're old enough.'

I smiled and slipped my hand down into his shorts and took out his cock. I stroked his manly shaft, kissed the tip and caressed it with my tongue. He tasted of honey. After a while he removed my clothing and mounted me with an urgency, I was dripping wet with expectation. He then proceeded to push himself into me at a rapid speed, for what seemed like a few moments, and then he grunted with relief. Apparently it was all over. He withdrew, kissed my forehead and lay beside me with a satisfied grin on his face. My body lay palpitating, longing for more of what had just started to awaken. But he rolled over and fell asleep. I lay awake wondering was sex just like Christmas, one more big fat lie?

THE BOMB

ELLA'S STORY

I was seven years old when I experienced my first bomb. I was quite oblivious to the seriousness of the war, more commonly known as the Troubles in Northern Ireland. Despite the constant voice of the media and the daily mutterings that took place between my family over the dinner table, or the daily habit of everyone being hushed by Nana to listen to the latest update on the news, I maintained a healthy distance.

To an extent, living in East Belfast allowed for that. The only difficulty was that I was a Catholic living amongst Protestants.

The Troubles were gathering more momentum as the Seventies kicked in. It was July 2Ist 1972. Security had tightened and the physical presence of the British soldiers and police were everywhere.

Earlier that year the infamous Bloody Sunday took place during a civil rights march in Derry; thirteen people lost their lives, seven of whom were teenagers. Jack and Nana attended the funerals. A month later, Jack went to the March in Dublin where they carried thirteen empty coffins and black flags to commemorate the deaths. He wanted to bring me along but Annie wouldn't let him. Jack had promised a trip to the Dublin Zoo after, I was very keen.

'I am sorry, I will take you another time Ella, it's just a march'.

Said Jack with his head tilted like a puppy towards me, he looked sternly over to Annie.

'It's important she sees some kind of explanation of what's actually going on Annie.'

'Jack she's just a child, didn't you say *'let children be children'*?'

'You promised dad, please Mum!'

'No. I will take you into town for a day out instead and that's my final word'.

Annie got her way again and she was right, as usual. They marched to the British Embassy peacefully, made their point, then some extremists threw stones and petrol bombs which caused the Embassy building to burn to the ground. Then all hell broke loose. The usual carry-on.

Some weeks later, Annie took me into to town. I was given clear guidelines as to where and what I could spend my saved pocket money; all of five pounds. Certain areas of the city centre were out of bounds. Each main entrance to the city centre was blocked by security checkpoints. These were permanent small Perspex tunnels that were set up by the army for people to walk through. Once in the tunnel a member of the British Army or the RUC searched bags and bodies. It was automatic, I stood up straight, arms out, legs apart, chin up, and they would search my seven year old body by gently running their hands along my innocent and nubile limbs, inside leg and all. Sometimes they would make me laugh but not with Mum there, she hated this procedure.

Annie hated men in uniform. She stood like a manikin, her arms and legs spread wide. She let them search her without making eye contact or verbal communication and because they sensed her dislike, they would always demand a thorough search of her bag. Often spilling her purse and jewellery pouch, displaying her private bits and pieces for all to see.

Annie was a shopaholic, but understandably nervous in town which meant that there was always a time factor that had to be adhered to. We made a plan on the way into town on the bus. We headed towards Boots to buy some agreed lip-gloss as long as it was transparent. I was excited at the thought of shopping with Mum, because we never had one-to-one time together. She knew how to break the rules, in a fashionable way. I didn't. She caused heads to turn, in her almost six foot model frame. Clad in a size eight, hand-woven, autumnal tweed trouser suit, a soft silk cream open necked shirt and with a perfected waltz in her heeled leather boots. She simply looked, and smelt of wealth. We first went to the perfume stand and sprayed every perfume tester available.

'Can I help you?' asked a young orange-tanned looking woman in a tight white dress, with eyelashes like yard brushes.

'Yes, I would like to sample the new Chanel Number Five please. I don't see it out.'

Off waddled Miss Orange in her strappy heels to find the hidden little bottle of perfume that she then insisted on applying herself to Annie's inside wrist.

'You try it Ella.'

'It's not for children.'

'It's Ella I was buying for, perhaps you need to explain that to your supervisor.'

So Miss Orange sprayed some on my inside wrist. I smelt it and gasped a little.

'What do you think Ella?'

'It's a bit too much.'

'Mmmm. Chanel should be used sparingly, my dear.'

Annie was excellent at finding bargains, which was economically pleasing to Jack as he was fully aware that for Annie, only the best will do. It was unfortunate Jack hated shopping and spending money, I wished he could see her now, Happy. We went into British Home Stores and she tried on some dresses, she had small breasts and didn't wear a bra, just a silk vest.

'What do you think?'

'It's Beautiful Mum.'

'Shall we go find you a dress?

It was a sunny day, as we walked hand-in-hand through the city of Belfast, laden with bags. It was a stunning city when the sun shone, particularly because one could see the Cave Hill Mountains between some of the buildings. The architecture was a mix of Victorian, Georgian and contemporary. It was a reflection of the wealth that British colonialism had brought to this island with a reminder that we lived in the beautiful landscape of Ireland, the contemporary a reminder of buildings that replaced the bombs. We decided to pop into Woolworths to buy Jack a little surprise, he loved surprises. Annie found a little leather book for him to file names in because she was always finding names and numbers on pieces of paper in his pockets.

Just as we were about to pay, a piercing alarm went off. A man's voice came on over the loudspeaker.

'*Evacuate the building, immediately. This is a bomb scare.... Please use the exits to the back and the front of the building.............. evacuate the building immediately. This is a bomb scare please use the exits to the front and rear of the building...*'

People hesitated, deciding what to do. Was it a scare or the real thing?

A loud bomb blast went off in the distance. Shoppers stopped in their tracks. Like lemmings everyone started heading for the front doors; some at ease, some in a panic, a crowd of mixed emotions. An announcement of a bomb scare was a common occurrence and eight times out of ten it was only a scare. Sometimes it was just pranksters wanting a day off work. Schools were tormented with kids making calls to get an afternoon off. This time however the tone of the man behind the message smelt of fear.

Annie's face was suddenly older. Another bomb blast went off in the not so far distance. She grabbed me, lifted me into her arms and held me as tight as she had ever held me. She rushed towards the doors of the shop, and we ran out into the busy street. People were coming out of all of the shops. The street was packed with men, women and children, not knowing where to go, all asking the same questions,

'What's going on?'

The preacher who stood outside with the signs of the gospel strapped around him, usually shouting through a loudspeaker, '*Ye shall all be dammed, if ye turn away from*

Jesus', was quiet for once. He suddenly became ordinary and joined the crowds of lost faces. It seemed everyone started walking up Georges Street, towards the bus station for home. Annie was weakly dragging me along in a hurried step.

'What about the book?'

'Another time, Ella. We need to get home.'

She started to run a little. I couldn't keep up so I stopped.

'Not now, Ella!' she shouted.

Then a blast-of-all-blasts went off. The bang was like the earth being hit by a planet many times larger than itself. It was a building in the next street, it penetrated my entire being. I was lifted off my feet and thrown physically to the ground. I landed on my back and when I opened my eyes all I could see were people's feet running past me. I then made out Annie in the distance picking herself up of the ground, she was in a shop doorway looking for me.

'Mummy!'

I screamed, but I couldn't hear myself scream.

'Mummy!'

I kept screaming and a soldier appeared out of a smoky nowhere and picked me up, I pointed to Annie and he handed me over.

'Get out of here! Get to fuck out of here.'

He shouted in a thick English accent before disappearing into an air filled with fog and dust amongst people's screams.

Annie held me again but this time her entire body was trembling. The sound of the bomb was still echoing through my ears when another blast went off. The new vibration caused everything to move in slow motion, almost like an apparition. The colour of the sky changed from blue to black with bursts of orange and red smoke. It was like the world might be coming to an end. Annie held me and I surrendered to her. I buried my head in her warm breasts and listened to her thumping heart, as another blast went off. Everyone was screaming. The police, the army, even the fire brigades, screamed with sirens. I lifted my head and all I could see now was white smoke. We were not moving. I could see silhouettes of people running in the distance. We were huddled into a corner, frozen in time. Suddenly the street seemed empty, the screamers gone except for a huge army vehicle, full of frightened young soldiers. One soldier jumped out of the vehicle and approached us pointing a gun into our faces. He looked about fifteen, he was terrified. Another one approached us from behind; he unlocked his gun, and stuck it into the side of Annie's head.

'What the fuck are you doing here?'

Annie was frozen. He pushed the gun harder into her head.

'Who are you? Where are you from?'

'Annie Lovett, East Belfast. I'm just shopping with my daughter.'

'Get out of here, now! Go to Oxford Street bus station! NOW!'

He looked around waving his gun before he jumped back into his vehicle.

Annie held on to me, I pulled her away, got her up on her feet and ran out into the smoke, suddenly another bomb blast, in the distance. Annie stopped again, froze on the spot and started to cry.

'Ella, I can't do this!'

I took her hand, and looked into her eyes. She was shaking uncontrollably.

'I'm sorry Ella'.

'Imagine you are running with me towards the sea, the sun is out ...'

'Ok. Let's go'.

'Which way Mum?'

She pulled me in the direction of the bus station. We eventually caught up with people, who were running and coughing, towards safety, holding on to their loved ones, helping each other out; Catholics and Protestants alike, some wheeling prams at speed. Just as we approached the station, another massive blast went off. Again, it was as if it was in slow motion and it seemed to be coming from the bus station itself. We were thrown to the ground with the force. Everything turned black. The sounds disappeared.

When I sat up straight I saw people running towards me, in a cloud of orange smoke, they ran in every direction, slowly, skirts flowing, people dancing, hair swaying with the wind like a street ballet. My beautiful scene was abruptly interrupted with the return of the sound of screaming innocent downtown shoppers. When I looked down, I could see Annie had been hit by a piece of flying rubble, her leg was bleeding, her face covered in black dust, she was crying, frantically, there were bodies all over the place.

'Ella!'

I got up shakily and ran to her. We sat on the pavement and again she took me in her arms, she was holding me so tight this time that I could hardly breathe. Her tears were soaking my dress. I could see shadows of shapes flying through the air, for a moment I thought it was people. I started to pray. Annie buried my face into her chest and put her hands over my eyes. She was wailing. I don't know how long we sat for. All I wanted was my bed, my home, my Nana. The blasts continued to go off but further away, and eventually they stopped. Slowly screams turned into moans and silent tears. Ambulances arrived and lifted the worst. The dead.

Luckily a taxi pulled up and took us in, he hesitated when he heard '*Stormont East Belfast*', he was already full but he brought everyone home to their door. Tears and stories shared, no fares required. She held me the whole way home as we dropped the various people off and I fell asleep like a baby in the comfort of her bosom.

When we arrived home Nana was waiting at the gate with Luke, she hugged us and took us in to the warm kitchen. She fed us both with small amounts of whiskey, whilst she dressed Annie's wound. Our clothes were destroyed with dust. Our new dresses long gone. Jack hadn't yet returned from work. We started phoning round the pubs and possible places he might be. Just when we had finished phoning the hospitals, he came walking up the drive. He looked like a ghost. He was covered in dust and his body was in a tremor. Annie took him in and Nana poured him a large drink. He cried, as he told us of the bodies and body bits he had seen that day. He was never quite the same after that.

As we watched the news that night; silent tears fell. There were shocking images of body parts being shovelled into bags, possibly some of the objects I had seen flying around earlier.

The IRA had exploded twenty-two bombs in the centre of Belfast in the space of seventy-five minutes. Nine people were killed and one hundred and thirty people were injured. It was later to be named Bloody Friday. It was, apparently, a response to Bloody Sunday.

ELLA'S STORY

THE ROCK

Belfast was overshadowed by the intensity of the H-blockers planning to go on hunger strike. Nana knew some of the young men planning to go on the strike. She had grown up with their mothers. So she insisted that we pray every night for them. Before the hunger strikers, it was nuns in Africa who worked with the 'Black Babies', and before that it was the priests in Mexico. As the tragedy of the H-block unfolded on our television screen, she became more distraught as the drama became a living reality. She wrote to newspapers giving her point of view with headings like 'Margaret the merciless', referring to the then Prime Minister, Margaret Thatcher. Each printed letter was cut out and put into a scrap book with photos of the men and women involved.

Annie tried to prevent her from involving us, but Nana insisted we needed to know the reality that we were living in instead of being kept in the dark. Jack inevitably backed his mother up.

I had planned to go out and celebrate turning fifteen, with notions of painting the town with Ali and Robert. But I was forbidden to go into town because of the riots which were causing the so-called 'police force' to reintroduce curfews which meant no-one was allowed to walk on the streets in the centre of town after a certain time of the day. So I settled for being dropped off to my friend Ali's house after my birthday cake which was, in fact, freshly made cream puffs.

Jack came home elated that evening, he had finally put the 'Shankhill Butchers' behind bars. The Shankhill Butchers tortured and mutilated people with butchers' knives. Apparently, they castrated their victims then slashed their throats. It was a known fact that Protestant terrorists were barbaric thugs. This type of violence, according to Nana, was different than that of the more humble IRA men and women who, like their grandfathers, were '*fighting for a cause*'.

Cream puffs were my favourite and took time and effort to make. Nana would have prepared the butter layered pastry the night before. She spread the cream and homemade raspberry jam on the pastries as soon as they came out of the oven. Then when you took a bite, the puff would immediately sink and melt in your mouth and you would enter a heavenly space. It was the small things in life that gave my youth meaning.

Jack was a little pissed when he got home. This was a common practice when he won a case, the giveaway being that his red and blue paisley bow-tie would be a little loose and tilted. Jack was a lean handsome six-footer with a shock of unkempt black hair. On his entrance into the kitchen, a place he referred to as the '*ladies' quarters*', he would offer a Japanese bow, before he took his place at the top of the table. Nana had made him Irish stew, his favourite. Annie entered the kitchen looking like she just walked off the set of a Bette Davis movie, wearing an autumnal-coloured, tweed, short, fitted dress. She made most of her own clothes and mine, much to my horror because they were obviously different to everyone else's and I really needed to feel like everyone else. She sat down beside him, as was her custom under his persistence, to listen to him unravelling his successful day at the law courts. There was an ease between them; Annie was too intelligent to countenance anything else.

Luke and I had eaten earlier, as usual, so while my parents ate Nana hauled us into the second kitchen, known as the 'parlour', and we knelt before the Aga stove with Nana to say the Rosary. Luke would do anything to get out of praying and tonight his excuse was possible detention at school if he didn't finish his science essay. Luke once told me he was a Devil worshiper, and that he was quite happy with the prospect of going to hell after he died. He had experimented with the idea of being a punk, but was now settling for nerdy hippy though he still had punk friends. So it was me and Nana again tonight.

To ensure I understood who and what I was praying for, Nana would show me newspaper clippings of the prisoners-of-war who were about to go on hunger strike. When she spoke of these men her voice filled the room with sadness.

We prayed for their mothers; we prayed for peace; and we prayed that the British soldiers would leave our country. There was never a shortage of things to pray for. I liked praying, it soothed me especially when it helped remove the black spots from my soul that the nuns at school warned us about.

Jack finished his stew and lifted his bowl indicating he would like some more and Annie got up to refill his bowl. Jack approached Annie from behind whilst she was at the stove stirring his stew. He stood for a moment before he began kissing her neck but she shrugged him away,

'Not now Jack.'

She whispered with a hint of melancholy. But he was in mischievous form and he tried again, this time she giggled, with his face stuck into her neck, and his body pressed up against her, she pushed her bum out to detach and swung around with a full plate of stew smiling.

'You're drunk'

'I had a pint in Mc Keevers'

'Sit.'

And he sat. Nana's praying became louder. There was a consistent distance between Annie and Nana but it was never challenged, just accepted. Nana had the upper-hand over Jack being his mother. Annie would have expressed concerns for Jack's appetite for alcohol but Nana consistently affirmed his need to de-stress after a hard day at the office. Denial was Nana's coping mechanism.

Annie was difficult to understand sometimes, she was private; a bit of a puzzle. A different breed to Nana and Jack, they came from poverty into wealth; Annie felt as if she had left her wealth for poverty.

Annie was powerless in her relationship with Nana and my closeness to Nana just added more acrimony. I was also Daddy's golden girl, I adored everything there was about my father; but Annie was a constant challenge. She was impossible to get close to, she never got close to anyone, even Jack struggled. Luke was the only one who seemed to stay in close proximity with her, in that they managed to spend time together in the same room without irritating each other, yet their intimacy was an unspoken one. I got my hugs from Jack, occasionally, quick and to the point; neither Nana nor Annie displayed physical affection. Nana produced her love on a plate and Annie gave love through whatever air of wisdom she had on offer.

After prayer, the warm smell of freshly baked pastries wafted through the kitchen as food for the soul should. It would take approximately three minutes for the aroma to reach Luke's untidy, forbidden-to-enter bedroom, on the third floor of our home. He descended the stairs, resembling a zombie after study, and took his place at the table to indulge in what he claimed was the only sane reason to stay home: Nana's food. Nana lit a candle on my extra-large cream puff.

'Okay, it's time for a birthday-girl wish, Ella.'

Nana switched off the light. Jack sunk in guilt.

'Ella, little bird, I didn't forget.'

I smiled knowingly.

'You're forgiven Daddy, Bob Geldolf and the Boom Town Rats are playing in the Ulster Hall next month and I saw purple Doc Martins with my name on them.'

'It's yours, all yours.'

I hadn't expected either of my parents to make a fuss of my birthday because they never did. If Nana wasn't around they would have forgotten. Annie sat at the top of the table with her head resting on her knuckles, niggled by how well I knew how to manipulate her husband. Nana burst into *Happy Birthday* with gusto, and the others, excepting Luke, droned along. Then we sat as a family, quietly together, eating delicious cream puffs. I knew our family wasn't quite the Waltons I longed for, but I also knew that I loved each and every one of them.

Nana smiled as she ate efficiently and watched the happy faces munch. Jack just put it into his mouth and sort of inhaled it. Luke, on the other hand, picked at it, ripping bits off and savouring it slowly in the hopes that he may be the last one holding a cream puff while we watched and drooled with envy.

Annie invisibly licked the cream around the edges with the precision of a cat; her sallow skin and honey-brown eyes made her look like a pre-Raphaelite painting, she was beautiful. She paused for a moment.

'I got accepted onto the Art course I applied for.'

Jack looked at her bewildered.

'And what course might that be, dear?' he asked, a little indignant at the idea she would need anything outside of the home he had worked so hard to provide.

'The degree in Fine and Applied Arts, darling. The one I told you about.'

She went to the fridge and took out a bottle of champagne, popped it herself, then proceeded to pour for everyone, except me.

'Mum.'

She poured me an unusually generous glassful.

'A day for celebrations'.

She handed me a brown parcel. She'd actually wrapped something up! I opened the parcel slowly, to savour the moment. It was a hideous brown leather waist coat. She lifted her glass, something had shifted in her, she was happy inside and it was visible in her broad smile.

'To Ella.'

She beamed, secretly knowing that this Art course was her ticket to freedom after many years of a suppressed depression.

'To Ella.'

I blew out my candles and we lifted our glasses.

Suddenly, as if in slow motion, we heard a huge bang and a large rock flew through the kitchen window, it sounded like a bomb. I got up and put my arms around Annie who was visibly shaking. Nana began calling on the Saints, Annie started wailing and Luke, predictably, had a delayed reaction and remained calmly in his seat.

'Don't anyone move.' said Jack, with a stern chill in his voice. We remained still because we knew from experience that another smash was likely; just like the bombs in town which came in succession. Dad ran to the front of the house to see some youths running down the drive way. A large rock wrapped in white cotton with the words *'CATHOLICS OUT'* written on it in black marker lay on the kitchen floor. We were now targets of the on-going Troubles because Dad had just locked some of the bastards up, and now they knew where we lived.

Belfast, '79 - the year Pope John Paul visited Ireland praying for peace. The year my father helped jail eleven of the 'Shankhill Butchers', who were each sentenced to life imprisonment for nineteen murders.

MY FIRST WALK

WILL'S STORY

Today the house was full of buzz as my father, my grandfather and I prepared for what was to be my first Walk. I had waited years for this,

It was the twelfth of July and I had never seen my respected Minister father look at me with such emotion, his watery blue eyes welled up at the sight of me; his thick white hair looked alive. With a broad smile he took in the sight before him. Even Sam, my younger brother, who had been ignoring me for the past few weeks, managed a smile which revealed a hidden sense of pride. There I stood, finally in my full regalia, proud to be an Orangeman.

I would have walked the earth to please dad. I had wanted to walk earlier but my father insisted that I had to be fully aware of my undertaking and that I would take to my position, with respect for the institution which I was representing. Hence I had to wait until I turned sixteen. Fortunately I was allowed to attend band practice before and I was given private flute lessons. My flute playing always pleased my father, especially when I played with the choir at his service in church.

I was aware that Sam was a little envious of me for two reasons; one being that I was first to make my father's dream a reality by following in his footsteps. The second was that I had finally achieved a black belt at our local karate club and he was still struggling with the brown.

Sam endlessly tried to please Father, but continuously failed; he simply tried too hard.

Sam was two and a half years younger than me. I knew how to influence him; it was easy and often not to his benefit. Like the time I sent him to Mrs Cricket's house to pick her prize winning roses as a present for Mum on Mother's Day. Mrs Cricket threatened to phone the police if Mum didn't keep better control. Or the time I had convinced him that Dad would be delighted if he was to wash his precious robes for Church on Sunday. That wasn't so funny, he got whacked with a belt for that and I had to suffer the guilt.

My mother smiled tenderly as I adjusted my collar. Everything about my mother was genuine.

Our Georgian home had a purity about it, a simplicity that reflected her, there was little-to-no colour, all was a soft white, except for the moderate floral arrangements she created. My father's imprint was evident in iconic pictures and written scriptures on the walls. I liked the fact that they didn't need things; oddly Sam collected everything from sweet wrappers to feathers. He would store stuff in boxes and under pillows, his little stashes were always secret; evidence that he didn't quite belong here. Mother looked over at me and her eyes welled with pride.

'I wish my father could see you now, Will, he would be so proud of you ... and you too Sam.'

She said gently gliding her neck around to Sam, so as not to leave him out. I remember vague little snippets about Granddad Ellis. He lived on a well-organised, modest farm on the outskirts of Belfast. He introduced me to the fact that food came from natural sources rather than out of a shop. He had chickens and pigs and every time we visited we would leave with a large sack of home-grown vegetables. His wife died shortly after he did. He was killed in 1969 when feeding his pigs; his killing was apparently in retaliation for a Catholic being shot the day before in the same area. No one claimed responsibility for his death. They broke into his home and shot him dead in front of his wife. He had no connection to any paramilitary organisation. He was just another easy target, a prominent Orangeman. Nana Ellis died from unknown causes about a month later. They were survived by my mother and her brother Niall; he moved to London and became a teacher in physics, and he never married.

Today, Nana Goodie and mother pottered about in the

kitchen fussing and clucking, whilst Granddad Goodie, my father's father, Sam and myself sat huddled around our small kitchen table which was adorned with fresh orange marigolds handpicked from the garden. We waited with anticipation on Dad's return with the blue velvet box that he kept in the bottom of his walnut wardrobe. The box we had been forbidden to touch since we could walk, but had sneaked glimpses of on occasion.

Dad set the box in the middle of the table and opened it like he was lifting the lid from a coffin. He took out a parcel wrapped in tissue paper. He unravelled the orange silk collaret, more commonly referred to as a sash. He handed it to my mother.

'Stand up then.'

She placed her Father's orange collaret over my newly fitted black jacket. Then he took out my Grandfather's white gloves and as I slipped them on, I felt Granddad Ellis's presence instantly; it was so acute, it was as if I had shaken his hand. The collective hush was telling; I wasn't the only one who sensed a presence. Mother placed the black bowler hat on my head and it sank below my eye line, breaking the eerie silence with laughter. Then my father did something very much out of character, he hugged me quickly and with warmth.

Walking was in our bones, our blood. Apparently our family had walked since 1795 when the Orange institution was originally founded; it was, literally, a family tradition. My great, great grandfather, my great grandfather, and my grandfather had all been Orangemen, so it was never doubted that the tradition would continue forever through the generations.

As early as I can remember, I waited in anticipation for the twelfth of July. The day we gathered as a family, got dressed up and paraded like peacocks, up and down the streets of Belfast, playing flutes, beating drums, whistling in unison, amongst the colour and vibrancy of all the other local and, sometimes, international Protestant communities.

Sadly, as the years passed it became a political landmark for many of the walkers, but for Christians like us it was a celebration of our deeply-rooted religious beliefs and culture.

Granddad Goodie and Dad marched every Twelfth, rain or storm. Over the years they had both played the wicker flutes with various groups. Their mainstay was with the Apprentice Boys, then with the Royal Black preceptory and then with the Donegal Pass Defenders flute band, now known as the Belfast Young Conquerors, which is who I played with.

Granddad Goodie was like an Orange Santa on the twelfth of July, he had a white beard and receding white hair. He stood around six-foot-one and had a round belly that usually protruded over his black pants. He had a great sense of humour and laughed a lot, especially at himself. He would smack his thigh and let out belly-roars each time he laughed. It was odd really because my father rarely laughed, certainly never out loud. Every Twelfth, Granddad and Grandmother Goodie would come and stay with us, so that Granddad and Dad could walk the walk together. Grandmother was a warm, small, five-foot-two, tidy, astute lady, always with a smile on offer, a face as rosy as an apple. She crocheted and was involved in various groups within her own parish in Five Mile Town. She was one of a group of women who founded the charity 'Grand Master Charity Appeal' for families in need within the Protestant community, this offered a confidential helpline and financial assistance to those less well-off. She was a practical, no-nonsense sort of woman quite like Father. Grandmother Goodie was Granddad's rock, his personal keeper, his platform that allowed him to be the family entertainer, which was a godsend when times got tough.

The Twelfth festivities would begin with Grandmother's home-baked delights, something my mother cherished. We started brunch with Grace, always led by my father and always a serious moment. Then the full Ulster fry of soda bread, potato bread, steak sausages from McCambridge's butchers, eggs, rashers and black pudding, swilled down with a pot or two of brewing tea, and after all that another little prayer or blessing for the attention of the walk ahead. The ladies would then clean up after the feeding of their loved ones and wait in anticipation on them coming downstairs in their walking regalia. Grandmother would cluck like a hen, fixing bowties, producing white gloves and collarets just starched and ironed. Her husband and son would stand to attention waiting on her approval, whilst Sam and I would watch with the knowledge that this tradition was one we would be expected to inherit, to pass on. Today was my day, and Mum took great pleasure in standing beside Grandmother, to poke and preen me.

At noon we would walk on the busy Upper Newtownards Road where we would be led to the gates of Stormont Parliamentary Buildings and grounds, then up to the bronze figure of Edward Carson, a Protestant middle-class lawyer born in Dublin, who was seen to be the arch opponent to Irish Home Rule.

Ironically, Stormont is now a parliament building that houses both sides of the community.

It was easy to tell where the Catholics lived along the road, there were only a few amongst the hundreds of houses that lined the Newtownards Road, and they would either have their curtains drawn or have vacated and gone down South. Occasionally you could spot a child peeping out through a window. That was how I first noticed Ella Lovett.

When Granddad Goodie passed us during the walk he would stop momentarily and throw us toffees. Sam would be loyal to his promise, and shout *'God save the Queen'* upon request as he approached, while I conveniently forgot my promise and would collect the sweets for myself and make Sam beg for one.

Today I stood alongside my father and grandfather as we joined the walkers *'Ulster's Chosen Few'* with the

Newtownards district, first established in 1795. I genuinely felt proud that day as I stepped out, to represent what I believed were a nation of people who were grossly misunderstood. I was nervous playing my father's old flute. Over the afternoon the street lined with supporters and they cheered us on. When we arrived at Stormont Gates there were some speeches and then my father was called upon to lead in prayer. We prayed in the glorious sunshine together and sang various hymns. After prayer everyone met in the grounds of Stormont some with picnic baskets, others with carry-outs of beer. We had planned to leave straight after our picnic as Mother didn't feel comfortable around people drinking alcohol. Both my parents were teetotal.

After the speeches, some Catholic protesters started throwing stones. They appeared out of nowhere. An elderly man got hit in the face. He was beside me and I noticed blood pouring from him, I went over to help him. I sat him down and took out a tissue to wipe his face, he was shaking uncontrollably.

'This will be my last walk.' he said. I looked over and saw Spider, the school bully, smashing a bottle and throwing it at the Catholics, others joined in. They ran after the perpetrators as if they were on fire, I then saw them beckoning Sam and to my utter astonishment he joined them in the chase up the street. They caught up with them. Kicks, punches, bottles, bites, man-screams. Mother was distraught that Sam joined them.

'Stop him Will, stop him!'

It was always the same, he got into trouble and I had to find a way of getting him out of it. I ran towards the rioting and thankfully I could hear the police sirens approach and the crowds started to disperse from the blood-stained road. That ended what was a beautiful day. Sam got off light with a graze or two to his arms.

It was difficult to discover, as I became older, the negative connotations attached to a tradition I spent much of my youth relishing. By the mid-eighties some families wouldn't stand on the side of the road to support their loved ones for fear of being attacked by Catholics with petrol bombs.

I was brought up to respect all of God's children, I had nothing against Catholics, except the fact that I was opposed to the Papal hierarchy that made Protestantism look like a walk in the park. I did my best to embrace the concept of cultural diversity and Ella was a distraction that weathered my commitment to my core identity as an Orangeman.

Nineteen-seventy-nine was the year that my brother Sam befriended Spider. The year I started to fall for a Catholic girl, Ella Lovett, much to my own internal turmoil. The year Protestants all over our community were still in recovery from the twenty-four bombs that were planted across the Province, seriously injuring thirty-seven people, some of whom were important members of our Loyal Orange Order. The year my father's cousin, uncle John, was killed in Enniskillen along with three other RUC men by the largest bomb ever known in the Troubles, weighing in at 1000 pounds; the year Louis Mountbatten was blown up on a family get-away on his boat, all at the blood-thirsty hands of the terrorist group called the IRA.

SAM AND WILL LOOK FOR TREASURE

WILL'S STORY

As kids Sam and I were inseparable. We were also black and white. He was chaos and I was order. But we complimented each other; we had a balance between us. I would have done nothing exciting without him and he would have ended up in a juvenile detention unit if he hadn't had me. Thankfully, we had the freedom of Stormont Park across the road. It was our sanctuary, because at home we lived under our father's canon. I never really knew how crazy my brother Sam was until the day he talked me into looking for buried cash in a vacant house four doors up. Sam loved adventure. He made our mother read Tom Sawyer to us four times over.

One summer's morning Sam came to tell me he had been told by a reliable source that the vacant house up the road had lots of money stashed in it. The owners of the house, a Mr and Mrs Page, had left for England shortly after the Troubles had started and had hoped to return when the Troubles had ended. They apparently hid the money as a nest-egg for their return. Sam had been informed that the money was either under the bed or under the floor boards. But the reliable source, whose name he was sworn not to mention, wasn't one hundred percent sure. I wasn't really prepared to steal anything but I was curious.

'How much?'

'One thousand pounds.'

'And how are we going to explain finding a thousand pounds?'

'We don't. We keep quiet about it. You could buy that new Scalectrix slot car you saw in Branigan's.'

I figured that if we found the money we could bring it to the police station and claim we had found it outside of the house and perhaps we would get a reward, or if no-one claimed it, they could give it back to us.

So we set off and when we got to the house we checked to see if the windows were opened. The green paint was peeling off and the wood underneath had gone rotten, Sam ran around the back.

'All locked.'

'Shush, for fuck's sake Sam, do you want a loud-speaker.'

We tried the back door, which at a gentle push would have fallen in. Locked as well, so Sam got the bright idea to climb up to the back bathroom window and see if it was open. It was, and he climbed in.

He opened the back door with a smile, as if he had been tenant in the place all his life.

'Welcome. Please do come in.'

'Sam, I think we should go home.'

'Bluck bluck, blk blk.'

'Shut up.'

'Look goodie-two-shoes, let's just take a look!'

The house smelt of the dead. Mouse droppings were scattered around the beige lino on the kitchen floor.

The living room had been left like they had just gone out for a walk. Two patterned armchairs and green patterned wallpaper from the forties, no doubt the latest thing in its day. A large dark wooden clock sat on the mantle above the cleaned out fireplace, it had stopped at six-fifteen, awaiting their return.

We climbed up the creaking stairs; they felt a little spongy as if they could collapse at any moment. The smell was getting worse, damp and shitty. We looked into each of the bedrooms and settled for the master bedroom overlooking Stormont grounds. It was interesting seeing it from a new perspective. Sam immediately lifted the mattress and out flew a large mouse, leaving behind a family of three baby mice. Sam jumped backwards into me, I fell over and landed on my arse twisting my wrist in the process. I was in pain and couldn't scream. Sam

37

laughed. The mice ran.

'I've hurt my wrist. It's bad.'

'Are you ok? Do we have time to look for the cash?'

'No.'

Sam pushed his hand into a hole in the mattress and frantically started to search. Feathers started to pop out and fill the room; the more he searched the bigger the hole became and the crazier the feathers became.

'Sam, that's enough! It's not here.'

'We haven't looked under the floor boards yet.'

He took a screwdriver out from his pocket and proceeded to start lifting the floor boards. I stood by the window with my wrist throbbing, keeping watch. I saw a grey police wagon pass and got scared.

When I looked around I saw that half of the floor had been lifted.

'Sam what are you doing? That's vandalism; I just saw a police wagon slow down. Look, my wrist is killing me.'

I got down and did my best to help him put the boards down. We left the house quietly and quickly. When I looked at Sam about to walk out unto the main road I saw his back, which was covered in feathers.

When we got home we sneaked in and went upstairs to get changed. We shared a room which I liked because we could catch up on the day. However Sam was very untidy and I had to constantly clean up after him. We planned our next visit with a little more precision than this one; we would bring a torch and some other tools. And we would put the feathers back into the torn mattress to get rid of any evidence that anyone had been there. But all didn't quite go to plan. The doorbell rang just before six o' clock tea, an unusual time for visitors. I could hear my mother talk quietly at the door, then Father joined her.

'Boys, come downstairs please.'

Two policemen stood inside the hallway, one wrote in a notebook and the other asked questions.

'There was a break-in, boys, number thirty-seven, do you know anything about it?' asked Father.

We both remained silent and then I realised that our silence was giving us away.

'No, we don't know anything.'

As I spoke I looked at Sam who had a feather sticking out of his hair.

'I hope not, Will, because two young boys who fit your description were reported to being seen breaking and entering the property.'

'It wasn't us Dad, honest!'

The policeman, a calm, gentle-faced man, looked at us and smiled knowingly.

'We'll be keeping a watch on that house, boys, so stay well clear. Understood?'

'Yes sir.' we said in unison.

So that put an end to our finding the cash. But it didn't end there because the boy that informed Sam about the stash was Spider and he became convinced that we had found it. He himself had gone in after us and completely trashed the place. As far as he was concerned we owed him. One thousand pounds to be precise.

MOTHER'S LITTLE HELPERS

ELLA'S STORY

Luckily, because of Dad's position we got police protection for the days after the windows were smashed. Annie was constantly nervous and began planning a mass exile again.

I was born in 1965, the day Annie's father, Charlie passed away. Just days before my birth, the UVF had issued a statement declaring war on the IRA.

The story went that Granddad Charlie was in Mac Keevers' pub, in town, a second home to him; it was run by his closest friend and colleague, Paul Butler. Granddad was his accountant. Charlie got his dinner in Mac Keevers everyday courtesy of Rose, Paul's wife of thirty-five years.

Granddad was tucking into a steak and kidney pie, accompanied by his daily pint of porter. The masked men burst into the pub armed. They paused as if looking for their chosen victims then opened fire across the room.

Granddad fell to the floor, when he came to he could see the ambulances arriving through the door. He didn't realise he'd been shot. He watched the paramedics approach and slowly he began to recognise familiar faces being lifted onto stretchers; one of whom was his now dead friend, Paul. He closed his eyes and awoke to the sound of machines attached to his nipples monitoring his heart. He had been hit in the leg which was easy to fix but he had apparently suffered a heart attack during surgery. While he lay silently in intensive care, Annie screamed her way through labour several doors up.

His wife Millie, a no-nonsense strict and emotionally cold woman, renowned as an excellent ballet teacher, sat in the grey corridor for an hour before any one came out to her. She had started Graham Green's novel '*Travels with my aunt*'. It was a young, blonde, female nurse, with pale skin that lit up, who came to inform Millie of her husband's deterioration.

'I'm sorry he's passing.'

She took Millie in by the hand to watch her beloved Charlie take his last breath.

I was born bum first which caused a delayed delivery and a third-degree tear.

Annie was exhausted and alone in the labour ward when Jack arrived in to meet me and deliver the news of Charlie, now laid in a morgue just a few floors away from her.

Annie spent days trying to feed me but the milk didn't come, her breasts froze with grief. My first two weeks were spent in a hospital, being nursed by nursing staff, and then Nana Lovett took me home. It was Nana who named me Ella, after her mother. When Annie returned home she took to her bed, she had missed her father's funeral and was bombarded by relatives doting over her new-born girl. Annie was a perfectionist but she didn't do grief well. Jack nursed me during the small hours until he was close to tears with exhaustion.

Nana dealt with the situation in an efficient manner, she agreed to move in with us temporarily, with Jack's relentless persuasion, which included promises of him easing up on the drink and being at her side every step of the way. Annie's mother Millie took off to America to visit her sister. We received postcards but never saw her again. Several years later we got a postcard from her sister to say she had passed away peacefully; causes unknown.

Nana's husband John had died of lung cancer a year before I was born. Grief was not such a distant friend. Rooms were kept tidy, to the extent that all the white linen was washed and starched, she needed to be in control for fear she might lose control, so she had the house running like a cruise liner with a briskness that didn't allow for any sign that things might be in disarray. Her consistency for order reflected the control she had over her emotions; her need went as far as mending frayed curtains and cushions.

She wore a starched white apron every day, a tradition she had become used to from working in the bakery with Granddad. I adored her, she was old-school, not one for hugs and kisses but a consistent love was delivered on a plate or in the warmth of the fresh cotton vests she would heat by the range before putting on us.

She occasionally visited her immaculately kept two-up-two-down brick terrace in Mary's Street on the Falls Road, to collect bits and pieces of clothing and relics or to hear the latest on the goings-on regarding the Troubles, from her tearful friend Biddy O' Connor from next door who smelt of brandy and pee.

Over time she boxed the memories of her past, keeping only her most prized possessions in her handbag, relics, photos, jewellery he'd bought her and snips of his hair wrapped in white cotton.

Each time she locked up the red front door on the two-up-two-down terrace of number 7 Mary's Street, she took another step away from what was once her joy. Each time she returned she thought she might just see him sitting there in his armchair with his newspaper on his lap.

Dad sat in the car outside his childhood home, with the engine running, rejecting the street that made him what he was. He was nervous of the presence of the armed British soldiers who paraded up and down his stolen childhood memories, pointing guns at our car with me in my little cot in the back seat; he was eager to return to his middle-class Protestant terrain, to the comfort of his denial.

Doctor MacMullet, who should have been retired, was with Annie when Jack and Nana returned. They drove up the sweet-pea scented driveway of the middle class mini-mansion, maintained by a gardener and cleaner who visited weekly. The doctor recommended three months rest and a diet of fresh fruit and vegetables with liver or kidneys as often as possible; he stipulated, in no uncertain terms, that she could not cope with any stress and stated emphatically that the consequences of stress would set her back. My mother's newly-diagnosed illness was

42

exhaustion, today known as postnatal depression. He left some '*mother's little helpers.*'

And so that's how my life began, by my Grandmother's side, soon to be strapped into a highchair by the Aga range, where I would watch her recite Rosarys, create cakes, jams and chutneys. Annie would make appearances, in her pale pink Japanese kimono dressing gown, nibble on something like an apple and retreat to her bedroom where she spent most of her waking and sleeping life. Sometimes it was difficult to figure out when she was awake or asleep because she often wandered about the house at night. The months fell into years, and a consistent routine developed where Nana took hold of the running of the house; the cleaner sacked, the gardener kept.

Jack worked very hard, sometimes not returning home until eleven or twelve at night whereupon he would be made to sleep in the office attic bedroom, on the fourth floor, eventually his bedroom. But he never failed to come and tuck me in with a story and a kiss goodnight. Jack lived and breathed his work and often when he came in he would tell me about the case he had in court.

Annie took to painting. Watercolours first, then oils. Her room was a bombsite, filled with these small little oil paintings of still lifes, eggs, onions, and bowls of various shades of blues and greens. Each painting focussing on the light that fell upon the subject. Her work mirrored her sense of stagnation. The still life as real as if photographed. I was forbidden to touch anything in that room.

Gardening was her other passion and she loved Alan, the young handsome gardener, whom she would shower with smiles and enthusiasm which we had not witnessed indoors.

Before Nana moved in Annie would have fed the family with little plates of snacks, raw carrots, apples, and celery, slices of cheese and crackers; the majority of the food put in front of my father was minimal and generally raw. She totally embraced convenience food. Angel

Delight being a firm favourite.

'Do you not know how to feed a man Annie?' questioned Nana.

'I like him just as he is Nana.'

They would move around the kitchen like cats, avoiding each other and protecting their space within it.

'You need to eat, if you want to make a full recovery, I can't stay here forever.'

'Nana, you can go home when you want, we will survive.'

This was usually followed by a sulking silence and later apologies from Annie, prompted by Jack who would insist she prove her remorse by sitting at the table and eating a full dinner with him.

Nana's diet consisted of fresh produce whenever possible. Liver and onions with champ was her favourite meal, she ate it regularly, the smell of liver would turn Annie's and my stomach, but Jack loved it.

Nana walked to Mass every morning which was a mile there and another mile back and she made new friends in the community quickly. Essentially I had two mothers and a father: Nana with clear boundaries, with punishments carried through; and Annie with a no boundaries, learn by your own mistakes method who, when disappointed in me, punished me in a psychological challenging way like long-term silence. But because of their own power struggle over who had the upper hand over me I was occasionally able to find a crack.

When I refused to pick up my cars and crayons scattered across the floor, Nana put on her real fox fur scarf and she threatened to get the fox to bite me if I misbehaved.

'Well Fox, what do you think, has Ella been a bold girl?'

'Maybe just a little nibble.'

And she would sneak towards me with his mouth open, and it would actually nip, and she would laugh, and I would cry. This was her method of maintaining control over me, and it worked.

Eventually Annie and Nana found common ground when they shared their grieving. Sipping sloe gin and looking at old black and white photographs of Nana and John dressed to kill for a Ball or Annie fishing in Donegal with Charlie. Each photo bringing the men back to life. Annie soon became seduced by the irresistible flavours of lamb, garlic and rosemary, or chocolate lavender truffles. Nana's herbal drinks kept the depression at bay. Occasionally it would knock on the door again like an unwanted visitor. When it returned, she was like a geisha, wandering about the house in her silk dressing gown, wearing bright red lip stick and fake smiles that framed her unwashed mass of auburn locks like a bunch of daisies someone had forgotten to put out. Silence followed her everywhere with a racket.

Nana never gave up trying, she bought her a beautiful new apron and a Mrs Beeton's cookbook, in the hope that someday Annie would take over and she might return home, to her little two-up-two-down in Mary's Street, but it was not to be. Each time she threatened to leave, Annie would have a relapse and lock herself away in her bedroom. Annie tried to mother Luke and me, but it didn't come naturally to her. She would let Luke read his comics in her room while she painted. I was forbidden to come near her when she painted because of my clumsiness. Luke adored her. I felt as if I belonged to someone else but still I missed her. I would wet the bed when Nana left to visit her sister overnight.

Nana had won all of our hearts through our stomachs. I later became the mixer of butter and sugar and, in due course, the creator of the chocolate toffee and Rice Krispy biscuits. The kitchen was my safe haven; the fuel for my soul which kept me relatively normal. It was also where the conversations that mattered took place.

It was in the garden that ultimately Annie and I established a sort of mother-daughter connection. There was a large acorn tree at the back of the house and, when I was not required or just when I needed some comfort, I would sit with my back as close to the trunk of that tree and imagine it was hugging me. Sometimes she would join me. I would bring out lemonade with biscuits, she liked that. I would watch her with Alan, chatting among the lush green vegetable patch. They had a tender contentment.

When she was fed up with me she would say '*Poor Ella darling, Mummy has a headache now run along*' and so I would take myself off, usually to Stormont across the road. In my mind, just another extension of our garden. I would run up to the old forest on the hill and search for fox holes, and poke sticks down them or I would bring empty jam jars down to the little streams and fill them with tadpoles that I would keep on the kitchen window, and feed bread to. When Luke returned home from boarding school, Annie would like nothing more than to visit art galleries with him, I was usually excluded from these outings but if I heard of visits to the cinema or the Museum I stomped my feet until I was included. I loved the Three Musketeers. When we got to the Museum, Annie and Luke would immediately get the lift to the fourth floor where they exhibited the art. I would go to the second floor where they had an interactive science show which would lead into the Natural History exhibit. I could have happily lived in this part of the museum. It housed a real Mummy, a small female Egyptian Tukabuti who lived during the 25th dynasty. She lay in an original hand-painted casket wrapped up in bandages.

I loved Stormont, its mighty statue of Carson, and its forbidden castle where people worked. I was told not to go near any of the buildings, they were government buildings, which meant they were Protestants and I knew, that as a rule in general, it was safer to stay away from the Protestants.

Finally, number 7 Mary's Street was sold. Nana handed her keys over to the emotionless middle-aged over-worked salesman who checked his watch every three minutes and smiled with yellow teeth. She took one last look around at the empty building which no longer was home, and stepped outside to a gathering of familiar Catholic faces who had lived through troubled times. Amongst them, the nuns from the convent whom she had befriended and envied. The parish priest himself made his way down to the gathering, with his own personal blessing. This reduced her to tears, albeit silent ones. She smiled through the hugs she took from her friends and neighbours with promises of return visits that never happened. She climbed into the new engine-running car with me in the back welcoming her into our world, in Protestant East Belfast. She didn't look back at the car wreckages that lay along the roadside or the burnt and bombed-out homes that she had visited as a child, she didn't even see them. She just blessed herself, waved to her lifelong friends who had been through the wars with her and as they went out of sight she began to pray.

THE ORANGE ORDER:
A POLITICAL STATEMENT

WILL'S STORY

Our institution came up against attack on many levels, either from Nationalist thugs or via the media which portrayed us as the thugs. The main gripe being that we were opposed to Catholicism. Since the foundation of the Orange Order the rule has stipulated the qualification that *'the Orangeman should strenuously oppose the fatal errors and doctrines of the Church of Rome and scrupulously avoid countenancing any act of Roman worship'.*

Almost all religions outside of Catholic faith are indeed opposed to Catholicism; it would be idealist to think otherwise.

With this in view, it was interesting that Father ensured that we were brought up to respect others' rights to worship their own religions, even with their far-fetched ideas and idealisms, especially that of Catholics and the likes of the Virgin Mary stories. Orangeism is just an extension of our Christian faith with Christianity being our main source of inspiration and guidance. And so it is disheartening being constantly reminded of the negative forces that tarnished the good name of Orangeism.

As early as the 1678 rebellion, when many Roman Catholic Churches were burned in Co. Antrim, Orangemen condemned such antics which in turn led Orangemen to rebuild them.

It was widely claimed in various media publications that the Orange walk was just a platform; used only for the intent of provoking the minority Catholic community of Northern Ireland.

I felt that the majority of walkers, religious moral men and women who believed in their cultural birthright, walked simply because they were proud of their Christian cultural identity. It is part of who they are and the walk is a custom of celebrating their Protestant identity, a custom that gives grounding to their true Christian beliefs.

The Orange Lodge is an international establishment that celebrates, above all, a Christian gathering of like-minded people with high moral standards.

However, for some, over time the organisation did become a political platform to air political views, and also for the purposes of seeking revenge on Nationalists. The revenge was displayed in a variety of vulgarities, like insisting on banging Lambeg drums outside of selected Catholic homes, or by way of creating riots to gain media exposure.

The minority who chose to use the Order as a stage for their own political agenda were viewed by many as men who stood against everything that the Order stood for. These people came from troubled backgrounds, they were the wounded and they were tolerated because of it.

Rarely would the media comment on the music, the costumes or the charitable organisations that the Order consistently worked with. The focus became the routes and the riots and it remains so till this day. The fact is we are proud to be Northern Irish. I believe everyone who lived through the Troubles became affected in some way, some more directly than others and, through this process, people have developed a bias and it is bias that keeps the conflict alive.

THE STINK BOMBS AND SMOKING

ELLA'S STORY

I loved it when Luke came home; one rainy afternoon I caught a rabbit by the hind leg on its way down his hole. I pulled him straight out of the hole and held on tightly. When I handed him to Luke he jumped several feet backwards.

'Chicken!'

I teased. The rabbit ran for his life.

'Idiot!' Luke sulked, and he got up and started for home. I was also better at catching frogs than Luke; unlike me he was actually a little scared of things in the wild, a better observer. Unbeknownst to him I once sneaked a frog home, killed it and opened up its insides; admittedly, it was disgusting, but fascinating at the same time.

When Luke came home Annie transformed into something that actually resembled a mother. Nana knew my vulnerability and she always kept a close eye on the family politics, empathising with me when needed. And when required she would take me by the hand and sit me up on her knee and let me hold her rosary beads while we recited the Rosary, praying for whatever was the current most needy cause, which in my private opinion was me . I put Annie's favouritism towards Luke down to the fact that she just preferred boys. That was probably why I hated dolls and preferred action men. Fortunately I never let it come between Luke and I.

Sometimes when we were bored we would walk over towards the Stormont Government Buildings and spy at the windows with Dad's binoculars. Usually we just saw people behind desks typing, or people getting in and out of cars. Luke always exaggerated these spying incidents and claimed he could see terrorist spies with guns passing documents to each other. I didn't like this game so much because he never gave me the binoculars. I was also a little afraid of terrorists. I was aware that they were the ones planting the bombs.

We would continue to play the spy game from the tree house in the acorn tree because we could see the cars and people entering and leaving Stormont. Sometimes we could watch Annie happily pottering in the garden with Alan.

'Do you think they're doing it?'

'Doing what?' I asked innocently.

'The business ...?'

I looked over at them.

'Yeah, I think so.'

I was thinking that their garden industry was indeed a good business.

When we were really bored we would go and visit the empty house up the road. There was a rumour that money had been stashed in it. We gave the place a thorough search but reckoned someone got there before us because there were feathers everywhere. Sometimes we just sat in it and ate sweets in a contented silence.

Luke was tall, sallow and thin with dark auburn wispy hair like Annie. He had large, round brown eyes that could sometime have been mistaken for black; he was always messy and always covered in bruises. He hated school and all his teachers except for Critters, his English teacher whom he said he could talk to. His excuse for passing his exams was that there wasn't much else to do in '*The Hell Hole*', as he called school. He hated wars and people who got involved in them. But he always knew his history and who was at war with whom. He hated the British Army with a passion; he would bring his toy soldiers over to Stormont and we would pretend they were the British Army and ambush them, sometimes torturing them with my pocket knife.

Sometimes we would bump into the local Protestant thugs on our way to McMinn's sweet shop. One of them had an amateur tattoo of a Spider on a web which climbed vulgarly up his neck, he was known as Spider. I hated him from the very first day I saw him. When I saw them approaching from a distance, I would just ignore them and imagine I was walking through a zoo. I was a lioness and they were the resident hyenas. When they flung comments at me regarding my identity, *'fenian bitch'* I would roar into myself and proudly walk on. Luke wasn't as accustomed to this ritual as I was because he spent most of his life at boarding school. One day while we were walking to the shop I heard someone shout,

'Anyone get a bad smell?'

I continued as usual, almost immune to his pathetic taunting. I was nearly at the shop before I realised Luke was no longer by my side. He was standing behind the sniggering Spider and his gang. I ran back up and stood beside Luke.

'Come on, Luke.'

'Hey, look boys. The smell was bad enough with one Fenian, but two Fenians, well that's just not fuckin' on!'

Spider paraded a number one haircut and a sharp angular face like a Samurai warrior from a cartoon. He was tall and skinny, to the point of being slightly emaciated looking. When his father was on leave from prison, he tattooed a Red Hand of Ulster on Spider's right upper arm for his tenth birthday.

'Fuckin' stinkin'' added Simon, who had a big face like a bulldog attached to what seemed close to a malnourished body, which didn't quite match the head.

The young tidy innocent-looking boy with a soft face, called Fred, looked at his feet. Fred didn't quite fit in with the others. There were a few other stragglers I didn't know, but you could tell they were all from the same gang.

Spider stood in front of us, blocking us from walking any further, a head taller than Luke, his nose almost touching his face. Luke froze on the spot.

'Fuck off.' I said nervously.

Spider stood up and laughed at me.

'I will when you hand me over the money.'

'What money?'

'The money you stole from that house.'

'What house?'

'You know exactly what house, you filthy Fenian.'

'I never stole any money, from any house.'

'How much money have you got?'

'Five pounds', said Luke.

'That's a lot of money, we could buy half the shop for that.' said Fred, excitedly.

'Did I ask you to FUCKING speak?' hissed Spider with a hint of a lisp.

'Sorry.'

Luke put his hand straight into his pocket and handed them whatever he had. I tried to snap the fiver out of Luke's hand before he handed it over. I was too late.

'Yours too, big mouth.'

Spider's face in mine.

'You can fuck off, I don't have any money, and if I did I wouldn't give it to you.'

I caught Luke's astonished face.

Spider grabbed me by the arm; he pulled me into his foul-smelling breath.

'You watch your fucking mouth, and give me what you have'.

He then slipped his greasy hands into my trouser pocket. I was just about to surrender and hand over the fifty pence piece I had hidden in my shoe, when I heard a voice of authority,

'Spider, back off.'

He let me go instantly. Sam and Will, from number 22, were approaching. They lived in the Minister's house. He preached in the little Church of Ireland on the corner of our road. Will was lean and tall with feathery brown hair, handsome. Sam was a little smaller with lemon-yellow hair.

'Right Sam, how's it goin?'

Sam stopped, and greeted them with a nod and a smile,

Will stopped and looked at me and nodded at me to go on. Spider backed off slowly and let me and Luke go.

'Why don't you pick on someone your own size?' I heard Will say as we walked away.

Later that afternoon when Luke and I sat up in the tree house munching on the little packet of mixed penny sweets I purchased, he quizzed me on the thugs.

I told him everything and we waited until it was getting dark the following evening before we decided to take action. We found Spider's address in the phone book. We walked silently under a washed-grey sky that threatened to soak us. We entered the estate with trepidation, knowing we didn't belong here, like walking into the zoo with the cage doors open. The gable walls at the entrance displayed stunning large hand-painted murals of Protestant historical figures, one atop a white horse waving his hand in the air victoriously. The little streets were lined with the British Union Jack flags, hanging out of windows or mounted on front walls, bunting hung from telephone poles and the pavements were neatly edged with painted red, white and blue stripes. Spider lived at the end house, a rundown council house, with a fresh Union Jack hanging from its front window. There were trees and bushes at the end of his gable wall which led onto the back road again, we hid in there. We watched Spider's house for about an hour; Luke worked out our exit carefully. We even did a practice run just in case. The moon peeped out behind the black stretch of cloud and smiled down on us. Luke put his hand into his pocket and took out a packet of stink bombs. We each threw several bombs at his front door and waited for the smell to arise. When we were gagging with the fumes and well enough back, Luke threw a stone at the front door; he hit it bang in the middle first time. We buried ourselves amongst the bushes frozen with fear and delight. Spider appeared at the open front door in a vest and tracksuit bottoms. He gagged instantly at the pungent aroma surrounding him. We did our best not to laugh, as we watched Spider look all around him, totally bewildered.

'Ma!'

A slim lady about five-foot-four with short hair, a hard face and arms tightly folded around her chest appeared in a dressing gown. She took one whiff and for a split second the hard face said it all. I could feel Luke bobbing beside me in giggles as we huddled together like hamsters, it was contagious and came to a sudden stop when Spider's eyes seemed to be looking straight in our direction, his eyes squinting like cats.

'Bastards!' he shouted.

And for a moment our hearts stopped. We were, after all, in the lion's den. Thankfully he continued scanning and again shouted into the air.

'Bastards!'

Then his older brother stumbled out, got attacked by the smell and smacked his younger brother with some force across the side of the head, sending him back inside. The door got a similar smack with a boot from the inside.

Luke and I sat perfectly still for the next half hour before we made our way out of the bushes for our return trip home. Our adrenalin high, our bond tightened.

We laughed hard that night atop of Luke's bunk bed as Luke repeatedly described each and every facial expression on Spider's face.

It was like one big happy family when Luke came home from boarding school. Jack made an effort to come home earlier, encouraged with a little emotional blackmail from Nana, with regular comments like:

'A boy needs his father, Jack.'

I suppose the yellow summer contributed to the holiday atmosphere. The garden was abundant with fruit and vegetables that Alan and Annie had so tenderly guarded and Nana was contented to prepare home produce. Luke and I managed to avoid the thugs by accurate timing as they did seem to have a pattern of gathering at certain times of the day.

But like all good things summer came to an end and

winter set in again.

Jack's work load continued to increase as the Troubles became more intense, and he was often absent at weekends as well as weekdays, but that went unnoticed. That's what dads did then. They worked.

Every day the radio would deliver messages.

'Three men were killed in a bomb attack, and seven more were injured, on Tates Avenue, two of the injured men are in a critical condition in hospital, it is believed that the IRA are behind the bombing' or *'The UVF claimed the lives of three men when they opened fire in the O'Connor's bookies off the Ormeau Road, one of the men is said to be in his teens, six others were injured .....'*

There seemed no end in sight. Every journey into the city centre was different in that buildings disappeared or new ones appeared. Jack was convinced the glaziers had a deal with the bombers as their business expanded. My constant fear of the never-ending whispers among the young and naive citizens of Belfast that the minority Catholics may all have to be shipped out of the North and posted down to the South remained a possible reality. Daily riots, shootings and bombs were an everyday part of life now, though thankfully not on our doorstep, which allowed us a little distance from the actual realities of a war going on. I was slowly becoming immune to the reality that I was living in a war-torn society.

It was impossible to ignore the constant presence of the British Army, the Royal Ulster Constabulary (RUC) and the Ulster Defence Regiment (UDR) whose presence patrolled and controlled our city on a daily and nightly basis. Uniformed men had been given authorisation to question or body-search us in and out of town at any given opportunity. There was some notion that this uniformed presence was to protect us all from the doings of the IRA and the like, but it was evident that their duty was fuelled with a bias and a precedent to protect only the Protestant communities.

Annie began her Arts degree, in 1979 at the University

of Ulster, with an already established reputation, not to be sneezed at, for her perfected, slightly surreal portraits which had a knack of revealing honesty to the sitter that wouldn't otherwise be seen in the flesh. The paintings were already selling like hotcakes. It was uncanny and I was happy for her; she needed an outlet but what I didn't know was that I was yet to meet Annie, the woman my father had married.

Annie took to her course with the enthusiasm of Hitler and her work possessed her to the very core of her being. She surpassed Jack's dedication to his work and he watched from a distance, in fear of her newfound energy. There was nothing he could say or do to stop her. He was afraid of losing her. He sacked Alan the gardener because he arrived late one afternoon, Annie didn't argue with him, she sent her apologies to Alan with excuses for Jack but it made no difference because Annie would always have admirers. She watched Alan leave the house weighed down with grief, with his bag of tools, wounded but accepting of his fate with an air of understanding that only verified Jack's suspicions.

Success was inevitable. She would sell a piece of art and the money would be spent on champagne, caviar and smoked salmon.

During this time I was becoming a young woman with my own values and beliefs. The more my parents engaged in their careers the more they came apart. Consequently, the more freedom I gained. The more my mother shone, the more my father withered into an insignificant background. He was wise enough to know not to try and stop her but his objection was made obvious after he retrieved his old saxophone from a box in the attic. Night after night he blew his anguish into this vessel, oblivious to our interrupted sleep. Annie was a liberal, feminist, atheist, Jack was a practicing Catholic driven by conservatism.

I was sent to the all-girls Grammar school, Mary Magdalene's, situated in North Belfast in the hope that I would eventually follow in my father's footsteps or in Nana's dreams that some young handsome Catholic gentleman who had studied law would take me in for his wife. I was saved from going to boarding school because my best friend Ali was also going to Mary Magdalene's.

I was a Catholic in the sense I was brought up as a Catholic but most of my indoctrination and teaching had gone by the wayside, probably because I just couldn't help but commit sins on a regular basis. I started to sin at around twelve years old, with small sins like lying to my mother about the fact I had started smoking. I had just stubbed out a Marlboro which I had stolen from Dad, earlier that morning whilst he slept on the living room armchair. I never felt guilty for dipping into his pocket for a few quid or a couple of cigarettes; he had, after all, awoken me with unwanted rhythms on the saxophone the night before. Usually I opened the large sash window in the bathroom which looked out unto the busy traffic with a view in the distance of Stormont Castle. I would sit on the generous outside sill and let my feet dangle below, while I puffed contentedly, witnessed only by the passing traffic which I imagined were taking great pity at the sight of a young neglected-looking girl. But today it was lashing rain outside and I barely opened the window because I was being attacked with shards of ice-cold rain every time I put my head out. I could hear Jack and Annie arguing downstairs but fortunately not clearly enough to hear the abuse they were hurling at each other. I reckoned I had plenty of time to risk smoking inside, while blowing the exhaled puffs through the slightly opened window. I did catch Annie shouting:

'I'm sick of living in this goddam place'.

I knew how she felt, I often thought how wonderful it would be to live in a castle with cooks and butlers, I dreamed of sprawling across four-poster beds indulging in my latest fantasy. I had almost finished my cigarette when I heard a loud banging on the door. It was Annie, I knew the knock.

'Ella! Are you smoking in there?'

She hollered with a crack of anger in her voice.

'Open this door, now!'

And I quickly opened the window, plastered half a ton of toothpaste in my mouth and frantically shook smoke out the window with a towel, with a gush of wind and rain blowing in on me.

'Right now, Ella!'

I opened the door, and stood indignantly facing her.

'You were smoking, I can smell it.'

'No I was not smoking! I don't smoke Mum, how many times do I have to tell you? I don't smoke!'

She grabbed me by the arm and pulled me towards her, as I tried to continue in my stride.

'Let me smell your breath then?'

I opened my mouth in her face whilst holding my breath.

'Have you no respect for yourself, no boy will ever want to kiss you, all dirty, and cigarette-stained? Not to mention lying about it, Ella. '

'I wasn't smoking.'

She tightened her grip on me.

'Let me go!! You're hurting me.'

I shouted loud enough for anyone to hear, thinking she would instantly let go but when I looked up at her she was white with anger.

'Were you..., or were you not...., smoking cigarettes... Ella? This is the last time I will ask you.'

'No!'

She looked through me and slapped me across the face, full force.

'Get into your room and don't come out until I say', she said with venom through gritted teeth. Mortally wounded I ran all the way to my room and buried my head in my pillow, I was inconsolable. It was clear to me now, I hated my parents.

I was fourteen when I got my first job in Flannery's, the hippest pub in town. They supported Bluegrass and a mix of alternative Blues, Jazz and Rock musicians who were brave enough to come to Belfast. I told them I was seventeen and I got paid fifteen pounds to pick up and wash glasses until last orders were called, the time of which changed nightly. I told my parents I was babysitting. It was a haven for bikers, hippies and anyone who needed to escape the war zone for peace and love. It was the beginning of my social life and a place to spot the very limited male talent that existed in the North. It also attracted students, Southerners and foreigners. Like-minded people gathered around tables and openly rolled joints, occasionally displaying their goods by way of little white tablets or tabs under the tables and no-one was objecting. The owner, Tom Vestible, was a handsome, young, hip son of a well-known barrister. Tom knew I was underage but ignored it because he liked the illegality of it. He kept a close eye on me. I felt quite protected; often he insisted that Kermit, the leader of the Hells Angels' brigade who was a permanent fixture in the pub, drive me home after work. Kermit was six-foot something and must have weighed a ton; he had a round happy face and a grey beard that fell into a point. He would drop me off a few yards down the road so I could maintain the lie.

Annie soon discovered my workplace because she had been tipped off by one of her arty friends. She made a dramatic entrance with Alan one evening after an art opening. It was unusual to see Alan dressed in fancy clothes, he wore a black velvet jacket over a pale pink shirt and black jeans and they looked well together. I had only seen him as a gardener up until now. She triumphantly sat at the bar and ordered two gin and tonics. She then waved over to me with a smile of almost approval. She knew that she was losing control and for some reason she didn't try to stop me. I didn't mention she was out with Alan and she didn't mention my new job. Nana often tried to step in more and take control but Annie made her motherly boundaries clear which prevented Nana from laying down the law.

By my mid-teens the sins got worse, in particular Robert Gallagher. I met Robert in my Scouts group. I was fourteen and he was sixteen. We got away for weekends to go camping and hill walking; it was a Godsend having a mixed-sex scout camp.

Robert was a gorgeous almost six-footer, with broad tanned arms and a generously proportioned body, his face was square and sallow, framed in dark brown locks of hair. It was difficult not to notice him. He walked with ease and confidence, alert, with darting dark brown eyes that jumped straight into my heart.

He was confident making his first move, I wasn't sure whether he liked me or not. One night when we were sitting cross legged in the local parish hall, telling ghost stories to celebrate Halloween, he sat next to me. It was a perfect opportunity for Robert, to slip his hand into mine, while still looking at Liam O'Malley telling us a ghost story, I didn't object as I had been fantasising about this moment for weeks. He went on to gently and discreetly caress my calf. Later that evening, he walked me home and gave me my first delicious French kiss, that left me walking on air. That was the beginning of my realisation that sinning was in fact a pleasurable activity.

Despite what the priests or nuns may have preached at my weekly Mass or my daily religious class at Mary Magdalene's, I had no doubt that God would have no problem in forgiving me any of my little sins. God, in my opinion, was all about love and that's exactly what I was up to.

Despite Annie's disapproval of Robert, she still managed to make an effort to be nice to him when he was around; she was welcoming in a warm manner. She had kept her tongue regarding our obviously developing relationship, partly because she was using reverse-psychology, because it would have been predictable for her to object, and she was also feeling guilty about the fact she wasn't around much because she spent most of her time in Donegal.

Before Robert I was quite a saintly young girl, I even fantasised about becoming a nun. But there were too many contradictions. I especially had difficulty believing that Mary had conceived a child without actually making love; I believed in miracles. It also had possibilities of being scientific. So did the floods.

I had particular difficulty with the sex part of the procreation of Jesus getting cut out of the story. I was a romantic. Why didn't Joseph kiss her and vow his undying love for her and she, Mary, fall into his arms and surrender to his uncontrollably manly passions? Why couldn't this child Jesus be an icon made out of love?

In my younger, more innocent years, I actually looked forward to confession; I prayed that my little soul would become pure white again until I was informed by a Sister Fidelma that only saintly people could achieve a pure white soul. For ordinary folk like me that wasn't a possibility so then I always had an image of this little white soul with a dirty mark on it. Sometimes I would sidle up to my friends on the pew and ask them what they were confessing and we would whisper our sins into each other's innocent little ears and suddenly everyone would remember that they had used a swear word or taken the Lord's name in vain, and off we would trot into our little dark box to confess our white lies to the rather enthusiastic Father Dumphy.

Ali, my best friend, always laughed her way through life no matter what. That's what I loved about her.

'Ella, have you been a naughty little girl again, tell me?'

And I would deliver my sins into her eager ears, with mischievousness.

'I like to wear my Daddy's knickers.'

She would giggle so much she would have to bury her head in her hands and pretend she was in deep prayer.

The idea of being married to God, none of the hassle of having to deal with men and marriage, did appeal to me.

One day I had been advised, again by Sr. Fidelma, after

being caught discussing the new nightclub in town with the school's resident young plumber *'that I was heading on a journey towards hell'* where the devil himself, in person, lived. I was in double trouble because I was caught coming to school wearing make-up and silky black knickers instead of the compulsory thick navy-blue cotton ones they insisted we wore, designed to deliberately deglamourise young women. The fact that they did spot-checks on our knickers speaks volumes in itself.

Despite my sinning, I believed in love. I craved it and pursued it with a passion. Yet I was intelligent enough to know, probably thanks to Annie and her feminism, that it was all fairy-tale indoctrination; princess meets her prince, they kiss, marry and all live happily ever after my arse sort of a story.

THE ELEVENTH OF JULY BONFIRE

WILL'S STORY

It was the eleventh of July and bonfire night. The neighbourhoods had been collecting for months, soon the air would fill with the scent of the salvaged wood. Sam was preparing for his first walk the following day. We all made the effort of making it a special day. Sam was making some breakfast for us this morning, as Mum was doing her 'hand of friendship' delivery run with the Lodge. Every year, money would be collected for those in need and then distributed by way of food, furniture or cash.

Sam enjoyed cooking, it came naturally to him. He always made the effort to make it nice. He spent a lot of his time in the kitchen with Mum, watching her prepare, then helping her. This morning we were having French toast with bacon, his favourite. Father joined us with his Saturday morning ritual of reading the Times without being interrupted.

'So Will, are you joining us tonight?' asked Sam with a grin of insolence as he dished the French toast on to a plate, pan in hand.

'Joining who, exactly?'

'Me and the guys from band practice.'

'No'.

'Why not?'

'Because I need to practice tonight, it's my first solo.'

Sam slammed the plate of French toast in front of me and then predictably sulked for a while; he often had difficulty containing his emotions.

'Where's your sense of loyalty, the one night we have to go out there and show those lot what we stand for.'

'Who?'

He smiled up at me,

'You know who ... Will....'

Father lowered his paper below eye level and gave him a silent warning with a scary stillness.

'What?'

'We need to educate the Fenians'.

I admired Sam's courage, he made me laugh. Father folded his paper slowly and meticulously.

'Sam that's quite enough! Remember your first loyalty is to your Maker, which is whom, Sam?'

Sam quickly responded with.

'Our Lord Jesus Christ'

But he said it in a tone of sarcasm.

'Yes Sam, Our Lord Jesus Christ, who accepts all people on this earth regardless of their religion or creed, there is always room for redemption. The Roman Catholics you are referring to don't require us to show them anything if it is not in their belief system'.

Sam interrupted him.

'And do they have the right to require that we don't march our designated routes, or celebrate our culture?'

Dad looked at Sam and focussed, coldly,

'Your loyalty is to Orangeism. It is not about showing Catholics anything; it is about promoting a true Christian Protestantism and the celebration of the memory of William of Orange. Your loyalty is to represent Orangeism with a Christian attitude. You will stay at home this evening and reflect.'

Sam went to speak again,

'But...'

'Your second loyalty is to your family, to love and respect the hand that feeds you. Try not to forget that Sam!'

He paused staring at Sam's impassive face.

'Now thank you for breakfast, I don't want to hear another word'.

He picked up his paper and continued reading.

Sam's fear of Dad was wavering. He was always harder on Sam than me but then I never challenged him, I had no need to. I took most of what he said as Gospel. He was an intelligent man, well-respected within his community - and community was everything to him. He couldn't afford to have unruly teenagers.

'I won't.'

Sam stood staring at father's paper, pan in hand, waiting for a response. Father looked up, with impatience.

'I won't forget my loyalties and neither will I forget that I live in a country where our people are being brutally murdered on a daily basis; where our customs are slowly but surely being stripped from us. I'm just defending my loyalties like I was taught to, Dad'.

Dad lowered the paper stiffly this time.

When we were younger, Dad would have slapped us hard enough to keep us in line but now we were big boys and slapping wasn't an option. His face was flushed.

'I don't know who is filling your head with this nonsense Sam, but you're getting your loyalties mixed up and, let me be clear on this, I will not tolerate sectarian biasness in this house'.

Sam smiled mischievously,

'But you are opposed to Catholicism.'

Dad was losing patience.

'I am not a Catholic, so I don't practice Catholicism.'

'Would you be opposed to me bringing home a Catholic friend?'

'No, I wouldn't be opposed. However, I think it's fair to say that under the current conflict, it would be wiser to stick with your own'.

After breakfast Sam and I went to band practice. I with my flute, he with his drum sticks. As we walked down the Newtownards Road we saw the rather large piles of firewood that had been collected, old bedsteads, chairs, anything really; each area competing hard to outdo the others. Wooden pallets thirty feet high, some with a tri-colour flag on top. It was a beautiful day; the sun had blessed us. I prayed that tomorrow we would be blessed again because I had my first solo flute performance on the

66

scheduled walk.

'We could go to the cinema after band practice if you want. Stars Wars is out, I suggested.'

'Yeah, maybe.'

Band practice was buzzing with anticipation of the events ahead.

Spider was in particularly good form. He had got a new skinhead haircut in preparation for tomorrow and it exposed his scrawny face with darkened sockets for eyes. He was almost oriental looking, sallow, with gray blue eyes. Oddly enough the local girls would fight over him, or so I was told. But I just saw him as a disturbed individual who was in need of help, and I couldn't understand his hold over Sam. When we finished practice, with an enviable emphasis on my solo, we packed up our gear. I was in top form, until Spider intruded on us.

'Sam, are you coming over to mine? '

Sam looked up at me knowingly, he was afraid of my disapproval but his fear of not pleasing Spider was even stronger.

'Yeah sure, will you tell Mum I'll be home later? Sure why don't you come with us? he added as an afterthought.

'No. What about Father, you know how he feels about the bonfires?'

'Fathour'

Mimicked Spider, in a posh accent.

'Don't you start.' laughed Sam.

And off he went. It was fair to say Spider was a nasty, dangerous imbecile - a bad influence on my brother. But I was ever so slightly jealous of Sam's loyalty towards him and his determination and ability to live by his own rule.

When I returned home Mum and Dad were out in the garden. Dad listening to Radio Four Gospel, Mum tending to her flowers.

'Where's Sam?' asked Dad.

'He's going to practice some more with some friends'.

I lied. I had heard many a fun story over the years about bonfire night, but they did seem to attract a certain crowd, some genuine Christian people and some not-so Christian. Drink was the bigger of the evils and appeared to play a huge factor in the concept of having fun, but having come from a family tradition of teetotallers, alcohol held no appeal for me. I too would become teetotal for life.

My form of escapism was with my flute. I tidied my bedroom and opened my bay window carefully so as not to disturb the growth of red Virginia Creeper. I always tidied before I played. I opened the window so that Mother could listen whilst in the back garden, I could hear nothing other than the song of the starlings.

Sam didn't come home that evening as requested by Father. Instead he returned home around four in the morning, he woke me with a stone hitting the window from outside. I looked out and there he stood smiling up, I could tell he'd been drinking by his unstable stance.

'Let me in, I don't have my key!' he whispered loudly.

'Shussh.'

I got up to let him in but just as I was about to leave my room I saw Dad leaving his room. He put his finger up to silence me. He sneaked down stairs and opened the door to Sam, at first I just heard mumbling, then shouting, and then a large smack, a scream and a bang or two followed by a silence. My fear froze me. My fear always froze me. I always felt the need to protect Sam and my inability to do that drowned me in guilt.

I was envious of Sam because he was better-looking than me, warm-hearted, smart; he wasn't predictable like me, no fuss or worries. He had the balls to stand up to Father, and Mother adored the very ground he walked upon.

Dad, Granddad Goodie and I had breakfast and got dressed for the walk. We all wore black and white with our Orange collarets. Sam didn't appear at the breakfast table; however he did appear just before we left for the walk, dressed in his suit and Orange attire sporting a swollen black eye. Mother gasped when she saw him.

'What happened?'

Sam ignored her and looked over to me then up to Father. I looked away, stuck as to what to do or say, pulled in two directions. Father stood upright and looked straight at him.

'You're grounded.'

Mum went over and examined his eye, touching it as if it burnt her fingers. He had drawn blood this time.

'Sit down son; I'll put an icepack on it'.

Nobody else made comment. We left in a silence. I wanted Sam to be with us but I knew he couldn't.

A NIGHT OUT WITH SAM

WILL'S STORY

Because of my mother's growing concern for Sam's safety and my experience from the week before on a night out with Sam, I had agreed to take him out for a drink with some of my mates from the Youth and Bible Studies group, for his birthday. We were tall, handsome young men, and we had no difficulty getting into places. When living in a city that was riddled with terrorists, one often allowed for a little rule-breaking.

I drank my lemonade and Sam drank pints of Guinness. I watched him closely.

Sam was the only one drinking beer and unfortunately he sat beside Annemarie, a girl I was quite keen on, who, as the evening moved on, was visibly growing tired of comments like:

'University is just for poofs.'

Annemarie was set to study veterinary at Queen's University; she was also a product of a mixed marriage. Her mother was a Greek Anglican and her father, Church of Ireland.

Sam was quiet and observant at first but, once the beer kicked in it was like he was plagued with a personality that resembled something that was dragged out of the slum estates of West Belfast. It masked the real Sam; the funny, kind, intelligent Sam.

I did get to sit next to Annemarie and Stephen managed to distract Sam away from us.

She was interested in history, my favourite subject, so we discussed the early plantations coming to Ireland. She was genuinely impressed with my level of knowledge on the subject. We discussed Cromwell and Shakespeare. The Troubles.

'So what else do you do other than swot over books?'

I'm a black belt in karate and I play the flute, for the Lodge.'

She smiled.

'Cool, an Orangeman, my Dad has been a member forever.'

She seemed relaxed so I asked her would she like to come to the movies with me next Saturday.

'Yeah that sounds like a plan.'

I was ecstatic but I managed to contain my emotions. Then she bought a round of drinks. Sam asked for vodka and I watched him down it in one after he wished himself a happy birthday. I should have taken that as a warning sign but I was too engrossed in Annemarie. She was telling me about her grandmother in Greece and her regular summer vacations there. She talked animatedly about the horse riding school her uncle had over there. We were shut off from the rest of the table around us chatting in a comfortable space, and when I looked up I discovered Sam had been left alone. He was staring at Annemarie like a stalker then he started winking at her with a cheeky grin on his face, she was clearly mortified and so was I. He looked straight at her with a large stupid grin.

'So you're good at riding,'

'I think you've had enough Sam, we best go.'

He smiled up at me playfully.

'Horses, for fuck sake, lighten up.'

The others talked amongst themselves again but I wanted the floor to open up in front of me.

'No Sam, it's time to go.'

'One more drink before we go?'

I got up and put my coat on as he lit another cigarette.

'Will, stall, I'm only having a laugh.'

'No, we're leaving, now Sam!' I grabbed his coat 'Come on, let's go!'

Stephen appeared again and quickly got my drift and put on his coat.

'I'll give you a hand.'

We stood waiting on Sam.

'Mr fucking perfect Will, never does anything wrong.'

He looked into Annemarie's face a little too close with that mischievous look. I gave him his coat.

'Sorry, Annemarie, I'll call you next week, see what's on, okay?'

'Okay.'

'Did you know Will keeps girly pictures under the floor boards?'

When I looked at Annemarie she laughed. I shook my head, no, but I knew she didn't believe me. Stephen pulled him up and directed him outside. Stephen was six-foot-two and was also a black belt at karate. When we got sufficiently down the road, I threw Sam up against the wall and he bounced off like a rubber doll. It was pointless hitting him. I knew he wouldn't fight back. I put my hand into my pocket and pulled out an envelope with a pair of tickets to go and see UB40.

'Happy fucking birthday.'

I threw the envelope on the ground. He knelt down to pick up the envelope, he looked inside. He loved UB40.

'Will, I'm sorry.'

'No you're not! You don't know what the meaning of sorry is, you moron, but you will be sorry Sam..'

I walked away, I hated him. Stephen stood between us. I stopped at the top of the road and saw him pushing Stephen away. Stephen left. Sam sat on the dirty ground against a wall that read in bright red painted letters 'Brits Out'. I stood and watched him for a while, I looked at him and wondered what had happened to the Sam that broke his neck to catch the frog to take home as a pet. Father had always forbidden pets. He fed it lettuce and water before he set it free again. I flagged a taxi.

I watched him as he pulled out the UB40 tickets again and deliberately smacked his head against the wall twice with full force. I felt his pain. I took him home in the taxi and managed to clean the bleeding wound in the back of his head. I got him to bed, unnoticed. The girly magazines didn't exist but I knew he had stashed a tin box under the floor boards and I found a magazine of his, stuffed away behind the box, but to my horror and surprise it wasn't a girly magazine I found. Father would have died of shame.

Needless to say, I didn't phone regarding a night out to the cinema.

The week before he came out with me I had stupidly agreed to go out with him and his mates, he wanted to prove to me that they were okay and I had promised Mum and Dad I'd let them know who he was hanging out with.

Our night out began with a bad start in Spider's house. Spider lived in a heavily decorated Protestant estate in Dundonald, with his wretched, skinny, over-worked mother who had raised him single-handedly along with his older brother who was a bully and fought for the cause. About six of us squashed into Spider's small box bedroom that smelt of dirty socks. He rolled a very long joint, that took almost a packet of cigarette papers stuck together to roll. The bedroom was decorated with his various symbols including the swastika, Union Jacks, and slogans that various friends had written on his wall over time, like, '*Wiz woz ere*' or '*Long live the UVF.*'

Dirty underwear, used plates and cups lay about the floor and under the bed; it was enough to make me sick.

'So, Will, are you here to keep an eye on your baby brother or are you just bored of the good life.'

'Bit of both.'

He handed me a joint, which I mistakenly refused.

'Does Mammy's boy stay off the grass.'

The others laughed.

'I don't smoke tobacco.'

This was an even bigger mistake.

'Ah, no worries, I have just the thing'

And he whipped out a little brass pipe and proceeded to fill it with what seemed like a small mountain of hash, he lit it and passed it on to me and I puffed it like I had seen Granddad puff his tobacco pipe. My throat and chest went on fire, and I coughed for what felt like ten minutes; I was now the established joke. Sam was enjoying every minute of it. Later we all headed into the city centre where we met some friends of Spider's, who were standing outside the City Hall building, a classical Renaissance design where the Ulster Unionists Parties would hold their elections. Police vehicles would crawl past us keeping an eye on what was going on; turning a blind eye to the dope and underage drinking.

It was a large enough crowd, about fifteen of us. Most were clinging onto plastic bags with their night's supply of drinking cans; the atmosphere was jovial yet tense. I stayed with Sam and tried to relax a little, but it was difficult. I was afraid. The dope made everything a little weird, everything was too weird anyway and I didn't like it. The drink and dope didn't seem to reach the desired outcome for Spider; it seemed that each joint just fuelled a need for another. I watched Sam chatting with a couple of girls and he was smiling like the Sam I knew.

'I know what you need.'

Said Spider approaching and he whipped out his pipe again and proceeded to fill it with brown hash. He lit the pipe and handed it to me with his hand carefully covering the top of it. For some reason I was too afraid to say no perhaps because I had made some kind of peace with this guy with this pipe business. Perhaps because I wanted him to mind Sam.

'Lift your hand off when you go to inhale, don't waste the smoke man.'

He said in a sincere sort of a tone, I did my best to inhale it but again I spluttered and coughed to everyone's delight. I couldn't stop coughing this time.

'He has asthma.' said Sam. He took the pipe from me puffed it like a professional smoker and passed it on. The drink supplies rapidly ran out and then the mood started feeling edgy. Spider hollered:

'Let's go.'

I looked over to Sam,

'Go where?' I asked naively

Spider looked at me with a smile.

'Let's go get us some Fenian wee bastards.'

He took off up the street as proud as a cock, confident he had followers.

We walked about a mile to the Maysfield leisure centre, close to the Short Strand, a predominantly Nationalist area. Another joint rolled, another pipe loaded. The walk was very pleasant; everything looked a little more beautiful. The city lights shone; the buildings stood in their place of heritage. I felt proud to be a part of this city with its old Victorian and Georgian architecture. Sam walked beside me and I could see he was happy, I was with him, he was wearing a continuous smile.

'See, they're not all bad.'

'Who was the young one playing with your hair?'

'That's Jess, she's nice but I'm not interested.'

We walked on in silence, afraid to burst the bubble of content. I noticed Spider observing us, he looked jealous. He always looked around him as if someone was following him, always checking, always on the move. A trail of army vehicles and police wagons drove slowly past, guns pointing at us. A young solider jumped off the back of one of the trucks and approached, his gun pointing straight at us.

'Where are you coming from? Where are you going to?'

'East Belfast. We are just heading over to a mate's house, for a few cans' said Spider with authority.

'Where does your mate live?'

'Newtownards Road, we were in Maysfield leisure centre having a game of football'

'No trouble tonight guys, alright.'

He jumped back onto the green truck and it headed off.

We walked into the Short Strand, a place I would never have even dreamed of setting foot in. The two-up-two-down terraces looked quiet and quite peaceful, the streets asleep and bare. These were the homes of the IRA, I felt totally out of place.

'Sam, I think we should call it a night.'

'Look, it's only messing, we won't hurt anyone. Mind you we don't usually come this far.'

'Fine. Do what you want, but I'm heading home.'

I turned to walk away when swiftly we were all hushed under commando Spider's wave of a hand. He was in his element, he was in control. Just around the corner I could see a group of young people who looked about fourteen sitting against a wall clinging unto their cans and smoking joints.

He shushed us all with his hand signals, and held up the hand again as if stopping traffic; he sneaked around the corner by himself.

'Drop the bags, leave the dope on the wall!'

They looked at each other for a moment and then one looked straight at him with a smile; it was a pretty blonde girl, dressed in pink flares with a pink hoodie that said Grease across the back.

'Fuck away off.'

She made a run for it, followed by the others, back towards their own territory, bags held tightly under arms. One unfortunate dropped his bag of cans, and quickly tried to retrieve them and make a run for it. He looked around and saw our crowd chasing him and dropped the cans again. Most of our crowd stopped chasing him and picked up his offering but Spider and Dave ran for the kid. It didn't take long for them to get hold of him; he looked a young thirteen, a clean blonde blue-eyed, cherub sort of face.

'Hold him.' ordered Spider.

Dave grabbed his arm, the kid screamed.

'Let me go!'

'Where are you from?'

'The Lisburn Road' replied the kid, lying.

Spider slapped him across the face, hard.

'Don't lie to me.'

'I'm not'.

Spider kicked him in the stomach, the boy let out a painful yelp.

'Where are you from?'

'The Short Strand.'

'Right answer.'

Spider slapped him across the face again.

'Say the alphabet.'

'The what?'

'The a, b, c or don't you fuckin paddies know it?'

'a, b, c, d, e, f, g, h.'

Spider laughed,

'Wrong answer' he said, the others laughed too, even Sam.

'That's not right boys is it? Tell him how we Prods say our hs.'

He said in a thick English accent.

'It's ache'.

'Get up.'

And the boy stood up.

'Shall we go for it boys?'

'Yes, let's.'

'Sam, Fred, you keep a look out.'

'He's just a kid, Spider.' offered Fred

'Did anyone ask for your fucking opinion arsehole?'

Spider charged the kid. Sam headed up to the top of the street to keep watch; I stayed out of curiosity more than anything. I felt numb. I watched them in a daze as they kicked the kid until he seemed almost lifeless. Dave smiling as he sunk his heavy boot into the young motionless body. Spider waved his hand to stop, then unzipped his pants and pissed on him.

'Leave him alone.' I shouted, and they took no notice,

'Leave him alone!' I roared loud enough to get possible unwanted attention. Spider looked around at me with pure evil in his face, the others stopped at the wave of his hand.

'Did you want a go?' he asked.

I looked down at the young kid who was a mass of red mess.

'Or, are you a just papal lover, Will?' he asked with a cold anger.

I walked over to the kid and lifted him up.

'Are you okay?'

'Yeah.'

I saw Spider make a move towards me and I jumped into a protective karate stance. He laughed.

'What, you're going to attack me and let the Fenian run, you're fucked up man!!'

I helped the kid find his feet.

'Thanks' he muttered as he hobbled towards some of his mates who were standing watching at a safe distance.

When I turned around Spider and the others looked like they were going to jump me but I didn't care, I was ready to fight back. Spider approached me, he grabbed the collar of my shirt. I wanted to put my hands around his scrawny throat.

'Stay away.'he whispered.

I looked through his glassy, dull, grey eyes

'You stay away from my brother.' I whispered back.

Sam stepped in, and pulled me away.

'Leave him' said Sam.

'Let's go' ordered Spider.

They followed their leader. Sam hovered on the spot, he looked frightened.

'Sam, come home with me.'

But I knew when I looked at him he was lost in all of this. I had to let go.

A small crowd of older looking boys could be seen, walking rapidly towards us.

'Run' ordered Spider and we all ran like hell.

I got stuck into studying for my A-levels and I got a job in the local sweet shop at the weekends. I prayed that Sam would eventually see the light.

ELLA'S MORTIFICATION

I grew up curious about the Orange marchers who paraded up our main road towards the gates of Stormont. I had annually observed the Twelfth of July march through the gap in the middle of the annually-closed red velvet curtains of our drawing room window. I would wait to see Orange Lil, my favourite part of the show. Lil was a middle-aged woman, who dressed differently every year; perhaps an orange tutu with a fitted Union Jack top, matched with an orange parasol and frilly orange knickers that she would every-so-often flash, to the beat of the Lambeg drum. She would dance in and around the well-groomed walkers, waving her brollie in the air to the rhythm of the music, intoxicated by the abundance of flutes, accordions and drums.

Inevitably, it was only a matter of time before I would feel the disapproving hand of Nana, angry at my defiance, because she had warned me repeatedly not to go near the windows on the Twelfth of July. Only two sets of curtains were closed on our road, so they knew we were Catholics, this encouraged them to stop outside our house and beat their drums even louder. I in innocence thought this was for my behalf because they knew Nana had closed the curtains.

Every morning without fail, whilst waiting on my school bus, I was subjected to verbal taunting from the Dundonald High School boys. They waited across the same main road as I did for their school bus. Fortunately the road was always busy, and it had a width of four car lanes, so we were kept at a safe enough distance. We Magdalene girls dressed in green uniforms and the boys were in black. There were three of us and usually about ten of them. Margaret, Ali, and I waited at this stop.

Ali and I ignored them most of the time and Margaret would occasionally throw them the fingers just before boarding our bus. We all gave them the fingers once we were safely on the bus.

As the seventies progressed it became more apparent Catholics were not welcome in the area, or in fact in Northern Ireland. Annie did everything in her power to try and persuade Jack to sell up, but Jack was stubborn.

They painted *'Catholics out or else'* across the front wall of our home. It was painted in bright orange letters. I saw it as I was leaving the house on my way to school. I felt as if I had been attacked and I ran in and told Nana exasperated, but she calmly threw her eyes up to heaven and ushered me out again. When I got to the bus stop, there were smiles of triumph from across the road and indecent arm gestures from Spider. I gave them the fingers back this time, and Will who stood a little apart looked over at me with a sympathetic look.

Spider put his fist into his inside elbow and drew his arm up. Luke explained later that that meant he wanted to fuck me.

The worst was when I was sent to the local shop, Batemans, for messages, which was almost daily. The shop was long and narrow with the cash counter at the top. Designed so that there was no lurking behind hidden shelves.

Batemans went through an assortment of shop assistants, on a regular basis, because the owner Billy Bateman was never fit for work. He was either busy with paramilitary activities or he was sleeping off a drug-induced hangover.

Will was working there part-time which was a relief. Will threw his eyes to heaven when they called me names, his courage excited me. They were just kids but their elders were probably members of groups such as the UVF or the UDA, I was used to it by now and almost immune to it. I could see through them and I was aware that they came from troubled working class backgrounds. I would smile a nervous smile through the taunting, 'rise above Ella, they have small minds, small dicks', I told myself, 'they don't know any better'.

'I smell a Fenian bitch who could do with a wash,'

'Fuck off' I said under my breath.

'Hey you, Fenian girl, you something to say?'

It was Spider, the dirty wee four-foot, skin head, with a face like a prune. He was no taller than me. He wore drain pipe jeans and a blue Lynnfield football shirt two sizes too big for him. He was grinning with blurred eyes, his hands in his pockets, probably out of it on glue or hash and, as usual, I ignored him and went searching for my goods.

Today I had the ultimate teenage girl embarrassment of having to purchase my own sanitary towels because my mother, unlike everyone else's mother, wouldn't buy them in bulk for me. The nearest chemist was about three miles away. I was mortified, today of all days, eight Protestant boys stood either side of the shop counter, four aside. Will's brother Sam was among them. Spider put his foot out as I approached the counter with my sanitary towels that I hoped were well hidden inside my Beano comic. There were sniggers all around when they saw what I put on the counter. Then an awkward pause.

'Fi Fi Fo Fum, I smell the blood of a Fenian one', sang Spider, and they all laughed, even Will let a smile break, I waited for Will to put the towels into a bag and he did.

'When are you going to understand that you don't belong around here?'

'Spider, leave her alone' said Will and they looked at him in disgust but let it go as they knew he had the kudos to get away with it.

Will smiled over at me, and to my internal-most horror, I blushed. His words gave me the strength to pick up the towels and make my exit. I had just reached the door, hugging the paper bag with my towels, when I heard and felt a disgusting spit hit the back of my shirt.

'For fucks sake Spider, wise up.' I heard Will say.

'Fuck off and stay out of it, Fenian lover'

'Get out Spider before I call your big brother'.

Spider's face changed.

'Does Will fancy a bit of Fenian action? You dirty wee

bastard.'

This was followed by more titters from the others. Will, unyielding, retorted with

'I've no problem with Catholics.'

Again Will's words gave me strength and I turned around and walked over to Spider, silently shaking with nerves, ready to tell him to fuck off for once and all but he spat at me again, this time at my face and out of nowhere my hand flew up and smacked him across his right cheek, leaving a red and deeply shocked wee Prod dumbfounded. I wiped my face and stuck my face into his and announced clearly:

'I'm proud to be a Catholic.'

I turned and walked out of the shop. I continued walking till I got past the shop front window and then I ran for my life. They'd have come after me but I think they must have been in a state of shock. Needless to say I was unable to return to the shop for weeks after that.

THE LIBRARY

By chance I saw Ella one day in the Linen Hall Library. I purposely sat as far away as I could but not so far away that I couldn't get a good view. When she lifted her head out of her Shakespeare's sonnets, I buried mine in 'The Art of Politics'.

I was distracted. Ella was very attractive, beautiful really. She had light auburn hair that sat in gentle waves just below her shoulders, sallow skin, and dark brown eyes, almost foreign looking, different from the girls I knew at school. Today I saw a softness about her. She sat back in her chair as if there was a roaring fire in front of her with one foot nestled under her thigh carelessly, boldly. She appeared to be the focus for the light in the room. I was mesmerised. The following day I would probably see her across the road again and we would go through the usual ritual of Spider making rude gestures over at her and she would continue to ignore us until the bus arrived, whereupon she might politely give us the fingers. She looked up at me staring at her, and I quickly buried my head in my book again, I could feel the blood reach my cheeks. Finally, she packed her bag and left and I could start studying.

I was sickened by bigotry. I toyed with the idea of becoming a lawyer, or a policeman. I wanted to help innocent people who had been affected by the troubles. My grandfather Goodie, a police sergeant in Ballymena was shot one night when he was on patrol. Luckily he was wearing a bullet proof vest but it unnerved him.

Before he was shot they would write on the walls of his home, 'RUC BASTARD OUT' usually in bright red paint. They re-housed him twice for safe-keeping but it was inevitable they would find him again. When they set fire to my father's church he became so distressed that the doctor had to give him pills for his nerves. It was ironic that the majority of victims during the Troubles were innocent hard-working-class Protestant people.

Dad and I practiced playing the flute in harmony, in the drawing room. It was a still room, unlived-in as it was kept for guests, eggshell blue walls and mahogany furnishings. '*Here Lies a Soldier*' and then in preparation for my solo I played '*Paint The Clouds*'. I could have played the flute all day without noticing the time pass, which is sometimes what I did do. On a Saturday I would start practicing at six-thirty in the morning and finish around two. I was determined to join the Ulster Orchestra one day.

'Lovely, Will'.

I continued playing and he sat silent and relaxed as the notes swam around the room, I finished off with '*King Billy's March*' the very first tune he taught me. He smiled at that.

'We'll just leave the walk if there's any sign of trouble, it's not what it used to be you know, we used to have such fun on the walk. To be honest I'm not sure there's much point in it anymore, it's a tradition betrayed.'

The morning glow of sun was peeping through the clouds before we set off. Other than Orangemen walking up the road, the road was as quiet as a ghost. People had stopped coming out to wave their loved ones on, for fear of possible attack. Most Catholics evacuated for the annual holiday. It was a pity really because, idealistically, I wished they could see us celebrate. Why not, don't Catholics play flutes, drums, accordions and whistles; don't they wave iconic paraphernalia, don't they dress up for dancing fetes like we do, and wear colourful costumes like ours?

'Wouldn't it be great if we could all celebrate together?'

Sam laughed when I made this point.

'They hate us, and we hate them, what do you not get about that simple equation'.

As the drums beat into my soul, the walk began. I played my flute with potency. Spider walked alongside Sam, Sam's large Lambeg drum, could probably be heard several miles away. Father walked alongside me. As I walked a strange thought came into my head. I wished that Ella would come out and watch. I don't know why. I was approaching her house, and I wanted her to see me in my full regalia. I suppose I was curious to see her reaction. The curtains were drawn closed. Thankfully, she wasn't there. When the band stopped outside her house, they beat the drums louder, they stayed a little longer, the music crescendo rose to an all-time high. Drums rattled and vibrated through the air. I caught the look of ecstasy on Spider's face as he watched Sam beat the Lambeg drum with every ounce of pathetic strength he had, in the hope of making some kind of point.

LOSERS QUIT WHEN THEY ARE TIRED AND WINNERS QUIT WHEN THEY HAVE WON.

ELLA'S STORY

I loved it when Jack would tuck me in at night, it wasn't often but if he came home early he would patiently sit on the armchair beside my bed until midnight making sure I understood my equations, pies, and squares. He made maths and science fun. Once we made a toy plastic boat behave like a submarine by filling it with baking powder and submerging it in water, every now and then it would pop up and then dive back down into the water. He was relentless in pushing me until he was satisfied I understood everything at task. When he went over my Tables I would fall back into the pillow and try and change the subject but he never gave in.

'Ella, losers quit when they are tired, winners quit when they have won.'

This was always his way; he was consistent with his belief in having a good education, whatever the costs. It wasn't until he was assured that I had covered my work that I would be granted a story. I lived for my stories, he was so convincing, with his voices, the bolder the character the better. I preferred his made-up stories because they always involved very bold characters, who did things like lock their grandmothers in cupboards, or little girls who created havoc in the schoolroom with magic.

We both thrived on Roald Dahl. We moved from Dahl to Graeme Greene and then to Austen and Jane Eyre. My appetite for such fantasy was endless. I adored my father in a sort of fantastical way. I boosted his ego and he mine, our bedtime ritual was a safe zone for us to share any intimacy we had for each other. We were mates. I simply adored him for who and what he was and he simply adored me for the same reasons. I made him promise me that even if I was asleep he was to come in and waken me to read to me and I promised him that when he was old and mouldy I would return the favour.

Things changed when Robert came on the scene. Jack tried to hide the fact that he disapproved of Robert. One Saturday evening he marched into the kitchen at eight-thirty and sat down with Robert, myself, and Nana. He looked to Robert with a smile.

'I think it's time you went home Robert.'

Just like that, no reasoning, in a tone only a father would use. He suggested that we keep our 'play dates' to weekends only. What was equally surprising was that Robert immediately stood up, chest out, bum in, and left, dutifully, not even a smooch goodbye. How gallant was that?

Some days later we were sitting in the kitchen with Nana having tea and Jack came in. Robert stood up.

'Sit down Robert.' ordered Jack. He stood over us with his glass of whiskey slightly tilted in his hand wallowing in his authority.

'Isn't it near your bedtime Ella?'

'I'm just giving them a quick bite before Robert heads home, Jack, sit down and join us, I've just made some flapjacks' said Nana.

He looked puzzled for a moment torn between the flapjacks and the imposter, wanting to obey his mother and wanting to regain control. So he sat down opposite Robert, saying nothing and Robert smiled nervously back.

'So Robert, what do you intend on doing when you finish school?' he asked.

'Medicine or Law'.

'Oh very good, very good. You'll be wanting to put your head down then , no-one gets to Law school without hard graft, what age are you now?'

'I'm seventeen, sir'

Jack grinned like a monkey.

'Not legal yet.....to have a drink that is, no hurry I hope?'

'No sir, there is no hurry.'

Nana approached the table armed with flapjacks straight from the oven.

'Now folks, tuck into those.'

I wondered had she put something into those flapjacks because Jack and Robert talked for ever about everything and anything, snooker, golf, tennis, bridge and the joys of being a lawyer in Belfast. Nana and I became so bored we went and watched television, until we were falling asleep. I went to bed after kissing my boyfriend and father goodnight on the cheeks and leaving them to it. I was too embarrassed to ask Dad to come and read me my bedtime story, because I knew in my heart of hearts I was much too old for such indulgences. That night Jack cleverly managed to convince Robert that he and I needed to stay focussed during the week for study.

Denial was a way of life for all of us. To fully absorb life in Belfast was impossible. It was like calling the war that was going on 'the Troubles' a simple phrase that was developed to try and underestimate the reality that was our everyday lives. The dictionary's definition of a war is '*a conflict carried on by force of arms ...to war with a neighbouring nation.*' To deny a reality only promotes an ignorance and lends to the concept of living in a fantasy.

Jack and Annie had got to the point where they were starting to avoid each other. When Annie was home, which was less often, they would, as was customary, retire into the drawing room and engage over a drink fuelled with political discussions. These chats now only lasted for half an hour before one of them would storm off. Politics was Jack's fuel for life, he lived and breathed the news and media and Annie wasn't interested anymore. The current media fascination was with the hunger strikers at the Maze Prison.

Up until 1972 Paramilitary prisoners in Northern Ireland were treated as ordinary criminals. A special category status was introduced after forty prisoners went on hunger strike. This new status allowed the prisoners to be treated like prisoners-of-war. This meant no uniforms, no prison work, access to books and media, and open communication amongst prisoners. In 1976, the British government put a stop to this special category status because of the on-going conflict inside and outside the prison. After many failed negotiations to overturn this decision the prisoners began a series of protests which led to the much publicised hunger strike. Relationships between prison wardens and prisoners broke down, violence was an everyday occurrence. Nineteen prison officers died over the five year period of the protests. The protest began when prisoners refused to wear their uniforms instead they wore their blankets hence '*the blanket protest.*' Then prisoners refused to leave their cells because of the on-going conflict with the wardens. This meant they didn't use the communal bathrooms provided, hence '*the dirty protest*'. Prisoners smeared their shit over the walls of the cells they inhabited. Then the Hunger Strike. By 1980, the strike got international media coverage winning huge sympathy for the paramilitaries. It wasn't until two days after the tenth man died of starvation that the British Government agreed to make changes, one of which included that all paramilitary prisoners would be allowed to wear their own clothes.

Annie wanted to move anywhere that wasn't Belfast. She was pushing for Dublin, where her art work was gathering a name for its self but Jack was getting more and more steeped in the cause.

'I'm no chicken, I won't run.'

Was his mantra.

Nana knew some of the families affected by the hunger strike personally and stood by her son.

'Running away will never make you free Annie.'

So Annie ran away every week-end to her little holiday hideaway in Donegal.

I spent my requisite evenings in, with Nana in the

kitchen creating new and bolder recipes; sometimes Robert joined us. These were very treasured times; my safe haven, Nana, was my rock and my police.

'Don't throw it all away on the first fella you meet, Ella.'

I put our garden raspberries into the mould of pink cream mousse.

'Is that what you did Nana, with Granddad Charlie?'

She looked at me and smiled.

'Charlie took his time, I have no regrets'.

We continued quietly pottering about the kitchen, pausing comfortably with our thoughts.

'Perhaps I would have liked to have worked, but I wasn't driven, I wanted to be a good wife and mother. I look at women now though, like your mother, and I admire them for getting out into the world and making their mark, being someone. Get the icing pipe, love'.

'Don't get me wrong Ella; I'm just saying that you are in no hurry.'

She poured the whipped cream into the decorating pipe.

'Don't you like Robert, Nana?'

I asked nervously as the openness of our conversation was moving into rocky waters. She looked up at my innocence.

'Do you love him? '

I thought for a moment,

'I think I do Nana'.'

She smiled knowingly.

'Well then, Love will conquer all.'

Mum conveniently inherited the holiday hideaway in Donegal from her Uncle Tom. He designed some of the art nouveaux style cinemas in Belfast. A few of his creations left a reminder of his mark on the planet after he had gone. Some were blown up. Jack had hopes it would become their occasional love nest but instead it became a place of space and refuge for Annie. Jack never found the weekends he promised to her, and Annie never found the right reasons to stay in Belfast. Weekends turned into weeks and months.

She transformed Tom's bachelor pad into a haven fit for a harem. Donegal bachelors were soon discussing the local artist over a pint of the black stuff. She was the woman Jack had fallen in love with all those years ago, and to him she didn't look a day older. He watched in amazement whilst he continued to fund her lavish lifestyle faithfully and foolishly in love. Denial was his saviour, that and Bushmills.

THE GALLAGHERS

ELLA'S STORY

Robert was a keen rugby player, a popular Catholic boy who wanted to study sports but was slowly being coerced by his parents to consider studying medicine.

On the night of my fifteenth birthday we went babysitting for his uncle Peter. Robert presented me with a single yellow rose and declared his undying love for me. When he told me he loved me I believed him and I believed I may have been in love with him too. I needed to love someone.

Robert looked so sexy reading to Thomas, his little five year old nephew, kissing him on the forehead before leaving his ship-themed bedroom. He had a nice warm fire lit downstairs. He lay across the white shaggy rug beside the fire his shirt open and loose. I had, by now, discovered the key to good sex was through guidance and endurance from the female and willingness and patience from the male. I removed my shoes and lay down beside him. He leant over and melted his lips into my mouth. His well-manicured hands seemed to take on a mind of their own, as they wandered with the skill of a cloth cutter over my breasts. My intentional wrap-around dress fell to the floor and his mouth travelled around my body with the urgency of an animal. He seduced me with neediness for love that met mine.

His father Norman, a tall, reddish, weathered-looking man, was a health inspector and was rarely at home. Alice, his mother, shared her son's good looks, albeit fading fast. Her straight black bob was thin and her light touch of makeup revealed a face of someone who didn't really give a damn anymore. Happy to sip a Schweppes with gin, no ice or lemon required, in front of her reliable companion the television, with the knowledge that the first thing

Norman would do when he got home would be to pour an already inebriated Alice another large gin and tonic and himself a large whisky. Then he would retreat to the immaculately sparse, architecturally designed, white dining room while she remained glued to the various soaps on television. Everything in the house was white, everything.

When I probed Robert about the 'whiteness thing', he said he hadn't really noticed. When I probed him about the silence between his parents, he said:

'We are not a perfect family, but we are perfectly happy, Dad is a little emotionally switched off, but it works for them, they never fight.'

Maybe they were happy, maybe they didn't need to communicate and maybe Jack and Annie communicated a little too much.

Alice and Norman rarely spoke to each other, other than the deliverance of essential information such as '*I phoned the bank*' or *I've booked the car in for a service*'. They were not so much irritated with each other as bored in each other's company. She, too, had studied science with intentions of becoming a pharmacist, but gave it up when Robert arrived.

Robert, being an only child because of birthing complications, was the golden boy. He was often used as a go-between for family entertainment. They hung on to anything and everything that came out of that delicious mouth of his; Alice lived for his existence. He would be quizzed on what he got up to at school, or the rugby club, with incredible detail. Boundaries were often crossed between mother and son; she wanted to know every facet regarding our relationship, anything that might inject a piece of life or passion into the sterile place they called home.

Unfortunately his mother's needs often clashed with my need to be his one and only. Scarlet O' Hara would have commended me.

Alice's garden was covered in concrete, with a little

weed stretching out for life here and there, a few controlled shrubs, and a small manageable well-maintained lawn. Quite Protestant, really.

On a more positive note, it was easy to have sex unnoticed at his house; after gin number two, in his white bed-room, in his clean white sheets and his crisp white duvet.

My suspicion in regard to their dysfunction was confirmed when I bumped into Norman at the cinema one afternoon strolling out with a blonde woman half his age, carelessly too close for comfort. It was pouring with rain and he stuttered some pathetic explanation in regard to this woman being his secretary and scurried off with her. I said nothing to no-one, why spoil the fantasy? It was sad really, Alice not wanting anyone to steal her youthful bundle of hope, Robert. The only remaining affectionate hold she had on her husband.

Despite her coldness towards me, I actually grew to like Alice over time, perhaps even love her. I felt sorry for her above all else, she was trapped in a marriage of loneliness and she did try very hard to keep it all together. She was very intelligent, husband excepting. It gave me the insight to reflect on my own mother and see her in a new light.

Annie didn't like or approve of Robert, probably because of the age concern. She knew we were having sex, because she left a leaflet under my pillow with information on contraception alongside a packet of condoms.

I was until now getting straight A's in school in almost every subject, but my last assessment was tainted with B's.

The little control Annie had over me was dwindling. In fact if I needed a talking-to, for coming home in the early hours of the morning, she would just ask Jack to do it for her, which was a pointless exercise because I knew how to make him forget what it was he was giving out about.

One day I was peeling spuds in the kitchen whilst she painted her nails.

'Do you fancy a week-end in Donegal Ella?' she asked.

'No.'

'Don't pretend you're studying.'

'Yes'

'Is it anatomy you're studying by any chance?'

'I do have biology, actually.'

'Don't lie to me Ella, you know I can't stand a liar.' she snapped as she lashed dark purple paint onto her long strong nails.

'I'm not.'

'I don't really care what you do Ella, just don't come running if you fall.'

'I won't.'

I had tried to get the Pill from the family doctor but was refused on the grounds that my parents had not consented, so we got condoms when we could, which was seldom because they weren't available in chemists.

It was sometimes difficult to maintain a sex life under the atmosphere of disapproval but we managed. Sex was pretty much all we thought about.

The tension of Troubles had increased. Checkpoints were everywhere, the army presence, bombs and shootings and curfews all became a part of everyday life.

Unfortunately this posed a bit of a hindrance to my social life. I finally looked old enough to go to pubs and clubs, but when things got bad Troubles-wise, I would be grounded. It was just too dangerous to go into the town at night. During curfew, in the city centre the street lights would be extinguished and the only people to be seen were men in uniforms.

So, during curfew, Robert would call over to our house which was intolerable, because my parents could be either in a full-swing row, or Jack pissed.

It was okay when Annie was in Donegal, because Jack hid upstairs. Only Annie had the nerve to barge into my bedroom, ignoring the 'please knock' sign I had pasted on the door with black gaffer tape. I'd attached a new lock to the bedroom door and as a ploy I started wearing short skirts, so that we could have sex without me having to take any more than my knickers off.

Sometimes we would just lie together and listen to music. Robert would arrive with his heavily laden school bag over his shoulder, with murmurs of intended studying. He was a much more convincing liar than me.

Robert never took much notice of my bedroom; he usually just wanted to get straight to business.

I had scanned every item in his whiter-than-white bedroom by the second time I was in it. It was sparse other than his dirty washing which lay strewn across the floor. It had the sense of early-teenager managed by mum. Shirts his mother ironed hung to the left of his modern closet and matching socks slept cosily in one drawer above the fresh smelling briefs below. Rolled posters and an old collection of cars and magazines lay on the floor of the same closet. He had a cool music selection stacked in various piles on the floor which housed Jimmy Hendrix, the Stones, and Judi Zuke. His white and blue cotton duvet smelt of sex and looked like something from a toothpaste ad. His window sill was covered in emptied-pocket bus tickets and sweetie wrappers, but what I loved most about his room was the wild careless Golden Virginia that climbed across the top of his double glazed bungalow window. Robert was forbidden to hang stuff on his walls but he was given a little cork wall hanger to pin things on, and it was laden with concert tickets, badges, travel tickets and pretty women. A passport photo of he and I peeped out from the top right-hand corner.

My bedroom was a calming shade of violet. It was the tidiest room in the house. It had a bay window that had white silky curtains with embroidered birds and flowers on them that made shadows on the wall at night when closed. Purple Doc Martins sat under an old pine dresser. Clothes hung organised. The walls were adorned with a signed photo of me and Bob Geldof, alongside the French painter Matisse's 'Blue Room' and Picasso's 'Woman pissing' - presents from Annie's London excursions. I had a framed black and white photo of Robert and I on the dresser, he noticed that.

I had a heaped collection of blankets, because I was always freezing cold, topped with an old patchwork quilt.

After sex we would usually get hungry and head down to the kitchen, where we would find a trusting Nana sitting by the range, reading the paper whilst listening to the latest update. She had a particular soft spot for Bobby Sands. Tonight she was delighted because he won the first Nationalist seat in Westminster. Nana was comfortable with Robert.

'How's your Mum, Robert? I saw her at Mass last Sunday.'

He would look over at me first and then make his reply, 'Oh she's great.'

But Nana knew better, because I had filled her in with the not-so-rosy details. Later she would ask me to update her and I would divulge my version of his home environment.

THE MISTAKEN PROPOSAL

ELLA'S STORY

For Robert's seventeenth birthday we dined in 'Valencia's' – a chic new Italian pizza restaurant, manned by young sexy Italian men who looked like they walked straight out of the Mafia. Perhaps they had, it was Belfast. The pizza was lovely, not your typical cheese and pepperoni plastic, it had a really thin base and new exotica like artichokes and anchovies with a homemade olive taste to it; the seafood pasta Robert ordered melted in your mouth. I had decided we would return for my sixteenth birthday. Robert had just got the A-Level results he needed to apply to do Law at Queen's University. We got dressed up for the occasion, me in my little black denims and purple silk top and Robert in a crisp white shirt and black jacket with his nice velvety black jeans.

'Do you think we will ever get married and have kids?' he asked casually and genuinely.

'I can't believe you asked me that, we're just kids ourselves, Robert, ... I mean it's not that I wouldn't want to, at some point in my life........actually I don't know'.

'Which get married or have kids?'

'Either. I don't really believe in the whole marriage thing. I think it's a little over-rated.'

He looked wounded.

'I hope you're not thinking what I'm thinking you're thinking'

I had lost him.

'You think I'm asking you to?'

'No, no, no, no, don't be ridiculous'

I was mortified.

'I didn't mean tomorrow, or ever, for that matter. I was just testing the ground. I don't know if I believe in marriage either'.

He looked over to me and laughed, with relief and disbelief, realising what he had said.

'Well then, that's great, neither of us believes in marriage. So be it.'

Then he relaxed a little and sulked a little. Then he got stuck into his seafood pasta. I watched him and as I watched him something happened; I saw the man in him, that brutish male and for a moment I loathed him. His sexiness disappeared as he swallowed his creamy mussels, and stringy bits of wet fish, his lips covered in sticky wet pasta, his neediness spilling out everywhere.

'Look at our parents, my aunts and relatives, all the married ones are miserable, all except mum's cousin Eileen who lives in Dublin with her partner Liam. A man ten years her junior.'

He looked up for a moment from his plate of pasta and he replied with his mouth full,

'My parents are perfectly happy...'

I played with my pizza. My only thought was the Pill. Tomorrow. We ate our food, in silence, followed by another silence. Eventually after coffee, I regained my ability to actually look at him without feeling like I was sitting with a stranger. He looked at me.

'You're a strange fish, Ella Lovett.'

'Stop sulking.'

'I'm not sulking.'

'We are supposed to be celebrating?'

I filled our wine glasses to the top.

'Happy Birthday to me'. He wiped his mouth on the crisp white napkin.

'What's wrong with you? You're not serious about the marriage and kid's thing are you?'

'I think you've said enough.'

I shoved a large piece of pizza into my mouth. I hadn't realised until this moment that the idea of marriage and kids was enough to make me feel sick. I wasn't sure where these feelings where coming from. It was unchartered waters.

'You have made it clear that you have no intentions of committing to this relationship, Ella.'

'That's not what I said; one doesn't have to have a poxy piece of paper to commit to a relationship.'

'Is that what marriage means to you?'

'No. But I believe it's a very orthodox way of sealing a loving relationship, and it is no reflection of a loving partnership.'

'I think you think too much.'

I looked up to the ceiling.

The restaurant was an old Victorian building with hand-painted Renaissance scenes; naked men draped in white linen, some baring all, frescos of golden cherubs adorned the vaulted ceilings. Because Robert had returned to sulking I decided to pour more wine from the silver chilling bucket of ice which prompted a waiter to come over.

'Is everything okay Madame?'

'Yes thanks, compliments to the chef, is he Italian?'

'Franco is one hundred percent Italian and I will pass on your compliment.'

He cleared our plates.

'Dessert menu, Madame?'

'No.' said Robert, not looking at the waiter.

'Yes please. Thank you.'

The waiter bowed at Robert and smiled at me and left.

'Congratulations on passing your exams, I could be married to a handsome lawyer one day' I said as credibly as I could.

'That's unlikely.'

'Oh yes. I forgot neither of us believes in marriage.'

'I forget how young you are.'

'I'm two years younger than you'

'Look maybe we need a little breathing space.'

'Take all the time you need! Breathe away.'

The waiter arrived with the menu and as he did a bomb went off, close by, totally unexpected, all the beautiful crystal chandeliers shook, along with the plates on our table.

'Dios mio' whispered the waiter as he wandered about aimlessly.

The new double glazed windows at the front of the restaurant shattered, falling gently to pieces on the floor. We looked over at each other, and he quietly took my hand in his, whispering 'I love you, Ella Lovett.'

The waiters held each other, terrified. Someone shouted *'don't move'* and instinctively everyone remained still, as if we were waiting on another blast, sitting ducks.

The Italian proprietor came out of the kitchen, walking around his palace, alone, lost and panic-struck as he looked around the debris, dumbfounded. He was unable to console his customers with comforting words or sound advice. All he could do was mutter Italian prayers. Then some unassuming stranger stood up and wrapped her arms around him, she was a young American lady clearly more emotionally moved by the trauma than the majority of immune Belfast customers, some of whom had returned to their plates with ease.

Robert looked at me calmly.

'Are you okay'?

I smiled back because that's what I always did when I was nervous.

'Yes I'm fine, look I'm sorry, I didn't mean to spoil your night.'

'No, it's me who's sorry.'

The front door was kicked open and an entourage of British soldiers and RUC men came running in pointing guns at various individuals, demanding they get up and go and stand by the wall near the back entrance.

We were escorted outside. The bomb had been in the frequently bombed Europa Hotel. The blast was significant enough to damage most of the surrounding buildings.

I snuggled into Robert on the bus home; there was a silent distance between us. We passed the Europa Hotel and I saw a young woman in a blue silky evening dress lying on a stretcher. Some thugs at the back of the bus joked and laughed as they passed. We saw Nationalist black flags hanging out of two-up-two-down house windows in sympathy with the hunger strikers along the Short Strand area. I had never seen Nationalists display flags before. Up until now I had only seen Union Jacks on display. Robert got off at his stop and I got off at mine.

JACK AND ANNIE

ELLA'S STORY

It was not uncommon to see my father's face up on the parish walls, or occasionally in the Daily Telegraph for some charity he worked with. He was conscientious about his status in the parish and seemed genuinely concerned for the welfare of other people. His knowledge of world hunger gave us a healthy, constant reminder of our state of privilege. When I refused to eat the fried liver, that he and Nana would devour contentedly. I would be reminded of the little starving children in the world who would give anything to eat the slimy sliver of meat I had in front of me.

Jack was a political man in the sense that he never accepted the hypothesis of the Ulster Plantation. He resented that he had to live in a post-colonial Ireland; Ireland being the separate chunk of land that lived next to England. He was distressed by the destruction that ensued over a political conflict, unnecessary injuries and deaths, a conflict which tainted his treasured personal identity; his Irish heritage. He claimed he was open to the concept of a shared Ireland. But really he wanted a united Ireland.

He proclaimed he wasn't a bigot and preached an each-to-their-own policy, but when he saw the Union Jacks being erected and the pavements and poles displaying their red white and blues, he got irritated.

'Bloody thugs and their paraphernalia.'

He hated the large murals which decorated the city walls illustrating political events throughout our history. He also hated traditional Irish music.

He supported the political party Sinn Féin because he said they had worked hard towards supporting the Nationalist communities whom he perceived as the most vulnerable in our society because they had no trust in, or protection from, our police force. He believed Sinn Féin ultimately promoted the concept of having peace on the agenda, despite their attachments with the IRA, he thought the Irish and British Governments had let the North down.

He maintained he had nothing against Protestants but it was clear he loathed the English. This would become apparent when a rugby or football match came on the television; he would support Mongolia before he would support England. It was the same with the Eurovision Song Contest he was delighted when the French voice would announce '*England un point*'. He had become a victim of bigotry to the on-going conflict, as we all had.

When Annie had suddenly become a human being, no longer the miserable lost cause, it was difficult for Jack to embrace. I quite liked the new woman I saw appear, I think it was more difficult for the men in the house.

Jack was losing the woman he married, and he was conflicted because he was turned on by this new woman living in his home, yet he had lost all control of her, she was no longer dependant on him and she almost rejected him because he was seen as the entity who kept her prisoner from being whom she needed to be in the past.

She started to sell her work, which gave her some income. She no longer had to wait for her weekly allowance that went on food and the upkeep of the house. Dad was well off but he didn't squander, except for the expensive suits he wore and the flash car he drove. Annie now regularly arrived home with caviar and champagne that she would share with new friends outside of the family. She was reacting to his years of holding on to the pennies. During her transformation she let go of me and Jack was so distraught at losing her that he let go of me too.

THE SYCAMORE TREE COMPETITION

ELLA'S VERSION

Every year the Cubs and Scouts would pick two names out of a hat and the lucky winners would be sent off on a cross-border outing, where middle-class Catholic and Protestant kids got to mingle for a weekend. The Cubs and Girl Guides would go on an adventure weekend, and the Scouts would act as leaders to the various groups.

I hadn't taken any notice of the competition, because I had no interest in going. Robert had left the Scouts at this stage and I continued going because I was habitual by nature and because it got me out of the house. Sadly, this year I was the lucky winner.

Robert hadn't phoned since the night we went out for dinner; he was still sulking with me. I had left messages with him to call me but got no response. I was happy for the breath of air, because it was all becoming a little too intense. I knew in the pit of my stomach that we were over, but I knew that as soon as I saw him that he would give me his come-to-bed eyes and I would fall for it. My head and my heart were sending mixed messages.

Annie was sitting in the kitchen with Nana. Often Annie would sit with her little box of water colours and paint whatever came into her head. Nana was knitting a hat for the parish jumble sale.

'Does anyone want tea?'

'Yes' was the unanimous reply. I lifted the already boiling kettle off the range. Nana sat at one end of the old oak kitchen table and Annie sat at the other. Annie was sketching some pears she had placed on the table. I put the cups out.

'There's a wee treat in the fridge. Be a love and put them out.'

I went to the fridge with anticipation and was a little

disappointed at the sight of a plate of flapjacks.

'Did you think any more about the cross border trip, Ella?'

'I did, and I decided not to go, it'll be full of Christian Prods and Catholic do-gooders'.

'Sounds like just the thing you need.' Nana sneered,

'Meaning what?'

'When is it?'

'It's from Friday to Monday, and I just said, I decided not to go, Nana'

Annie looked at me and smiled.

'I think it's a great idea, Ella darling. What do you think Nana?'

'I don't see why not, as long as she can behave herself, Annie.'

'Well, I'm sure there's not a lot they could get up on a peace camp.'

'Hello, I'm here!'

'Ella you know those new boots you wanted. Well?'

'The ones you promised me you would buy me?'

'The ones I said I would buy you, if you were good to me.'

'I'm always good to you.'

'Well be a good girl and say yes to the peace camp.'

'Why are you so adamant, I go?'

'It will help you get over that boy you were with. What's his name?'

'Robert and what do you mean ....?'

I looked over at Nana who guiltily stuck her face in her sewing

'You couldn't hold water!'

'You have a point; it's quite common at my age! When are you going on this trip again?

'I will repeat myself, I am not going.'

'Oh yes you are'.

THE SYCAMORE TREE CAMP

WILL'S VERSION

A dramatic violet-grey sky shot rain that pelted against my bedroom window which was framed by the red tartan curtains I had picked many years ago from British Home Stores. I loved being in a warm bed when the weather was like this. Father had left several hours ago; he was amazingly disciplined and always took to his vocation with one hundred percent.

I forced myself up from the comfort of my duvet so as to get a bus to the annual 'Sycamore Tree Event' of Cross Border Peace Camps.

I had promised I would give a hand and I was keeping my promise. Annemarie was possibly going to help out as well and it might be an opportunity for me to redeem myself with her.

I was taking a bunch of local school kids who had been chosen from various schools and backgrounds to Tullymore National Park. Once there, we would meet with other young people, Catholic and Protestant, and engage in various outdoor activities and camp fires. It was actually quite good fun. The key was to forget the religious backgrounds and enjoy each other's company for the people we were.

When our bus finally pulled into the beautiful grounds of the park, after Orange songs had been sung, and several kids threw up, I was eager to disembark. The team leaders had already arrived by car. Annemarie was with them and she looked as gorgeous as always. I went straight over to her, possibly with a little too much enthusiasm and she was a little curt with me but not rude. I didn't blame her. She appeared to be very chatty with the team leader Dave, who was at least five years her senior. He was enjoying her attention so I went off to light a fire and sort out some kids with their sleeping arrangements.

We got settled into our bunks, and I was given a room overlooking the bay. When I opened the window I could hear the waves gushing in.

The Catholic bus pulled up and I went over to greet them. Their pale young faces disembarking the bus with the enthusiasm of a group being sent to the gas chamber. The last person to get off the bus was making a bit of a calamity and then she appeared laden with bags.

Imagine my surprise when I saw Ella Lovett step out of the bus, I didn't think she would recognise me, in fact part of me hoped she wouldn't, in case she would remember the taunting.

'Hey, aren't you the guy who calls me fenian bitch from across the road first thing in the morning?'

'Sorry?'

'It's Will isn't it? We met before'.

'Yes, Ella!'

I managed a smile and put my hand out; she shook it and smiled back.

'Ella, the girl you sometimes smile over at, except when in libraries.'

My face burned and she just kept her gaze and smiled coyly.

'Hi, Ella, welcome to the peace camp.'

Ella, like me, was an assistant camp leader to a group of fifteen kids or so that arrived from various Scout groups and clubs. There were sixty kids in total and four leaders. Ella wore her pale blue Scout uniform which I have to say was rather cute; I liked uniforms.

Our job was to pair up a Catholic with a Protestant and to keep an eye on things. I noted Ella was a bit of a loner but nurturing towards the kids. I had spotted her earlier tying a young boy's shoelace; she appeared to be a magnet for the kids. She played hopscotch and tidily-winks with them. After I showed off my knot tying skills I approached and her warm smile was inviting.

'I didn't expect to see you getting off the bus.'

She looked up at me silent for a moment.

'And why would that be?'

'I didn't think you would be into this sort of thing.'

'And what sort of thing do you think I might be into, Will?'

'You've got me there, I have no idea, but you're very welcome.'

'Whoopee.'

'It can be good fun.'

She threw the eyes to heaven and looked at her watch.

'Two days, six hours and around thirty-three minutes left.'

'Why did you come?'

'Because my parents made me.'

'I see. The orienteering can be a good laugh and we are planning a bonfire tomorrow night on the beach.'

'Will there be any booze?'

'Unlikely'.

'You don't drink then?'

'No, I made a pledge.'

'Bags of fun!'

'You don't need booze to have fun.'

'Is that so, oh wise one.'

'Why not give it a try?'

'Look, Will, I know you have good intentions, but the bottom line is I'm not really into this sort of thing, so can we leave it at that?'

'Fine.'

We had lunch; I gave out the rules for the walks, and went looking for Annemarie. She was setting up a tent outside with Dave, part of the skills programme. She was getting confused and Dave was laughing at her in a playful manner.

'Hi Will, want to give us a hand?'

She asked, I did and no sooner had I joined them, than Dave went into super tent-maker mode with the speed of light, Annemarie and I sat and watched. As we talked,

Annemarie relaxed more. I made an attempt to apologise for Sam's behaviour on the night of his birthday and I quickly reiterated that the magazines were not mine. She changed the subject to tent erecting. The kids joined in and we finished putting up another tent as an exercise and then we instructed the group to take it down again while we started preparing for the orienteering. Each team of boys had to pick a partner from the other side, preferably someone they didn't know.

The losing team would make dinner whilst the winners could lounge in the living room with a box of Cadbury's Roses and relax.

The rain came and went by way of heavy showers with short breaks of sunshine. Ella and I paired up with one half of the group. Dave and Annemarie went with the other half. Ella was good, when she saw the other team approach she got our team to pretend that we hadn't found the last clue which made them relax a little more and take their time. She worked out the clues in no time but she wouldn't tell the kids the answer and she encouraged them to work it out, we finished in good time and got back to base as the winning team.

Ella and the kids collapsed in front of the fire. Later I thought I might make the most of the nice part of the day and decided to head out for a short walk down to the nearby beach.

As I was leaving Annemarie caught me.

'Do you mind if I join you?'

She was dressed in a pristine white vest through which I could clearly define her ample, rounded breasts, and a rather short pair of shorts that equally defined the ample roundness of her buttocks. No wonder the young boys' eyes followed her every move. As we walked, she talked and talked, mostly about her love for school. And as she talked I kept noticing her cleavage, which was not good mainly because she had already labelled me as a porn freak and also because these glimpses were not good for my aspirations to remain totally celibate until my not-so-near coming future wedding day. I wasn't great around girls; I was, in fact, hopeless. What made matters worse was as soon as we clambered over the sand dunes and got to the beach, the sky turned black and opened up, drowning us in cold wet rain. This made Annemarie's breasts and buttocks unbearable to look at. I made a U-turn back for the house. She jogged behind me, up the said sand dunes, bouncing with every step and when we reached a particularly steep bit I held out my hand in case she would slip.

'Christ, my hair will be destroyed!' she said in a moody tone, as she wiped her mascara-blackened eyes. I held out my hand and helped her up the sand dune. She must have noticed me looking at her cleavage which had just been within reach of my nostrils.

'What are you gaping at, Will.'

'Nothing, nothing.'

When we got back from our walk and got changed for dinner, I found Ella sitting at the fire surrounded by the kids listening to her telling them ghost stories. I left Annemarie and Dave to the cooking. We had burnt sausages and beans on toast, in the 'Sycamore tree' tradition. The kids went to bed and we older ones sat up reading.

That evening I had to wait on Ella going to bed before me, as we had to share a room. I had insisted that Dave and I should share a room and Annemarie and Ella should share the other but Dave had had other ideas. When I got to bed at half twelve that night Ella was fast asleep so I didn't bother to switch on the light. I just lay and listened to her snoring like a hamster.

The following morning was a busy schedule; canoeing and archery followed by a nature trail in search of different species of plants and evident animal trails. I was good at all of the above. Annemarie, who was obviously a morning person like me, sporting a low cut pink v-neck tee-shirt and joggings pants, helped clear away the breakfast dishes much to the delight of the young boys whom I eventually managed to get into their life-jackets for the canoeing. Dave arrived downstairs with a broad grin which was clearly directed at Annemarie and she responded with a similar eagerness. He then swooped past her and I was sure I saw him gently stroking her buttocks as he passed; I lowered my head immediately. What surprised me though was that I wasn't too upset, I could deal with it. There was no sign of Ella, who was supposed to be giving me a hand organising the group. I waited until half ten and then I went up for her. I called out her name at the top of the stairs in the hope that she would shout back if she was still in bed. Nothing. I got to our room. I prised open the door and saw her lying there still asleep peacefully in her white lace vest, both hands resting under her right cheek, her sallow skin beautiful. Silent.

I quickly stepped outside the door for fear of being spotted.

'Ella' I whispered as loudly as I could and she awoke.

'Will?'

'It's half ten; we should be in our canoes.'

'I'm not going canoeing, didn't Dave tell you? I've never canoed in my life.'

I laughed.

'That's okay. I can teach you.'

Silence, followed by more silence which left me stuck. Was she up or not?

'You can come in you know, we do share the room and I am decent.'

So I stepped in and there she was standing in her little lace vest and matching knickers. I was instantly aroused. So I turned and walked straight out of the room and I know she knew because she was smiling. I went to the bathroom and threw cold water on my face, and when I saw my reflection in the mirror I snarled.

I went down stairs to the overly-excited kids who seemed to be jumping around like beanbags.

'Okay settle down! How many of you have canoed before?'

Three hands out of twenty shot up.

'Great.'

I give them my speech on safety and the importance of working as a team and they all yawned. Ella appeared and they seemed to brighten up. She grabbed some fruit and we headed out to the beach via the minibus. The kids took turns to get into the water; some highly excited, others terrified at the prospect, but we managed to get everyone in and I was impressed I managed to have them all canoeing without any mishaps as Ella sat on the beach and watched. By late afternoon everyone was in except Ella who was now being coaxed by twenty young little faces.

'Go on, you'll be fine. Will can mind you, can't you Will?'

'It's not that difficult, it's easy once you get started.'

But there was no movement. So I started the bluck bluck chicken rant gently much to the kids' great amusement, not so much to Ella's. She eventually gave in and got into the canoe. She was terrified, I enjoyed this. I strapped her in, which allowed me a few moments of closeness. I instructed her as best I could which was difficult between the whispers of:

'If this fucking thing topples over there will be severe fucking consequences.'

'Remember to keep the knees taut.' I replied with patience.

'You're fucking dead if anything happens!'

The canoe set off into the thankfully very clear, calm waters of a beautiful sunny afternoon with some ease, I paddled behind in my canoe. Nothing but us, the ocean and twenty onlookers. Ella seemed to relax, she was smiling and taking in the breath taking view of the Mourne mountains.

'Ease off on the paddling, we will head back soon.' I shouted from my canoe. She was positively glowing with pride.

'Cool.'

We paddled out into the blue water still and calm, I

looped around she followed and we headed back to the shore. All was going great until a speed boat went whizzing by about twenty feet away causing a sequence of rapid larger waves and she started to wobble.

'What to fuck Will... Will! Get me out of this fucking thing.'

'It's okay Ella, just stiffen your knees, stay still and let it pass.'

The canoe wobbled more and she frantically started using her paddle either side.

'Stop paddling Ella, relax and remember to ...' and in she went, the canoe capsized. I raced over and there was no sign of her so I upturned my canoe, dived into the water to find her and she popped her head up, spitting.

'Bastard, Bastard, Bastard'

I didn't know whether to laugh or cry; I finally put to practice my lifesaving skills and swam back with Ella, when we got close to the shore she struggled free.

'Are you okay?'

'What do you think?'

She climbed out of the water and continued to cough, she was visibly shaking. I took off her life jacket and wrapped her in my spare fleece, I put my arms around her and she started to cry, she was genuinely terrified.

'It's okay, you're safe now,'

I planted a kiss on her cheek and she sank back into my arms again. The kids came over and comforted her with me which brought back a smile.

'Will. The next time I tell you that I don't want to do something, accept it as a given.'

'Sorry.'

We were scheduled to go up the Mourne mountain trail for the afternoon, I suggested she take a break but she decided to come along. We set off in a mild drizzle of rain. The kids seemed to be bonding well and, despite earlier events, so were Ella and I. She wanted to travel, possible study nursing, a solid income, 'whatever it takes' being her very words; not sure on babies or marriage and she dreamed that one day there would be peace and we would all live in a united Ireland. I noticed Ella didn't really volunteer conversation unless I initiated it; she was quite introverted despite giving the initial impression of being extroverted. When she smiled a dimple would appear in her left cheek. I did my best to impress her with my mapping skills but she was way ahead of me.

That night, I was exhausted, so I decided to go to bed early. Ella looked like she was up for the duration.

I awoke at around one o-clock in the morning to Ella climbing into the bed beside me. She snuggled up. She felt so good. I opened my eyes and looked down into her face, she smiled up at me.

'Is this okay with you? I'm cold' she whispered.

'Yes.'

She was cold when she climbed in and I put my arms around her, it felt like the natural thing to do, in minutes the heat between us became intense, and I kissed her on the lips for what seemed like an eternity, our lips couldn't part. It wasn't hard and passionate, it was slow and intimate.

About an hour later I suggested we sleep because I was terrified as to what might happen next. She sensed my fear, kissed me on the nose, gently caressed my cock and turned over to sleep. I prayed for strength. We slept for about half an hour and I woke and kissed her. As soon as she touched my cock, I melted, this continued until I had no choice but to surrender.

I woke at seven, exhausted but alive as in really alive.

That morning we had to climb Slieve Donnard. We had mountain maps and packed snacks. We set off around nine and the sky appeared to be clear, the sun was strong. It was a beautiful day. We made it to the summit by half twelve; the kids were exhausted but quietly exhilarated. Shortly after our snacks on top the mountain, the grey sky turned blue and Ella convinced the girls to cover their faces in mud, claiming the benefits far outweighed the ridiculousness. She was the first to cover herself in mud, most the kids followed suit and they bathed in the sun beside the lake. Later they washed their faces in the fresh mountain water. I was slightly envious at her ability to let go and just be. She even managed to get Annemarie to cover her heavily made-up face in mud. The kids started to pretend to be animals; the game was to guess which one. It was verging on the absurd.

'What else do you get up to outside of school and karate? Do you listen to music?'

'I like to play the flute.'

'Oh, cool, are you with a group or orchestra?'

'Yes. I play for the Loyal Black Presbytery, for the Lodge.'

There was silence and it wasn't comfortable.

'You're an Orangeman.'

She was making sure we were clear.

'Yes.'

'I see, I didn't know you were involved in that sort of thing.'

I waited a moment.

'That sort of thing has been in my family for generations. It's not as bad as you think.'

'You don't know what I think.'

'I think you are not impressed I am a member of the Orange Lodge'

'You are right, I am not impressed, if you must know, I think they are provoking orange bastards.'

Silence followed and a distance as big as the Atlantic Ocean fell between the recent warmth.

We were first back to base camp, which caused even further awkwardness; she kept walking away from me when I approached her. I hated the fact that I had emotions I didn't want or didn't like erupting in my being because I had already developed feelings for this woman. She was like a magnet. All I wanted to do was kiss her again. I went up to our room while she was making dinner and I prayed. I tried desperately to get in touch with my inner voice; my Godliness. The voice my father had preached to us about since we could stand. He would advise impure thoughts to be given over to God who would dispel such things, God would then cleanse our souls and such thoughts would disappear.

'Evil will always lurk behind you but Jesus is always there ready to catch you, trust in Jesus.'

Trust in Jesus. She was sulking because I was an Orangeman. My inner voice started to activate logically. 'She's a Catholic; Mother would hate it, because Father would detest it. There is no hope or future for us, this is lust.'

When I came down to offer my assistance in the kitchen she had kids begging to help, one was in an apron putting the final touches on to the apple pie. All was done. Our dinner was homemade chips, with homemade burgers. She had made a pie with apples from the tree outside. She had the kids raid it. The kids were ecstatic. We were all ecstatic; we had been living on burnt offerings until now.

'You didn't mention you were a domestic Goddess' said Dave,

'I wasn't aware that I was one.'

She smiled at him as she handed him his plate. This caused me a pang of jealously that felt like a stabbing pain. I was out of control.

We had decided to build a bonfire that evening and cook marshmallows on sticks. Dave was expert at this sort of thing, in fact Dave was expert at most things when it came to displaying manliness. He had trained in the defence forces as a young adolescent. His youthfulness was eternal. His tight hair cut matched his tight jeans, his bulging biceps, and his hard-earned six-pack. His enthusiasm was a little frightening; he did everything at speed, swinging sledgehammers into large blocks of wood that split in two with one shot. Lighting the fire with a small bunch of twigs, as if by magic. I had spent the guts of an hour searching for dry wood and brought back wet wood that I had viciously tackled from a dead log causing minor injuries, Ella and Annemarie seemed impressed by

Dave; they stood by his side ready to obey any orders to keep the camp running smoothly. Annemarie was sent off for matches, Ella was asked to get the marshmallows. It appeared she was happy to oblige in anything rather than be around me. I gave up and sat with the kids.

After all the fuss of fire and food we relaxed around the glowing fire, it was a beautiful evening, the sky was a cloak of deep blue streaked with long strips of red. The big yellow moon peeped out of the scattered grey clouds. I did everything I could not to look over at her. I taught some of the kids tricks with knots on a rope. Dave brought out his guitar. He badly strummed a few well-known melodies slightly out of tune; he even attempted a song, but was booed off by the kids. He tried to get them to sing but they wouldn't. The moon lit up all our faces, and the sea could be heard in amongst the pauses. Some of the kids headed off to bed. I wanted to wait until Ella had gone to bed.

'Anyone need anything back at the house?' I asked.

'Grab me a jumper, if you're in our room!' shouted Ella.

Embarrassed for no rational reason at hearing those words 'our room' I left and wandered into the dark.

When I returned to the fire there was a silence, just the sea. I threw Ella my warmest jumper and our eyes met with a smile. Then I lifted my flute out of its case.

Much to her surprise I played 'Black is the Colour' a song I had learned from a Nina Simone album my mother loved. She played it so often I had picked it up by ear. Suddenly she opened her voice and began to sing. The words travelled into the landscape resonating back. Everyone around the campfire lay still and listened amazed at the magic of our harmony.

Two or three songs later, Ella went to bed. Shortly after, I followed.

LOVE IS IN THE AIR

ELLA'S STORY

Three hours of a nauseating bus journey with obnoxious kids making me feel suicidal made being met off the bus by Will Goodie a rather welcome surprise. He resisted being bold. But I did my best to persuade him. I have three problems. First problem is that Robert was waiting for me with a stupid grin and a bunch of yellow dahlias at the bus station on our return trip to Belfast which caused Will to think he was my boyfriend, which was partially true. The second problem and probably a little more serious is that Will is an Orangeman. I can't go out with an Orangeman. Repeat can't go out with an Orange man.

I feel nothing but contempt for the Orange Order. They have caused murders, provocation, and bigotry and widespread hatred. They have advocated animosity towards Catholics for generations. So I'm not quite so sure what he or I was thinking of. They burn Tricolours on top of their fires; I even saw a statue of the Pope once on top of one of those bonfires. Nana nearly lost her breath when she recognised the little head of John Paul sticking out atop of the piles of gathered wood.

'Bastards 'she proclaimed. 'Dirty rotten bastards' Nana never used that language.

And my third problem, which is the most serious of all, is that I really, really like him.

FRED

WILL'S STORY

I asked Ella to contact me when she had got rid of the boyfriend. I was in a confused state regarding what had happened. It had been almost a week, I was missing her terribly. I did everything I could to distract myself.

We walked our usual route on the Newtownards Road that morning in the bright summer sunshine, our heads held high. I received a great applause from the standing families for my solo flute. Sam was the only one from our Brigade given the Lambeg drum to play and we felt, I believe, proud as any family could feel for giving such a positive contribution to our community.

There had been a lot of media controversy and on-going talks surrounding the Drumcree route. It was becoming, ultimately, the platform for what I now see as terminal damage to the Loyal Orange Lodge. We understood well why the Catholics would oppose us marching up Drumcree Road. To be honest, I am confident we would have consented to a re-route except the only possible re-route in question was miles out and there was mounting pressure on our backs regarding our lack of courage and moral values, to stand our ground. We had walked that route for decades.

The walk got off to a good start. The sky was a clear azure blue scattered with clouds as if someone had spilled water unto a watercolour page. The atmosphere was light. The walkers were led by a large group from the Royal Ulster Constabulary otherwise known as the police, some of whom rode on silk-adorned horseback, with men clad in leathers and knee-high boots. Leading the walkers was the traditional Orange Lil, a lady who danced in her much anticipated costume of an orange taffeta dress, with orange accessories such as a frilled parasol occasionally lifting her skirts for the boys revealing the PVC Union Jack knickers to roars of excitement from the crowds lining the street. We passed houses and played our music and beat the drums in harmony. Some elderly neighbours came out with their flags in support.

We had been strictly warned not to pause outside the Catholic residences on the road. But, of course, the usual trouble-makers blocked us, keeping back the walkers behind them and beating their drums louder than ever outside these houses, vacant or occupied, always with drawn curtains. They paused outside Ella's house and beat their drums.

Ella lived in one of the big Victorian houses opposite Stormont gates. Ella's house was the nicest; it had a wisteria purple creeper climbing wildly over the front and sweet pea through the hedge. A large cherry tree hung over the front wall. I had often questioned why her family would choose to live in such a built-up Protestant area. As we approached her house, I looked for any sign of life but there was nothing, the blue velvet curtains were drawn closed. Then, out of nowhere, oblivious to our glory she tiptoed out the big front door still wearing her paisley-patterned pyjamas to collect the milk that had been left at the front door. She didn't look up; I wanted her to see me in my uniform. I wanted her to smile with approval, impressed with what she saw but I got a poke in the back from my father who was walking directly behind me. I had created a gap in the walk. I continued to walk and I looked back just as she was going back inside and she looked up, I saw her fear and I prayed she wouldn't see me.

Later that evening after the walk, we went up to the field as was tradition; we would have our picnics with our families and listen to speeches given by the senior Orange Lodge members. Occasionally we would have speakers from America or Australia, or other celebrities such as Dr Ian Paisley. We, as a family, never had alcohol, but usually had a few cheese sandwiches and chocolate bars with tea.

We generally listened to the speeches and then went home. Many others stayed for the fun of more music and beer after. Some were still drunk from the night before.

Sam had pleaded this time to stay a little longer. Mother had asked me to stay and chaperone him, much to my distaste, as I knew Spider would be in top form. However as thoughts of Ella flooded my mind I managed to relax a little, I even played a few tunes on the flute. The moon was almost full and it was a warm balmy summer evening. Spider lay on the grass, and listened to some of the others talk for a change.

Fred Baxter, a young impressionable, who was sixteen going on sixty, played the flute like a leprechaun. He captivated us in his tales of travels as a child. His father lived in the States, in Arizona and he got to see him, at most, once a year. His parents were separated, but when they were together they bummed it around the globe selling anything from dusters to fraudulent insurance scams. Sam joked about how it would suit him fine to see his father once a year.

'My father's in prison, he has been for the last ten years.' contributed Simon.

'When will he get out?' asked Fred.

'Five more years, and before you ask, he went down for murder. But it was self-defence. And more power to him, one Fenian less to worry about.'

The others smiled.

'What's he like?' I asked.

'He's sound, good on the old flute like yourself.'

'Do you visit?'

'No'

'My Dad's dead.' said Spider, lying in the grass, like he was talking about the weather. 'It's better, for all of us.'

A heavy silence filled the air. Silence continued and Spider lifted an unlit joint to his mouth.

'A light.'

Fred jumped to attention and lit the joint. The joint was passed and no mention of my refusing it.

I played a few mellow tunes and Fred joined in.

Fred would have jumped ten feet high if he could have gained approval from Spider. Fred lived with his mother in the same run-down estate as Spider did. Later that evening as we all walked towards the bus, he thanked me for the tunes and asked me if I could give him a few lessons on the flute.

'What's it worth?'

'Cigarettes, or I am good at fixing bicycles.'

'Bicycle, done deal.'

We shook hands.

We stood in our dog-eared uniforms waiting on the number twenty bus, tired and contented with the day's events.

A group of Catholic youths, out of their heads on drink and drugs, appeared and started throwing stones at us. One of the stones hit Spider in the side of his face, causing it to bleed. Sam had been walking alongside him but was, thankfully, unharmed. The general public dispersed and a fight broke out between us and them. Sam ran after the Catholic kids and I ran after him.

'Leave me alone.' he yelled

I pulled him aside and held him steady

'Sam, it's dangerous, they have bottles.'

We heard a yell and bottles being smashed, another gang of youths appeared from nowhere and joined in. We watched the youths attack each other viciously. Yelling and screams could be heard, then there was an eerie silence and our gang were circling a young boy lying on the ground. I could hear a police siren approach from the distance and then gun shots could be heard, again in the distance.

The young boy was Fred. He was white, his face slightly tilted to one side, his mouth slightly open, drawing in a little breath. I knelt down beside him, he was laid on his side, and when I pulled up his jacket I could see the gashes, he had been stabbed in the back. He lay in a pool of his own blood.

'Call an ambulance, quick. NOW!'

His eyes were rolling in his head. The Catholics ran, dispersed like rats. Fred closed his eyes.

I took his hand and I could feel his small warm hand grip mine gently, Spider knelt down beside me.

'Come on, Fred, there's an ambulance on the way.' said Spider, his eyes filling with tears.

'Tell my Mum, I love her.'

Spider took off his jacket and wrapped it around Fred's young body. But I could feel the warmth disappearing from his fingers. An ambulance arrived. Too late. Spider gently closed his eyes before they lifted the body into the ambulance. I put my arm around Sam and he came with me quietly.

Later that evening I questioned everything I believed in. This was cold-blooded murder and for what? Because of a walk. When I got home I went straight to bed and I curled up and imagined her lying beside me.

LIFE IS A GIFT AND IT IS YOURS TO LEARN HOW TO RECEIVE NOT TO EARN

ELLA'S STORY

Jack's disorder was apparent when he poured his daily glass of milk with raw egg for breakfast. His hand would shake so badly he sometimes didn't make the glass. This was followed by his morning scan of the rattling 'Times' newspaper.

Jack held his own can of worms close to his heart. At night when the house finally held its own with the occasional grunts or snores, usually coming from Nana's room, he would visit my room for his nightly story and goodnight kiss. I would sometimes have asked him about his past. But he would always give me a colourful picture of an idyllic childhood. I slowly gathered a more realistic picture from Nana. His father had escaped a bombing which had left a scar psychologically during World War Two. This had warranted my grandfather the nickname, *'the ghost.'* Jack's older brothers, Charlie and Marcus, immigrated to Boston America to work as labourers. Charlie moved on to real estate and married a nice young American girl, Emily, who turned out to be not so nice after all. Emily developed eating disorders which resulted in her not being able to conceive a child and after several tempestuous years they got divorced. Charlie lived alone in a down-town Boston apartment for the next twenty years, apparently with a bottle of Black Bush for comfort, until he died of cancer. He came home twice in all the time he lived over there. Marcus was different, he was the more confident brother, a trait Nana fuelled; he got into journalism in the States and wrote for a local paper. He then got a good job in London and moved to write for the 'London Herald'. Later he married Ying Li, a quietly-

125

spoken Japanese girl; and fathered a little boy, Christopher. They occasionally came over to visit. Annie and Nana liked Ying Li and occasionally Nana would go over to visit them. Dad never did because he never had time to go.

Jack's first childhood home, a small two-up-two-down, had once been burnt out in an arson attack as had the homes of many of his Catholic neighbours. The house at one time had temporarily sheltered IRA terrorists, as had most of the neighbouring houses in the area. It was compulsory to leave the front door unlocked in case someone on the run needed a quick exit from front to back door, a fast escape route. If one didn't, one would suffer the consequences. If one did, one was a possible target.

Jack was a late surprise for Nana, his brothers had reached their mid-teens when he arrived and Nana was determined to get it right with him. Jack was sent to the posh school in town, disciplined enough with the occasional whack across the knuckles but nothing like the regular abuse the others endured. The others were schooled with boys who would inevitably join up with terrorists. When Charlie and Marcus entered their mid-teens the pressure on them to join up was just another reason for Nana and Granddad to encourage them to emigrate. Granddad saved every penny he had to help send them over to the American Dream via an aunt of his who had emigrated twenty years previous. Nana did her best to try and shelter Jack from the realities around her, he was like her shadow, and she often took him into town or to the cinema.

Years later when Jack qualified as a solicitor he was inundated with requests from his brothers' old school mates. This was what prompted him to move across town, albeit into a predominately Protestant area.

Jack was often faced with a dilemma because of his Nationalist roots. His dilemma was *'the cause'*. He dedicated himself to the cause through his work as a solicitor defending Nationalists which put him at risk regarding his safety. He was very good at what he did. The cases piled up and the money came in, some clients guilty, some innocent. Success in winning cases was often rewarded with lavish gifts, like cases of whiskey; other offers included possible stolen goods, cars, or tickets to America. It was the opposition he needed to watch, they kept a close eye and let him know by way of graffiti or broken windows. He loved his work, but over time the pressure and concern for his safety took its toll. His frown-line visibly deepened and the permanent black bags under his eyes signalled his resistance was cracking. He was reliant on tablets and alcohol to keep him functioning. He began working more often at home, more for his safety than anything else. He got regular phone calls during the night of bogus bomb scares in his office in town which would mean he would have to get up and go into town in the small hours of the morning and wait with the police and bomb squad to give the all clear.

After the Shankhill Butchers case, Protestant paramilitaries made several attempts to burn his office down. They even managed to break in and steal important documents he had filed on prisoners. He started becoming paranoid about being followed and would often quiz me and the rest of the family about the possibility of us being followed. Sometimes I would start getting paranoid because an army truck might follow me walking up a street in town and point a gun at me. Nana started watching her back also and would hurry about when she was out shopping; keeping a close eye on everything around her. Annie and Luke were oblivious. Slowly the stress crept up on Jack and he would binge drink. He rarely made it to bed when he binged. Annie disappeared to her hideaway in Donegal and would return every now and then and pretend that all was wonderful. Denial was her coping mechanism.

As the months passed his paranoia became more evident, with little tell-tale signs that all may not be well. He would come downstairs from his attic office and close the red velvet curtains in the living room and drawing room by six in the evening. So the front of the house was in darkness. He sipped whisky slowly and methodically throughout the day and got short-tempered at the slightest little things. He lived in his own world and very slowly anyone else's became irrelevant.

We were forbidden to leave our bicycles or any indication of our identity outside the house in open view. Jack insisted I was to be driven to school in the morning. This was difficult as Annie was rarely at home, Nana had stopped driving out of fear and Jack was usually so hung-over that he, in reality, was more of a risk to me than any Protestant thug. I hated his lifts to school; I had developed a zero tolerance for the after-smell of his alcohol fuelled solitude from the night before which had become absorbed into the leather seats of the now aging Mercedes Benz.

When Annie returned without any warning, for another brief visit, delighted to see us all, she would tidy and decorate with ease, which would totally transform the dull but organised home that Nana had spent the week perfecting. Suddenly large white lilies or exotic fruits would appear. Occasionally new works of art would appear on the walls.

We just accepted her conduct without question. I had made attempts to challenge her regarding Jack but was met with bouts of sulking. Conflict was a no-go area in our household, it was too explosive. Nana, in particular, held the belief that it was best to '*let sleeping dogs lie*' as it meant she could maintain some kind of control. In earlier years when Annie challenged Jack about his drinking, although Nana agreed, she still tried to defend him.

'Isn't a man entitled to wind down after a hard day's work Annie?'

These words would be swallowed later with lament. Annie would sometimes try and persuade Jack to join her for an art opening or a ballet but he declined so often she just gave up. He would insist she was mad going out on the town in such precarious times. She maintained her attitude expressing that if we didn't go out and celebrate life we were letting terrorists win. And the more he would try and dissuade her from going out, the more determined she would become. Sometimes I accompanied her, I liked going to the art galleries and I liked looking at art and seeing her mingle, and being happy. Sometimes I felt a bit like an accessory.

Nana didn't understand how a wife could neglect her duties the way Annie did. Such behaviour would not have been tolerated in her day. Nana clandestinely blamed Annie for Jack's decline. She would make suggestions to Annie on a regular basis and always with a polite smile.

'Jack needs his shirt ironed for his big case tomorrow.'

'I don't iron Nana, besides; he has specifically requested I don't because I do it the wrong way.'

She didn't iron her own clothes, and oddly nothing ever looked liked it needed ironing when she wore it. Silk didn't need ironing. So Nana added the job of ironing to her already overloaded list of chores.

Sometimes she would change her mind and stay in. But instead of him entertaining her as he used to in the drawing room over a few drinks, he would retreat to his office in the attic. She would sit with us and watch an old movie or play a game of scrabble. As I grew older I began to admire the woman I called Annie, despite her lack of hugs.

Things came to a head on May 4th 1981. It was a Saturday night and Annie had bought two tickets to see Van Morison, because she loved him. Luke had inspired Annie to listen to Van, and Jack was looking forward to the concert; he had managed to recreate some of Van's music on his saxophone. He was working on a case involving a guy who was wrongfully imprisoned. This was an area he was growing passionate about. He believed that a substantial number of Nationalists prisoners were being put inside to simply keep them off the streets. He apparently had the evidence to prove it, this was his big day in court and we all had our fingers crossed that he would win it because recently he had lost a few cases, which seemed to set him back.

Robert and I had agreed to see each other occasionally, as mates, with less emphasis on being a couple. He arrived early. He was eager because we hadn't seen each other since the day he embarrassed me outside of the bus stop on my way home from the Peace Camp. I hadn't heard from Will either. I wasn't one for chasing.

Robert was looking particularly attractive this evening. He was wearing the black shirt I had bought him for his birthday which matched his soft black corduroys that he had worn on the night of his seventeenth birthday. When he stood beside Annie they looked a perfect match. She too was dressed in black, a slimming black dress and heels. She looked amazing for her age. I felt a hint of jealousy; I knew she looked better than me because she made the effort and I didn't.

'You're looking exquisite tonight, Robert.'

'And you are looking lovely, Mrs Lovett' Robert smiled teeth showing, like a monkey.

'Where are you two off to tonight then?'

'Has Dad not got back yet?'

'No darling, late again, unlike Robert, who is always on time, tea Robert?'

At that I threw my eyes to heaven and went off into the kitchen to find my faithful friend Nana, who was sat, glued to the radio waiting for the latest news on Bobby Sands. She put her finger up to her mouth to hush me when I went to speak. *'Police and army have detonated three bombs in North Belfast today, the bombs were intended to target the Lyons club a well-known Nationalist club....'*

So I then went up to my bedroom and sat in front of my mirror at my dresser and applied a little eye shadow. This plain Jane looked back; pale-skinned and washed-out looking. Then I heard a knock, and Robert walked in without waiting for a response, he prowled around the room impatiently.

'Are you ready to go?'

'Should I put on some makeup?'

'No.'

'Why don't you go down and chat with Mum. Two more minutes'.

'I told Michael we would be in Fox's by eight.'

I went through my wardrobe and everything looked miserable, greys, purples, and blacks hung alongside the putrid green school uniform. So I went into Annie's bedroom and went over to her wardrobe and found myself a little green dress which she no longer fitted into and I put it on. Then I sat at my Mother's dressing table which was covered in bottles and tubes of everything a girl would need and I began covering my pale face with foundation then powder and rouge, then eye shadows and liners, finished off with a mix of expensive perfumes. Then when I looked into the mirror I saw a young woman who resembled a young tart looking back at me. Just then Annie walked in.

'What are you doing Ella?'

When I stood up and looked at her she laughed so loud, I wanted to hit her; I wanted to kill her.

'What's so funny?'

'You look absolutely ridiculous Ella; you're not going anywhere looking like that.'

She walked over to me and made me stand up and look at myself in the long mirror.

I saw a sad innocent little girl, dolled up like a geisha, grown up before her time.

'I just wanted to look nice for Robert.'

'For Robert? Ella, you are beautiful just as you are and if Robert doesn't see that he's a fool.'

'Can I not look sexy too?'

Feeling like an idiot, grabbing the cleansing wipes from her dresser, I wiped away my face. After a momentary silence she looked at me more carefully, doing her best not to smile.

She went to her wardrobe and pulled out a pair of pillar-box red patent killer heels and out of nowhere she pulled out a little black velvet dress and handed them to

131

me.

I put them on and they both fitted like a glove.

'Sit down.'

For once I did as I was told and she got a wad of cotton wool and cleansers and wiped away my tart pout and rosy red cheeks, she tested various shades of brown and pinks on the back of my hand,

'What do you think of that one?'

I didn't really notice a difference between them, but responded with anticipation,

'Yes, that's nice.'

Like a true artist she transformed me. Her long manicured fingers, made gentle brush strokes of pink rouge across my face and I could feel her warm sweet breath go down my neck as she applied eyelash tinted paint and eye lid shadows of purple and pinks. It was like magic.

The Victorian white dresser we sat at had a round mirror which she had adorned with movie star light bulbs; a few old black and white photographs of her and Jack at a dance, both looking beautiful lit up in their romance; another one of her when she was a child of about four, a cutie with masses of blonde curls on her father's knee, both waving to the camera. A little black and white photo of her dead mother taken before she died and, to my surprise, a little photo of me standing by the apple tree when I was about six, stuck in the crevice of the mirror. None of the wonderful Luke, I noted.

The room was luxurious in the sense of no order with beautiful things lying everywhere. Her walk-in wardrobe was an array of stunning shiny stylish and crazy garments: sequins and sparkles, ribbons and bows of every colour; garments she particularly liked would hang out over the door of the cupboards, like paintings. Each corner of the room was like a little Annie altar, her character held captive. Her disguises lay bare. It brought back memories of when I hid between the dresses to feel the comfort of my mother.

Dad's garments were nowhere to be seen, obviously hidden in drawers and cupboards in order, as he liked them.

A red and orange Basil Black Shaw abstract painting of a wild horse hung above the bed. It had been a sweetener present from he to she for forgetting yet another anniversary.

When she finished, she looked at me in the mirror with the warmest of smiles,

'Now go girl,'

When I stood up and looked at myself in the long mirror, I was shocked, totally shocked. I looked stunning.

'Thanks Mum, I, I look...'

'Sexy'

And no sooner had she said it then she stomped out of the room, almost embarrassed by her own admission.

'Robert, Nana, quick, let me present, the one, the only, the one and only, Ella Lovett'

I took one last look in the mirror and walked as best as I could in those heels, peeking every now and then at Robert as he feasted his eyes disbelievingly at what was approaching.

'Jesus, you look amazing.'

Nana forced a smile as she always did, when she was afraid she may spill out something she shouldn't.

'Well Nana, don't you approve?' asked Annie,

'Yes, she looks lovely dear, just lovely.' said Nana, continuing a forced smile. We all waited in the kitchen on Jack's return home. He fell through the door at precisely eight o'clock; he stood facing Annie still wet from the rain, his overcoat dripping, as he clutched on to his brown paper bag. Annie stood in stillness opposite him, he didn't even notice me.

'You're late Jack. Let's go'

He smiled at her.

'You look beautiful, as always. I lost my case, but if at first we don't succeed, we try and try again, let's have one for the road'

'We need to go.'

'Just one, and then, we'll go, okay.'

He trotted off into the kitchen, only to arrive back into the hallway with two glasses of whiskey, one with ice but no Annie in sight.

I was standing in the doorway because she had asked me to bolt the door after her, as he swallowed the disappointment.

'Can't stand that whining bastard Morrison anyway, come on Ella you join me for a glass of something, and you too Robert' he said pleadingly,

'No, Dad. Why don't you go after her, you know where she'll be.'

He downed both glasses and went back into the kitchen, grabbed the bottle and headed upstairs to his attic room. Robert and I went to Fox's for a pint, with some of his mates who gabbled about football most of the evening. So I went home but before I did Robert kissed me goodnight and there was no ignition.

It was five o'clock in the morning when I heard the thumping sound at the front door. I thought I was dreaming at first. I heard more thumping so I climbed out of bed and headed down stairs. I could hear voices outside the front door.

'Who's there?'

I shouted before I opened the large walnut door, a ritual I had become accustomed to.

'It's the police' I opened the door and two uniformed police men stood in front of me, I was slightly scared of the police.

'Sorry for disturbing you, miss, is this the home of Annie Lovett'?

'Yes?'

'Is Mr Lovett at home?'

I shouted upstairs with the fullness of my lungs 'Dad!'

Nothing stirred, I shouted again and Nana was walking down the stairs.

'What's happened?'

Quietly, she ushered them in through the hall.

It was amazing how she never got fazed, always under complete control. She brought them into the drawing room and closed the door on me. A few moments later she reappeared a little pale but stoic. She walked the two armed police to the front door.

'Your Mother is fine. She has been in an accident, now go and get your father up.'

'What's happened Nana? '

'It will be alright just go and get Jack. We need to go to the hospital.'

I jumped up the stairs. He wasn't in his bed so I went up to his attic. When I opened the door he sat facing me with a gun pointing at me. His stare was rigid and steel. He put his finger up to shush me and I quietly shook my head, no. He hadn't been to bed yet.

'Dad, it's the police! Mum's been in an accident, we need to go to the hospital now.'

He looked at me calmly as if he had been expecting this news, put the gun back into a drawer and came quietly down the stairs. His stained white vest looked awful, he was unshaven and stinking of whiskey. Nana faced him.

'She crashed into a wall, she got caught between joy riders, she's in the intensive care unit at the Royal Victoria hospital but she's stable, Ella get dressed, Jack take a cold shower.'

We all quietly went to our rooms got dressed and headed for the hospital. I didn't quite know what to expect.

The intensive care unit was busy and filled to its capacity. There had been a riot, earlier. Two young soldiers had been shot. The unit was guarded by armed soldiers.

Annie lay unconscious between the two men who had been shot. One of them looked so like Luke it was scary. Annie was naked excepting a paper gown and attached to her body were a multitude of wires that connected to machines that beeped and ticked. She had a ventilator stuck down her throat and a drip inserted into her arm. One side of her head had been shaved. Despite all of this she maintained her beauty. I sat with her and held her hand, swallowing the tears. Dad stood looking at her blankly for about ten minutes and then left. Nana came in, kissed her head and sat beside her mumbling prayers, in a trance state. I started to tell Annie what had happened, where she was, what she was attached to, her eyes were closed but flickered occasionally. When something continued beeping a nurse hurried over and switched wires and pushed buttons on machines. And then someone else's machines would start to scream and off she would go again. It was a while before Jack returned, holding coffee, I got up to let him in and as I did I saw the side of her head, revealing a large gash. I went out, and stood outside the glass-fronted unit and watched Jack, choking in his emotion, suffocating in guilt as he sat with Nana to pray. As he stroked her hair his hand shook and the love flew out in whispers, not knowing which direction they were headed.

'Annie, my love.' was all he could say again and again.

'Annie, my love.'

His whispering was making me angry. He just seemed so useless. He should have been with her.

It was early morning before we spoke to the doctor. He spoke with us in the corridor outside the intensive care unit. Dr George, a tall, skinny, over-read, self-important consultant who had lost touch with the human side of his profession. We stood huddled together powerless. Nana, Dad, and I. He checked his watch before he spoke. He spoke with a calm but eerie, authoritative tone.

'We fear she may have had a stroke. We cannot assess the damage yet. She did bang her head during the accident, which may also suggest an acquired brain injury. We are keeping check on the fluid gathering around the swelling of the brain. We cannot establish whether she had the stroke before the crash or after it. The recovery in these circumstances is unpredictable and slow. She will have an MRI when the swelling goes down which will give us a clearer indication of the damage caused.'

We were all speechless.

Jack forced the question: 'Is she going to be all right?'

Dr George spoke to him almost as if he was speaking to a foreigner or a child, clearly and slowly pronouncing each word with clarity,

'It's difficult to determine the prognosis; at present Annie is in a comatose state, we cannot say whether or not she will come out of it, if she does it will be a slow recovery. We will be able to determine better once she has had a MRI. She is too ill at present, but hopefully over the next few days, if she stabilises, we can scan her. Be assured we are doing everything we can to keep her stabilised.'

His beeper went off, he checked it.

'I have another serious injury in surgery, I'm sorry, I need to attend to it. I'm sorry I can't tell you more, I will talk with you tomorrow.'

He stopped his beeper and turned to walk away.

'Has her brain been damaged in any way, Doctor?' asked Nana clearly and loudly, focussed on the reality of the situation.

'Yes, how serious it is we cannot yet determine.'

Silence. Numbness. Brain damage. Vegetable. We watched Dr George continue down the corridor, not a care in the world, oblivious to our disintegration. We avoided each other's gaze, terrified of acceptance. We had had enough information; we neither needed nor wanted any more.

'Let's go and have a cup of tea.'

Nana gathered us in her arms and calmly ushered us away.

Over the following nights Nana would sit in the kitchen with me telling me stories of her past. The Second World War, living in Belfast and the antics she got up to with the restrictions put on them; smuggling butter home on her bus back from the border in her coat; or the excitement that ensued when she discovered silk stockings, and how she got away with wearing them to a dance by disguising them under her woollen black tights. She would often tell me stories of Jack growing up, with his brothers who tortured and teased him because he was so much younger. They covered his face and hands in brown polish one day and wheeled him down to the local shop and spread rumours about a new adopted brother from Africa, she had to scrub his face clean with salt. She had never mentioned Isabel, her daughter, and I never asked. But one evening she was sitting by the old Aga stove, radio perched on her knees listening to the latest on Bobby Sands. The news reporter announced almost joyously,

'The controversial republican prisoner Bobby Sands currently serving a fourteen-year sentence for possession of firearms, has just won a seat in British parliament, with 30,493 votes, Bobby Sands, who is at present on his second week of hunger strike because of the British government's refusal to acknowledge the prisoners as political prisoners of war, is said to be elated at his news of being elected. Sands, a member of the Irish Republican Army, has won international sympathies around the world in his endeavour to get the British government to meet with the five demands regarding the Nationalist prisoners concerning the legislation brought in 1976 regarding the ending of the special category status for prisoners of terrorist crimes. Other news...'

'God help his poor mother, it's all very well him getting a seat in British parliament but it's another to lose a child'.

Nana hung her head.

'I know the heartbreak, Ella, and it's with me now as it was the day I lost her.........'

'Isabel?'

'Isabel. She was the happiest child, always giggling, at what, we never knew, nonsense was her middle name. Isabella nonsense. I'd call her. And Jesus, when Jack came along well, there were fun and games. God, they adored each other one minute and the next they would be killing each other. If one got socks, the other had to have socks too. Pass me my bag, Ella.'

I fetched the brown leather bag she had carried possessively for the last ten years and she took out a little brown wallet with a small black and white photo of Jack and Isabel standing in front of her old house, arm-in-arm, with smiles that would have lifted the earth.

'It was Isabel's Holy Communion day, she is beautiful isn't she. I made her that little dress, from my wedding dress; I put in the golden ringlets the night before. Wee brown eyes like saucers. Look at Jack in his tweed shorts and white cotton shirt and braces. A little man ready to take on the world.'

She looked at me with eyes filled with tears.

'Isabel was a great swimmer you see, no fear. She wasn't afraid of anything or anyone. Unlike her brother who would have jumped at his shadow. No, Isabel was fearless'.

She put the photo back into her wallet, but continued talking, not looking at me.

'Jack was with her when it happened, you see. He wasn't to know, he had been sulking with her over something stupid, she could always outwit him and he couldn't take it. So he would sulk as a protest and she would smile in her victory. But they were inseparable. We were in Newcastle at my brother Liam's house, God rest him. We often went up when Charlie had his one week off in the summer. Liam lived right across from the sea. It was beautiful up there. The sun was shining that day. Liam was being awarded a medal for bravery; he was a reserve police man, unusual for a Catholic those days, a good soul. Jack wasn't in the water with her, you see. We had to go, because Liam had no-one else to cheer him on. So Charlie and I set off with Liam. I knew it wasn't a good idea. I put her in charge; she loved to be in charge. She was only eleven. I told them repeatedly not to leave the house until we returned.

He just saw her disappear. He couldn't speak for hours.

We didn't know what had happened at first, Charlie thought they had maybe fallen out again and she took herself off. She was independent like you Ella. I knew as soon as I clapped my eyes on Jack that something awful had happened. We and the neighbours searched for hours. Then he told us that they had gone for a swim.'

We sat in silence for a moment.

'It was a bit like a bomb, except this bomb went off inside our hearts. It was God gave me strength Ella, never stray too far from God because you may never know when you'll need him'.

She put a shovel of coal on the fire, took out her rosary beads and we sat by the big red Aga stove and said the Rosary quietly.

'Hail Mary, full of grace, blessed art thou amongst women...'

Then we sat in her grief for a while, like wading through swamp. I stepped down as I sometimes did and gave her feet a massage. She fell asleep.

Luke came home from boarding school, and it was agreed finally that he would stay at home for good. He inspired me; it was like he had become a man overnight. He looked handsome with his brown shiny locks of hair, and his tanned skin he had acquired from playing school sport. His almost six-foot body made me feel protected when I was with him. As he knew no-one in his new school he got focussed on his studies during the week. At weekends wafts of hash would escape from his bedroom. He visited Annie in hospital occasionally for the first while. Nana visited in the morning after her daily Mass. She would bring clean underwear and old fashioned night dresses, fresh as the sea. She hung rosary beads on the posts of the bed and left little prayers and relics under her pillow. She also kept the nursing staff on their toes when they made an appearance. Perhaps it made Annie laugh inside.

Jack switched off to the reality of his wife's condition.

When asked how Annie was on his return from his nightly hospital visit he would almost inevitably say, '*She's fine*' and leave it at that. He continued to work his twelve hour days but the drink was taking a hold. After visiting Annie he'd feel useless because there was little to no response and he needed a drink. He would read poems or sections from a book he carefully selected for her, but he would read without the passion she was accustomed to. There were no little glimmers of hope except for the occasional blinking of the eyes or a body jolt as she lay in what looked like a foetal position. The doctors offering no information other than '*we will have to wait and see*' His only life-line being the nurses, kind words of comfort, '*I think she hears you, Jack*'.

Annie's accident changed everything. Home was like a vacant warehouse. No-one showing their emotions for fear of losing themselves. Luke lived in his bedroom. He convinced Nana that the smell of hash at the weekends was incense that he used whilst praying. She wholly believed him. Nana, exhausted from the hospital vigils, was fit for little when she came home. So I embraced the cooking front with the enthusiasm of a slave and the help of Mrs Beeton, Nana's other little bible. I kept desserts simple and to weekends only; apple pie or rhubarb crumble. My efforts made Nana smile, even laugh sometimes, especially when I decorated my pies with little motifs of love hearts or flowers. I managed well because I was efficient. I felt as if I could do something. I had a little bit of control over the situation. I discovered that cooking could be quite therapeutic. I would have done anything other than go to the hospital to watch this woman they called my mother lie there like a rag doll.

I liked having Luke around even if he didn't use verbal communication that often. We were alike physically, both had dark brown eyes and thick manes of dark brown hair, except his hair hung over his eyes, we were close and connected in our tastes. Hippy attire, Cohen, Dylan and Blondie.

Luke kept his distance as I was still his baby sister but he was helping out more, quietly lighting fires, brushing floors, changing light bulbs. Someone had to, Jack didn't quite know how to go about doing that sort of thing and Luke just did. We missed the flowers, the chocolate, the candles.

Luke was due to sit his A-levels in June; he had brains and didn't have to slog the way I did to pass exams. He walked around the house like a dog looking for his master; he moved his study from the bedroom to the living room table which looked out unto the entrance of the driveway, his books sitting in front of him whilst he watched the gate, as if in hope of her return.

I had my O-levels coming up and had decided to put my head down. I went into automatic pilot; my practical skills were sharpened and helped me hide the reality of what was going on.

REFLECTION ON WILL THE ORANGEMAN

ELLA'S STORY

I hadn't heard from Will since the peace camp; since I had melted, since he saw Robert waiting for me at Belfast Central Bus Station and assumed he was my boyfriend. We had been discreetly snuggled into each other on the bus journey home, we had chatted about everything. Then he saw a pathetic Robert waiting for me with a bunch of wilting yellow dahlias and I identified him as my boyfriend because I was shocked to see him there. Will almost instantly turned to ice. He was a serious kind of guy, I liked watching his lips as he spoke and he had a perfect set of clean white teeth.

We had agreed on the bus not to discuss his position with the Orange Lodge as we needed to agree to disagree.

'*Orange provoking bastards*' was how I eventually described my take on the whole Orange thing, and it was on that note, which was just after he had spent time patiently explaining the need for such a worthy Christian entity for Protestants, that he suggested we agree to disagree.

He spoke about his family with great loyalty but I could sense all was not peace and love. I knew his brother Sam was different to him, I had seen him regularly hanging out with the Summerhill thugs in the local newsagents. He stood out amongst them. He didn't look like a thug, the others did; it was genetic with them.

When they called me names he just looked on, lost in his inability to be part of a gang he seemed desperate to be part of.

'Why don't you save Sam from those idiots? ' I asked Will.

'Not you as well.'

143

He kissed me spontaneously. And when he kissed me it was as if he ignited something inside, like a gas stove being lit. It was just after that kiss that the bus pulled up and I saw Robert standing on the station waiting for me. He waved with the enthusiasm of an autistic child.

'Who's the guy waving at you?'

'Who?'

'The idiot with flowers Ella?'

'My boyfriend, I mean my ex...'.

'Your boyfriend?'

I smiled up at him hoping to win his puppy look back but to no avail.

'He's not really a boyfriend, he was my....'

But he threw his small bag over his shoulder and got off the bus. I didn't really care. I wasn't in love.

My emotions were in an unknown place. They flooded my being with too much power; my only option was to switch them off. I didn't want to feel any more. I was genuinely happy with my ability to do that. Burying emotion was a family trait that I was beginning to see the benefit of.

TIME TO SAY GOODBYE

ELLA'S STORY

I finally ditched Robert via a phone call. After the phone call he came straight round to the house and entered through the back door. No stranger. No hello.

'What do you mean you need some space?'

He said it out loud and clear sure that Nana would hear every word. Knowing that Nana adored him. I took him up to my bedroom and as soon as I closed the door he pinned me up against the wall. He looked into my eyes with urgency. I could feel his hardness press against my thigh and it sent a rush of hunger through me. Then I looked at him, so sure he had won me over, and I pushed him away.

'It's me. I just don't feel as if we are going anywhere with this. We are too young to be settling into a serious relationship'.

He looked at me, smirking at first. Then when he saw my now cold response he looked horrified. He grabbed me again with force and I felt repulsed

'Stop!'

But he held me in his grip, forcing me to look at him, his eyes dancing in his head with passion and fury, his cock still hard against my thigh.

'Let me go!'

He loosened his grip.

'I love you Ella, I want to be with you, probably for the rest of my life.'

'Well you have a funny way of showing it.'

'Is it someone else?'

'No. Robert we, we're just kids, having a bit of fun.'

'That's all I am too you, is it? A bit of fun?'

He sat on the bed beside me.

'Please don't do this to me Ella, please, I love you. Let's just go back to where we were then.'

'I'm sorry.'

'No you're not; you're cold and heartless Ella. You don't give a shit how I feel.'

He got up from my bed. He looked disappointed and wounded. He left in the same hurried fashion that he'd arrived in. He had a point. I wasn't committed; I wasn't in love. My sudden need for distance appeared to encourage him to want to commit more and oddly the more he devoted his undying love towards me, the more I seemed to want to push him away. I stopped answering his calls and notes and effectively cut him out. Another family trait I was beginning to see the benefits of.

ANNIE WAKES

ELLA'S STORY

It was a Saturday morning and the sky, cloaked in a grey mist, drizzled rain monotonously with no sign of giving up. Nana came into my bedroom and made her way across the shoes and clothes that lay across the floor, tutting disapprovingly as she went.

'Really Ella, I thought I told you to...'

'I'll do it Nana, later, after my study.'

'Ella you need to visit your mother today. I need to visit Aunt Margaret. They are doing a brain scan on Annie to assess the damage and we need someone to be there at all times, so get up.'

I had studied until two in the morning and my body felt like a bag of cement. I dragged myself to the shower and stood still under the hot gushing water until I came back to life. I was dressed and almost ready to go when Luke came into the kitchen resembling a character out of Scooby-Doo who had just seen a ghost. I made him some French toast and he decided to accompany me. Luke was in his moody mood which I was now used to, so I didn't speak to him but rather at him, and only when necessary. He made his way to the middle of the bus and sat two seats in front of Spider and his little cronies. I contemplated sitting on another seat all together but thought the better and sat beside my brother. They made sure everyone on the bus overheard their foul-mouthed conversation. It took extreme skill to concentrate on thoughts of my own.

Sam the innocent sat amongst them. He was probably oblivious as to who he was sitting in front of. Five minutes later I felt something hit the back of my neck, it was a rolled up piece of paper, followed by giggles, then the taunts of

'Fenian whore, can't get enough of it from her own

lot.'

Luke caught a piece of paper mid-flow and threw it out the little window beside us, looked at me and smiled.

'Do you know what they are talking about?'

'No.'

They continued and as each little ball of juvenile paper flew, Luke just smiled.

'What do you call an Orangeman with a fly in his head?' Luke asked me.

'I don't know.'

'A space invader'

We laughed out loud. The jokes kept coming from I don't know where and the paper balls ran out. Luke's ability to annoy the little bastards was inspirational and clearly aggravated Spider because when he got up to get off at his stop he hovered over Luke.

'You watch your fucking mouth boy'

The irritated bus driver slammed a little harder on the brakes than usual almost causing Spider to lose balance before he disembarked.

Nana had phoned the hospital to let them know we were coming. They had prepared Annie. She was still in intensive care but they had detached most of the wires, there was stillness about her. Luke sat opposite me like a statue. Annie didn't look so bad, in fact she looked quite beautiful and I know she knew who we were, because she was blinking her eyelids whilst keeping them closed and she sort of smiled. I started chatting to her about everything and anything. When I held her hand though, I felt nothing.

'Aren't you going to say something Luke?'

He looked at her as pale as ice.

'What's the point?'

Nurse Bridget came over. A tall, slim, sexy sort of a girl, with a softness that matched her long dark curls, she was lovely, not yet thirty.

'Hello Annie' she said in a Scots accent. 'Look who's here to see you Annie, it's that handsome son of yours, and your lovely daughter. They brought you some nice freesias.'

Annie's eyes were open now some of the time. Sometimes she looked straight at me but I wasn't sure if she actually saw me.

As I turned to look up at Bridget, I felt a little squeeze on my hand, that little squeeze filled me with hope, my eyes filled with tears,

'She squeezed my hand Bridget'

'Really? 'said Bridget excitedly 'Really that's very good news, Ella'

She saw my face fill with her enthusiasm. Luke remained still and pale, not quite registering the good news. Bridget documented the hand squeeze.

'Well done Annie. You're talking with us again aren't ye?'

'Hello Mum'

Annie squeezed my hand again.

After that day I decided to make more regular trips into see my mother, I read books to her at the same time covering what I needed to revise for my English Literature. Comic short stories by Frank O'Connor, poems by Maria Rilke that I'd got in the school library. The nuns would inform me of the various saints they would be praying to and I would remember their names and specific benefits. Oddly I became more focussed and together during this time. I lived in a different reality. I prayed with conviction and I was determined to do well in my O-levels.

Annie said her first word about four weeks after the accident, I was reading *Lady Chatterley's Lover* by DH Lawrence. When I finished the last chapter I sat looking at her, wondering what she might be thinking. I saw shaking her head a little, then she made a little moan and looked at me.

'Ella.'

'Bridget she ...'

Nurse Bridget shot straight over and she said it again. I

stood over her and kissed her forehead. It was strange being in the position of being able to love her freely and openly. I felt the mixed emotion of hating her for making me feel this love, for having pity for her, for seeing her lie wretched in a bed hopeless and weak but I liked her like this too, mostly for needing me.

Her room was more her own now, I had brought in her black Italian night wear and hung it on the back of the door on a black feathery coat hanger much to Nana's disapproval. I put her tiger-skin slippers under the bed and hung a water colour painting called Utopia that she had done, of a naked woman sitting by a window. I dressed her in a modest magenta silk nightdress with a little black floral Japanese bed jacket she sometimes liked to wear around the house when she was feeling jovial. I sprayed the room in her Chanel Number Five perfume to try and get rid of the smell of hospital. It was seeing her dressed like a granny that inspired me to move in and give her back some dignity. Nana wasn't impressed with my transformation but she didn't question it.

I had placed some beauty products on the little table beside her. I moisturised her face, combed her hair and then put on a little makeup. She always smiled after I applied the makeup.

The room was always dripping in flowers from various friends and, I presumed, some admirers. Jack's twelve red roses were delivered every five days without fail, each time with a different little note, the latest one read.

To Annie, my one and only love. Jack.

Annie had effectively turned the tables. I did wonder how she might have reacted if I had been the one lying in the bed. Would she be hiding in Donegal?

When I was six years old I caught the measles. I was so sick I couldn't eat or get out of bed; I had to have the curtains closed because my head hurt so badly. Annie didn't come near me, she couldn't bear to touch me. She said it was because she had never had the measles herself and she was worried that they might be contagious. I tried to believe her, but my lack of trust was confirmed when I got glandular fever about a year later and I didn't see her for dust. During those weeks I despised her because I realised she wasn't capable of being a real mother, not like my friend's mothers who would whisk them off to a doctor if they sneezed. To me she was a cold, self-obsessed, egotistical, needy adult who shouldn't have had children. And now, ironically, as I sat beside her bed bringing her juice and reading her books, like she should have done for me, I felt whole. And I could love her more than I had ever loved her.

When I returned home Nana and I discussed each possibility, plans for the future, how we would cope at home etc.

'I'll take a year out if I have to Nana, what's a year, you can't manage on your own.'

'You'll do no such thing Ella. You will become somebody, someone your mother can be proud of.'

The following morning, we would finally know what fate had bestowed upon us. I was at home studying again, Nana was getting ready to bring Luke to his History and Politics exam, Luke was sitting in a trance at the living room window. Jack was up and typically looking for some lost brown envelope in a manic sort of manner. Opening drawers, messing them up and slamming them closed again with bits sticking out. Lifting tidy piles of books and newspapers and leaving them down in a mess. We were all a little tense waiting for the call from the hospital. The phone rang and everyone looked at me, so I answered it. It was Will.

'Hi, is that you Ella? I was just wondering how you are, I'm sorry about your mum, is she okay?'

It was odd hearing his voice. I wanted to talk to him but not now, especially when my entire family's eyes were on me.

'Actually we are just waiting on an important call from the hospital Will, this isn't a great time.'

'Oh sorry, I was just thinking about you, I called a

couple of times'.

'She is doing better.'

'Look I'm here if you need me.'

Everyone was looking at me.

'It's not the hospital; it's Will, a friend of mine. Okay, I'll call you back. Bye.' I said and that was that. I had just put the phone down when I realised I didn't have his number.

'Who's Will? It's not your man who works in the shop is it?'

I looked at Luke and I wanted to strangle him.

'No, it's not.'

'Good, because he's an Orangeman'

Ten minutes later the phone rang again, and again everyone looked at me to answer it, I answered, it was the consultant.

'Hello Ella, this is Doctor George, could I speak with Mr Lovett?'

I nodded a yes, looked up at Jack, holding the phone in his direction, he was waving his hand and mouthing the word 'NO' dramatically.

'I'm sorry but he's not here at the moment, I promised Dad I would take this call as soon as it came through.'

'Ella, I would prefer if your father and yourself, and your grandmother, if she wants, come in and meet me this afternoon. Don't worry, it's just procedure, suffice to say there is damage to the frontal lobes, but there is also hope for a more positive outcome than we had previously anticipated.'

I put the phone down and looked at Luke standing at the back door, as thin as a stick, ready to battle his final exams.

'It's not as bad as we thought, in fact it's good news, there is hope of a recovery, and he's asked us to meet with him this afternoon.'

Luke breathed a sigh of relief and headed out to his exam.

We went to meet the doctor that afternoon, Jack, myself

and Nana. Minutes turned into hours, as we waited silently outside his office. Dad eventually slipped out and disappeared for a quick fix. Nana and I were called into the doctor's office.

'No Mr Lovett?'

'No, he was called out on important business, but he has asked us to go ahead, if that's okay.' lied Nana, efficiently.

'Yes, you know we can offer him counselling?'

'He will be fine, Dr George, it's just how he deals with things. But thanks anyway.'

'We have looked at the results. We believe Annie has had a severe stroke. We cannot, however, be exact in regard to the damage she has suffered; suffice to say it will take some time, maybe years, for her recovery. There is no clotting or bleeding, which is the good news. We predict the stroke will cause speech impairment and physical impairment. However, over time with regular physiotherapy, speech and occupational therapy, she will improve. We will set up an individual person-centred programme immediately with a goal towards getting her home but continuing with the programme in an outpatient day unit. Any questions?'

Annie came home two weeks after the diagnosis. Nana and I thought we were prepared.

I had to get through four more O-Levels in the next couple of weeks.

Jack didn't quite know how to deal with his wife, whom he now treated like a child. Her speech was slow and she slept fourteen to fifteen hours per day; she could walk little bits at a time but spent most of her time in the newly acquired wheelchair. Jack would talk to her in a patronising sort of tone. Then kiss her.

'Are we alright Annie dear, is there anything you need Annie?'

She looked like she wanted to hit him. She would do her best to respond but he didn't understand her new language.

'Alright. That's a good girl.'

Then he would wander off again. We got home-help in the mornings to help change and feed her. Nana and I were exhausted at the end of week one, mostly as a result of her waking up during the night, because she needed to turn. I would waken easily, but Nana would insist that I go back to bed. My final exams were continuing to be a main part of her focus.

Generally Nana would retire to bed straight after the nine o' clock news, trusting that Jack would get Annie upstairs, she would be snoring by nine-thirty. Luke would help Jack get Annie upstairs, and Jack would insist on changing her into her night-clothes, because he knew how she guarded her privacy. Often he would spray Chanel on her before putting her to bed but he would always spray too much. Eventually we made a bedroom downstairs, Jack wasn't the steadiest.

Luke was more comfortable and gentle around her now she was home, he made the effort to try and understand her speech. He got through his A-Levels and applied to college in England to study philosophy. I did my O - Levels, and the work paid off.

Over time, the reality started to sink in. Annie needed full-time care. I felt fragile and exhausted with everything, mentally and emotionally, everything felt like a chore. The tiredness was making me feel ill. I went to see the doctor, in the hope he might prescribe something to give me a bit of a lift; mother's-little-helpers, sympathy, anything but preferably in the form of a drug. He listened carefully, took some blood and urine tests, asked after Nana and the rest of the family. I waited outside the surgery for ten minutes, skipped through a copy of Woman's Own and thought about Will.

When I returned to the surgery, I noticed that the doctor was looking rather grimly at me.

I sat opposite him as quiet and as curious as a fox.

'Ella, you're three months pregnant.'

'Pregnant! No!'

Then I physically felt a jolt hit my solar plexus so hard that I wanted to go and throw up. He continued with a lecture about my age, my poor mother, my lack of consideration for this unborn child, but I could only see his mouth making words, my hearing literally switched off after he said 'I'll arrange a social worker to discuss your possibilities.'

He handed me a letter abruptly to give into the hospital and I managed to leave.

'Please don't mention this to Nana, I'll tell her myself'.

'Okay, but you need to tell her as soon as possible, or I will.'

I got on the number twenty bus for home. I sat looking out at the summer approaching. Pregnant: I can't be pregnant. I don't want to be pregnant. I'm too young to be pregnant. I'm sixteen years old for Christ's sake. It must be Will the Orangeman's. I hate everything he is and stands for. I could be carrying a little Orangeman in my belly. Nana will kill me. Literally.

I remember the first time I saw the Orangemen march outside our drawing room window. It was just after I had had the measles and I was demented with boredom. I took to lying across the top part of the sofa which rested against the front bay window in the drawing room. This faced the front garden which faced the main road. I could relax stretched out across it and see out of the window at the same time. I couldn't see much other than traffic at first and when the traffic eased I could see the giant trees sway over in Stormont. Sometimes birds would rest on the branches and chat amongst themselves and I would imagine what they would be chatting about. Occasionally a passer-by walked past and tried to avoid looking at me. A little girl with a leg over either side of the sofa her skirt probably hitched up revealing her knickers, not a care in the world.

At first I heard the drums beating loudly and in rhythm, getting closer and closer and then I heard the pipes and finally the flutes. The music stopped and I heard a man roar and then it began again, getting closer and closer louder and louder. The vibrations filled my body with rhythm and thrill, my excitement grew with anticipation. I sat up with my feet rested on the sash wooden window sill, waiting. I wasn't sure at first if I was imagining what I heard. Why had no one mentioned that there was going to be a parade? The sun shone and the sky was blue. As the beat of the drums filled the room I felt my body move in time to the beat. A few people appeared on the side of the road and then the horses appeared mounted by policemen wearing white gloves and leather trousers; each horse dressed up like the ones I had seen at the circus last year. They passed clip-clopping together in rhythm. A man passed in a black suit with an orange band around it, wearing white gloves and a rounded, hard black hat. He threw a long thin stick into the air and he watched it spin amongst the clouds, then caught it. He was followed by a fat bald man with a drum ten times his size which rested on his belly. He walloped the painted face of the drum so hard it vibrated throughout the house causing a tremor on the sofa I sat on. I saw men in blue and gold, red and orange dancing to their tune, men in black and blue, walking like soldiers. I saw a woman wearing a bright orange frilly puffy dress waving an orange frilly parasol through the air dancing on the road with the freedom of a bird in paradise. I wanted to be her. She was magnificent. I started to wave out at her smiling with the joy of it all and she saw me, gave me a curtsy, a smile and a wave. The excitement was too much. I got up to go out to join in when I felt Nana's hand grip my waist, drag me off the sofa with the force of a wind. She snapped the curtains closed and warned me not to go near the windows again in a tone that was not to be argued with.

WILL MEETS ELLA ACROSS THE ROAD

WILL'S STORY

I was to sit my maths A-Level this morning. I loved maths, I was confident. I waited for my bus. When I got to the bus stop I was surprised to see Ella standing across the road, I hadn't seen her since the peace camp. I had called but was told by her grandmother she wasn't in and so I left a message with my number with the request she might get back to me. She was on her own and I was in a bit of a predicament, if I crossed over Spider, Simon and Sam would see and I would have hell to pay. I took my chances. I did have a black belt in karate after all. I knew by the smile on her face that she was pleased to see me. So I braved it across the four lanes of traffic. I liked her in her uniform.

'You didn't call me.'

'I know. My mother had a stroke.'

'I'm, sorry'.

I put my arm around her and hugged her.

The verbal abuse reached us over the sound of the traffic. It was disgusting. For a moment I felt like I was one of them. A Catholic.

I glanced over the road and saw Spider's face white with anger. She caught me.

'Aren't you taking a bit of a risk?'

'Yes, but it's worth it. I can't stop thinking of you Ella, and I know, this is all a little crazy, but ...Give me a call when you can.'

'I would, but I don't have your number.'

I looked up and saw my bus approaching.

'I'll call you. Bye'.

I dashed across the road again and just made my bus. I sat beside Sam who turned his head in the opposite direction. Spider pushed the two young boys behind us out from their seats and sat down.

'I hope you told that little whore to change bus stops because I don't like the view.'

'Whatever.'

'Keep away from her Will. Or else.'

'Or else, what?'

'Or else you and your little whore will get what's coming to you.'

I sat my maths exam. It was fine. Only one more exam left, Politics, then I could escape to college and get away from this lot. I had applied to Queen's University in Belfast and Cambridge to do social sciences and politics.

On my way home I fancied a packet of crisps. I was met by an older bunch of guys, one I recognised as Spider's big brother. I had no hope. There were around six of them. They hauled me off to an alleyway at the back of the shops; I was thrown to the ground.

The tallest one stood over me with his foot on my chest. Spider's brother, currently a member of the UVF, took out a gun and pointed it into my forehead and cocked it.

'Take this as a warning, stay away from that Fenian bitch.'

He pressed the gun into my head. Then lifted me up by the throat and smacked me in the face. I fell to the ground again. Then they all started to kick, oddly I didn't even try to defend myself. I watched them as they walked away laughing.

When I got home my mother cried when she saw me.

'I need to get you to the hospital son.'

'I'm alright Mum, really.'

She washed me and as she did we had a heart-to-heart.

'We should press charges, Will?'

'Do you want me dead?'

'Do you love this girl, Will?'

'Yes.'

'Look, listen to me Will, give it time, get your exams over and when the dust settles, see how you feel.'

She hugged me gently.

'No mention of this to your father. We'll tell him you had a fall. We'll think of something.'

I sat my Politics exam the following day with possible broken ribs and a black eye. It was easy. I was driven. I would begin a new life as a student after the summer.

My father fell for a story about me falling off my bicycle.

ELLA SEES HER ORANGEMAN

He risked his life for me. He actually crossed over the road, the divide, in front of those morons, and he gave me a hug. He was wearing his blue school uniform and he looked lovely. He was about to sit his maths exam. He didn't know when he hugged me that there was another heartbeat in the mix.

FRED'S FUNERAL

WILL'S STORY

Fred got a respectable funeral. My father did the service. We, his mates, dressed in our Lodge uniforms. I played a melody I had composed with him in mind. I called it '*Belonging*'. When mum switched the radio on that morning, I actually heard it: I was so used to hearing words like '*two youths were shot dead*' or '*several people have been seriously injured*' it was daily, on the hour, dominated by the hunger strikers in H-Block, it was inevitably more bad news. But often it meant so little to me. When I heard, '*A young Protestant, Fred Baxter was murdered in a stabbing incident, after a feud broke out in the city centre last night, survived by his mother, Margaret Baxter of the Glenville estate*'... I heard it.

There his mother stood at the top of the church, broken. Surrounded by her sad and bewildered family. Good Christian people. People from all roads gathered. Some knew him, some were related, others came in hope that their support may send out a message of abhorrence. He got buried in a storm of thunder, appropriately enough. Spider couldn't look at me. Neither could Sam. When we returned home, Father gave us one of his talks.

'Stay away from those thugs, they are nothing but trouble'.

And like the news I heard him this time.

Later I had my own talk with Sam with my own simple message.

'If you go near that bastard Spider again, I'm no longer your brother.'

ELLA LETS SLIP

It took four months before my belly started to swell. I really didn't know what to do. I didn't want to be pregnant. I didn't want to have to travel by boat over to England to terminate the baby because I didn't have the money or the knowhow to do that and because it didn't seem like the right thing to do. I didn't want to have the baby adopted because I knew that I would spend every day of my life wondering where my baby was. Neither did I want a baby. It was easiest to just forget that I was pregnant which was what I had been doing up until now.

My dream of becoming a vet and settling down in the countryside was now fast disappearing. I hadn't told a soul. Annie was just starting to communicate better and walk with the aid of crutches. The grey cloud that had suspended itself over our home was lifting.

Nana was starting to cook decent food again. The colour was returning to Luke's face and he was disappearing in the evenings on a regular basis, with a pulse to his movements, definitely a woman. Jack was starting to breathe again; he eased off on the early afternoon vodkas and waited until around six before he poured himself a large well-deserved whiskey and ice. Even Jack could understand most of what Annie was saying which gave Luke a break from translating.

It was unfortunate that the evening he took his new girlfriend to see Stiff Little Fingers the new Belfast rock band, that he wasn't able to translate what she was trying to tell me before he left.

Her speech became more slurred with tiredness in the evening. My hearing became more selective and she got grumpy and frustrated when I couldn't understand her. Nana had gone up to bed exhausted again and Jack was upstairs in his attic room frantically typing; his engine running on the fuel of Black Bush. Annie lifted her hands and shook them at me, she kept shouting.

'Hakic!'

'Hake? you want some fish?'

'No! tabete!!'

She spat as she spoke with frustration.

'Tibet.'

She took a deep breath and threw the remote control for the television across the room, narrowly missing me. I'd tried. I wasn't in the mood tonight.

'Fuck off!'

I closed the door with a bang and left the room delighted with the knowledge she was stuck in a wheelchair. My head was exploding with fear of the prospects of the future, could this be it for the foreseeable future. I could hear her banging things as I started to make ginger snaps, my comfort food, I had been craving them all week. My O-level results were out tomorrow. Jack staggered into the kitchen with his glasses resting on the bottom of his nose, glass in hand.

'What's going on, can't you hear your mother?'

I looked at him and I realised I hated him too. I ignored him as he stood awkwardly in the middle of the floor demanding my attention, and carried on about my work while he watched my every move.

'Ella, my pretty girl, what's wrong?'

'Well you're getting pissed again, Nana is flat-out exhausted, Annie is doing my head in with her brain-dead talk that come ten o' clock I no longer understand and I'm making ginger snaps.'

He stood with a puzzled look on his face and a welcome silence fell.

'Ella love, don't be like that.'

He opened his arms for a hug. I ignored him, he downed his glass.

'Look love, it's all going to be okay. You'll be fine, you'll get your exams and you'll do okay for yourself. You're a smart beautiful girl. It's me who will be left with this mess.'

I spread the ginger nuts on the baking tray with

absolute perfection and slid them into the oven while he wallowed in his self-pity. When I looked up he had fallen asleep at the table, his head resting in his hands. I made myself a cup of tea in the good china cups kept for visitors, cut a little smoked salmon and brown bread while I waited on the biscuits to brown and when they were done I scoffed the lot.

The following morning I awoke to a rumbling belly and made it to the bathroom just on time. Whilst I was emptying my insides out, I heard a banging on the door.

'Ella is that you?'

'Yes! I'll be out in a minute.'

'Are you alright?'

'Yes.'

Another barf lifted my ribcage as if an alien was trying to escape from my insides. I stood up, wiped my face, flushed the loo and opened the door. Nana stood in her pink cotton nighty and white hairnet looking at me with concern.

'I've a tummy bug.'

'You're the colour of those walls.'

'I'm fine honestly.'

We heard the post drop through the front door and I suddenly registered my exam results had probably just arrived.

We both headed down stairs. I lifted the white envelope that had 'St Magdalene' marked on the front of it and handed it to Nana, who handed it back to me. St Magdalene's had in many ways been my saving grace. I loved that school, its functionality and consistency.

I opened it and read the results. To my utter amazement I passed everything on the list. Eight As and two Bs. I jumped up and hugged Nana. She put her hands around my waist and I could feel her belly touching my unborn child. She was oblivious. Jack came down the stairs spruced up again in suit and tie, smelling of aftershave. He had a big huge smile for me, as always, because as always he had no recollection of the night before. I excitedly waved my results in front of him.

'Well how did we do? Are we any closer to having another lawyer in the family?'

I handed him the envelope and his hand shook like a rattlesnake as he scanned the results. 'Well done Ella, an A in mathematics, that's my girl....I'm very proud of you.'

We hugged.

The phone rang, it was Ali. She failed several exams, but got enough to do the A-Levels. The phone rang again and again. I went in to Annie who was sitting up; she smiled for me to come in. She grabbed a packet of painkillers that lay beside her and said 'tabette' then laughed. I handed her my results and she scanned them carefully. Then out her arms flew for a hug, I hugged her and she held the hug long enough for it to feel like a real mummy-hug.

That evening I sat in, to watch crap television after the phone calls stopped. I couldn't face celebrations, not when I was conscious of my expanding belly and not if I couldn't drink.

'Penny for your thoughts' asked Nana, suspicious of my joining her yet again for an evening of Coronation Street.

'Oh, nothing.'

When the credits came up after 'Corry' I looked over at Nana and I was sure she was getting smaller. She looked old and frail clutching on to her rosary beads that had been blessed by Pope John Paul himself. I felt guilty, again an emotion that kept coming at me.

'Fancy a treat?'

'Is the Pope a Catholic?'

'Cheeky'.

I watched her potter about silently, diligently. Often we had comfort in each other's silence especially after we said the Rosary.

'Easy on the biscuits Ella.'

'Yeah' I mumbled, taking no notice. Nana stopped what she was doing which was rare.

'What's up?'

'Nothing.'

'Well for someone who has just got all the O-Levels she could dream for you're not very happy-looking. Is it man trouble? How's our lovely Robert?'

'We finished.'

'Oh, I'm sorry to hear that.'

'I'm not.'

'Still friends?'

'Not.'

'Don't you go worrying your little head over any young man. You're too young for that. And you have a Nana who loves you and is very proud of you.'

The tears welled up and I held my breath so as to stop breathing which might help to stop the unwanted tears I could feel emerging. But I needed to breathe again and out they came. I had to tell someone. I had to. She came over to me and put her arms around me.

'What is it Ella?'

I sobbed and sobbed.

'Ella, tell me.'

'I'm pregnant.'

'What?'

'I'm pregnant.'

She had heard me the first time because her face had drained itself of blood.

'You're pregnant? Pregnant?'

She blessed herself automatically and I had the sudden realisation that I had just made the second biggest mistake of my life.

'How did you get pregnant? Jesus, Mary, and Joseph.'

She scanned my stomach with her disbelieving eyes.

'I'm sorry.'

'Sorry....Ella, how could you?'

'I'm sorry.'

'You can't keep it?'

'I don't know that yet, I don't know.'

'Surely you're not thinking of keeping it'

'What? You think I should abort it?'

'Don't be ridiculous, that's murder.'

She sighed.

'Jesus, Mary, and Joseph.'

Jack arrived through the back door soaked in rain. He looked older with his hair stuck to his head. Nana straightened herself up quickly.

'Stay put.'

'Hello ladies.'

He beamed and came over to kiss me on the forehead.

'Are we very proud, Nana, of our bright little spark?'

He rummaged through several pockets excitedly then handed me a small package.

'Yes Jack. She did us proud.'

I opened up the little package which revealed a little gold locket. It was beautiful. He kissed me on the forehead.

'I just need to put these files away.' he said, guarding his briefcase. 'I'll eat up there if you don't mind.'

So Nana set out a tray for him and he headed straight upstairs.

Nana looked at me, softer now. Waited until she knew he was out of earshot and closed the kitchen door.

'How many weeks are you gone?'

'Twenty.'

'Are you sure? Have you told anyone else?'

'No.'

'Good. I'm sorry Ella. I'm just shocked. You're only a child yourself. You're like my own.......... Do you want to keep it?' she asked more gently.

'Robert's not a bad catch you know, if he gets through medicine he'll look after you.'

'No....I don't know. I really don't know.'

The truth was I really didn't know. I had this thing growing inside my stomach and my only connection with it was fear and grief, shock and sadness and deep down I just wanted it to go away.

'I am presuming Robert is the father, does he know

yet?'

'No.'

'No, what Ella? No he doesn't know or no he's not the father?'

More tears rose and I tried not to breathe again, unsuccessfully. The tears started to jump out like prisoners making a run for it.

'Answer me, Ella.'

'No. It's not Robert's, I'm finished with Robert. The father is called Will; I met him on the peace camp. I think he's the father. He's a Protestant.'

A poignant silence. She stood up and started to pace the room. Then a change of tone. Sharper.

'You think.....A Protestant... What kind of a Protestant? Jesus, Mary and Joseph.'

'I don't know. He's a Church of Ireland, I think.'

'You don't know, you don't even know what religion he is, and you did that with him! You need to pray child. You need to go to confession.'

She paced around the room, thinking, thinking too much. She found her rosary beads and put the kettle on.

'We need a priest.'

'I don't want to see a priest Nana, please, stop, I'm scared,'

'We will pray Ella.' she said with an eerie calm. We began with the Apostles Creed, the Our Father, the Hail Mary. We covered all twenty mysteries. It was a saviour.

'The Lord be with thee, blessed art thou amongst women. Blessed is the fruit of thy womb Jesus.'

Anything to appease her and appease her it did. When we finished she sat for a moment. 'Not a word of this to anyone. Not yet.'

We stayed in the kitchen for the rest of the evening, drinking copious pots of stewed tea. We read papers and magazines.

'We will get through this Ella!'

Despite her initial shock I felt that she really cared and that she would do her best to help me sort out the mess.

Dad and Luke kept coming in and out with trays for Annie or snacks for themselves.

'I will discuss this with your father Ella, if you want? I think it's best not to say anything to Annie just yet; she's not able for it. We don't want any setbacks.'

Later that night I lay in bed clutching the little patchwork quilt Nana had made for me out of the rags of dresses I had worn as a child. I finished my last chapter of George Orwell's 1984. Luke had given it to me and it helped slow my mind. I was able to breathe again with ease. I said a little prayer for the baby and I could feel myself finally falling into a sleep when I heard a gentle knock on the door.

Nana tiptoed in and sat beside me on the bed with curlers and hairnet intact. I sat up and looked at her aged face, frail and saddened. She looked vulnerable, older; it was the look of sorrow in her eyes that concerned me. She was always the face of cheer; the one who despite everything kept us on track. She was the rock we all swam to for safety. After the stroke she would constantly remind us of Annie's qualities. If she saw a frown she had a knack of distracting us into doing something that could make us forget. We were all so dependent on her. It had never really occurred to me that she might need some support.

She studied my face for a moment and waited a second before she spoke.

'I have spoken with your father. Don't worry. I've told him that I will look after this for you, and that there is no need for him to worry. I have put a suggestion forward that he is very much in favour of. I have a friend Ella, a very good friend, I went to school with. I have just spoken with her and she thinks she may be able to help. Her name is Sr Nula, she's a lovely woman, a good woman. They can take you in a week's time and you can have the baby there, they will look after everything for you.'

I was stunned for a moment, in my sleepiness slightly confused.

'Who? What are you talking about Nana?'

She smiled, comforted by her ability to find a solution to the catastrophe.

'It's a convent for girls like you. They will keep you until the baby is born and then they will arrange the adoption for you. It's all perfectly legal and safe and then you can get on with your life, Ella. You have your whole future ahead of you. Ella, you have no future in this country with a Protestant man. You would be putting your life and the baby's at risk. No other man will take you seriously with a child by your side. I know about these things, you must listen to me.'

I looked away, in disbelief. Maybe she had a point. But maybe she didn't, who needed a man anyway to get on in this world. In my opinion they appeared to be more of a hindrance than anything else.

'Ella, listen to me, you need to do this for your mother's sake, she has been through enough and she couldn't cope with this news. It could put her at risk.'

'Why?'

'Stress could set her back, she is still high risk.'

I was both horrified and tempted by her plan. Imagine if she knew he was an Orangeman. She kissed me on the forehead.

'Now go to sleep love and we will talk again in the morning.'

I put my head on the pillow and the thoughts started racing again. The same thoughts going around like a bicycle wheel going nowhere in particular.

WILL MEETS NANA LOVETT

I couldn't get Ella out of my mind; it had been months since I had seen her. I needed to see her. So I decided to go and visit. I cycled round to the house, parked my bike two blocks away in case anyone might have seen me. I locked the bike with the usual two barrel locks and walked the rest of the way to the house '*Stormont View*'.

I rang the bell, and waited. I quickly scanned the facade of Ella's home. It looked like a real home. Two painted flower boxes either side of the door. Bay windows with the curtains slightly askew, an old round table adorned with beautiful flowers and newspapers. The door opened abruptly. It was Nana Lovett.

'Hello. I was wandering if Ella is in?'

'No. Young man she's not. Whom may I say has called?'

'Will. Will Goodie.'

She stood staring at me for what seemed like a lifetime.

'Will.... Are you the young lad that worked in the local shop?'

'Yes, over the summer.'

'Indeed, well Ella's not here.'

'I see.'

'She's with, with her boyfriend, they're in Dublin.'

I felt as if I had been kicked by a horse.

I handed her a note, with my number on it and I made my way down the drive way. That was that. I would have to just find a way of getting her out of my system.

THE LAUNDRY

ELLA'S STORY

Two weeks after I told Nana, I was washing laundry in a convent in a border town off Sligo. There were about fifteen of us. All girls. Some pregnant, some sent by families because of inappropriate behaviour. Some never left after they had given birth. Their guilt keeping them prisoner, or their families had simply disowned them. All from different Catholic backgrounds. All with stories to tell.

We got woken at seven am by Sr. Mary, who walked through the shared dorm like a ghost with a bell that caused pain to the ears. We made our beds the way we had been taught. We had a porridge breakfast in the pristine kitchen that one of us had cleaned the night before then attended Morning Prayer in the little church attached to the convent. We were told to pray at least seven times a day every day for God's forgiveness for our sins of the flesh. After the Morning Prayer we did the household chores like laundry for the priests or polishing the silver. Dinner was served at three every afternoon, on the button. It was always a decent heart-warming meal. After dinner, evening prayer; then reading or time for reflection and a light supper before bed. No-one seemed to question the routine. We accepted our punishment in the knowledge that if we reacted against it that it would be to our own detriment. Generally, the nuns looked after us well. If someone got sick they would be given adequate rest.

Stories were passed on by the girls who lived permanently in the convent, stories of women who had tried to escape only to be caught and kept in solitary confinement in some dark area of the convent. They told stories of loved-up, forlorn young men sneaking into the dorms.

The nuns were convinced that they were fulfilling God's duty in helping these young women find deliverance and, in a way, that's exactly what they were doing.

Once I accepted my fate, I found the whole ritual quite healing. I became quite close to God in an affirmative way. My persistent questioning regarding my faith lessened. I felt as if God was by my side; on my side. I also felt a bit disgusted by my actions.

It was comforting to be surrounded by other young women, I felt as if I had sisters for the first time. No alcoholic fathers, brain-demented mothers, or controlling grannies.

I felt a release in working out my guilt. I began scrubbing the Holy garments with a passion and I started praying with heart for the first time. Nana would have been proud of me; each day, each chore became a vocation.

Sr. Nula was my favourite nun; she had a heart of sunshine. She was a little, round, hobbling, seventy year-old with wispy white hair and a soft calm face that was permanently smiling. She looked handmade. Then there were the not-so-nice nuns: Sr. Enya and her little side-kick Sr. Teresa. I did my best to keep away from them and took Sr. Nula's advice in avoiding unwanted attention.

I was eight months pregnant when I got a phone call from home. To date no-one had visited. I felt betrayed by this. However I later learned that it was the nuns' preferred route and it made it easier for all regarding the task at hand.

Annie had taken a turn for the worse and had been rushed back into hospital.

The following morning Jack drove up the convent's sweeping tree-lined driveway, kept in immaculate order by Charles the gardener. Jack was shocked to see me standing there in front of him with a belly the size of a hippo's. He didn't know where to look. Smiles exchanged with gifts of cakes and bread from Nana before we departed in the already running Mercedes Benz with strict instructions for my return the following morning. Not only did he find it difficult to look at me but he had difficulty in communicating with me. Suddenly we were strangers. I had hoped for a huge warm embrace and a gush of emotional comments on how much I had been missed, but it was clearly the opposite. He was driving home with a big ball of embarrassment.

'How are you?' he asked sheepishly, twenty minutes into our journey.

'Thanks for asking.'

'I'm sorry Ella. I'm no good at this sort of thing.'

'Bingo.'

I looked out the window and studied the rain falling against the window. I struggled with the knowledge that I was re-entering the real world. A world awash with judgment. We didn't speak again until I got to the hospital.

'Does she know I'm pregnant?' I asked as I approached her little private room.

'No. Her speech comes and goes.'

I walked in and saw a shadow of my mother. All I could feel for her was love. I wanted to climb in beside her and stay there forever. Eventually she opened her eyes and smiled. I sat on the bed beside her and she managed to place her hand on my pregnant tummy and she smiled.

She pulled me towards her with the strength of a bird, hand still on her grandchild; I snuggled into her and she kissed my forehead. Jack watched with tears running down his face. She fell asleep again. I stayed with her for about two hours until the machines beside her started to beep and a bevy of nurses started to fuss around her.

Jack brought me home. Luke had a similar reaction to Jack when faced with the pregnant belly. The look of disbelief when he saw me was mixed with both disgust and sympathy. Nana had cooked Shepherds' Pie and creampuffs to follow. But the celebration factor wasn't with us.

Luke visited me in bed that night.

'We could run away together!'

'Where to?'

'I don't know, somewhere sunny'

'Would you be willing to change nappies?'

'I got accepted into London. I'm going to be a philosopher.'

'Good for you. Promise to write.'

'I promise.'

He bent down and kissed me on the cheek.

'I'll be home soon, it will just be like old times.'

'Yeah.'

I was numb. I was empty.

The following morning, Nana took the phone off the hook; Annie's admirers had been persistent. She made me French toast and bacon, and then packed a large basket of goodies; it was bursting with hours of home-bakes. Jack sat down to breakfast, unshaved, unwashed and sporting what looked like a concealed black eye. He pretended to be cheerful, and functional, but his shake could be heard. Nana grabbed the car keys.

It was pissing rain outside and a single magpie sat on the gate to wave me goodbye.

'It's for the best Ella. I promise.' whispered Nana with a hint of doubt.

The best for whom, I wondered as I sat silently in the car beside her with no fight left in me.

Sr. Nula was waiting for me at the front door and received me with a warm hug. I was allowed to be excused from chores for today. I went straight up to my room and climbed into bed. I was nauseous from the drive and the emotion.

I lay and listened to the rain pelt against the little skylight above me. I could hear rumblings of thunder and then a flash of lightening lit up the grey room.

I felt my baby kick inside me, kicking for life, I put my hand down and I could feel the outline of the baby's foot, I stroked it gently and it kicked again, it felt strangely amazing. I looked over at a statue of the Virgin Mary and the baby Jesus. As I studied it my thoughts started to sound more like my own again. Why should I feel guilty, when all I did was engage in an act of love with a man? Surely God, who was after all a symbol of love, approved of the concept of sharing love?

Each night as I collapsed into my little single bed I would start to wonder what in hell I was doing here. Why was I letting myself be treated like a criminal, locked up, in a convent; unable to visit as much as a shop. Forbidden to attend to my sick mother. Forbidden to mention the baby. No visitors, except under exceptional circumstances, and no outings. I wasn't even sure as to where I was other than it was a cross-border town near Sligo.

I began to realise that all I needed was some loving family support. I wrote a letter to Nana asking to come home. I explained that I didn't want to give up my baby because I knew it was a gift from God and that we would all manage fine. I got no response. I spoke with Sr. Nula but she just gently explained that this was normal, and that most of the girls felt like this at the last hurdle. She did her best to convince me that my baby would be loved and better off with the new adopted parents.

I went up to my room that evening and I lifted that statue of the Blessed Virgin and I threw it across the room. I confessed to accidently knocking the statue over. I was sent to confession, and given fifteen Hail Marys, ten Our Fathers, and the Rosary. I did it all. Most of the other girls didn't want to keep their babies, with a few exceptions. Some were relieved to hand over the unwanted child with their conscience cleared and with hopes of striding back into a new life with a new and stronger conviction that all men were bastards.

Some struggled, like Caroline Murphy, a young fifteen year old girl I befriended, whose mother had warned her that she and her entire family would disown her if she entertained the idea of keeping her baby. Caroline wanted to become a primary school teacher.

'I love kids' she said before she could hear herself.

Caroline was a buxom bubbly almost six-footer who chewed gum consistently. She was a natural beauty. Large green eyes and golden locks framed an unblemished rose pink complexion which could have lit up a darkened room. She had a short fling with a local man twice her age of whom she spoke fondly. She claimed he wanted her to keep the child. She told him she wanted that too. He was married with four other children, one as young as two. Bastard.

The stories that unfolded bonded us for life in a union of understanding that we were being judged by a society full of hypocrites.

After kitchen duty, we helped ourselves to a few biscuits, almost a mortal sin. We ate them slowly on the one and only window sill in our dorm after lights went out. That was probably the height of it, regarding excitement. The kitchen staff including Sister Nula, because she was the chief baker, who usually turned a blind eye; but Sr. Fidelma, an old grumpy nun who smelled of mouldy dishcloths, caught us one evening and took us into the utility room. She made us scrub the toilets the following day. The others got to scrub the conservatory floor on their hands and knees, for not informing her that there was a thief in the house. It was worth it though. We needed to be bold to remind ourselves who we really were.

My Catholic faith was being tested along with my reaction to Annie's illness and I began to reflect on my childhood. Oddly only sweet memories of Annie came to mind like sitting out under the cherry tree stuffing our faces with cherries, or making daisy chains in the sunshine in only our knickers on the newly cut grass lawn. Memories of her freedom and her boldness gave me strength. I'd forgotten her harshness and lack of warmth. I remembered things I had pushed away to serve my discontent. I knew in the depth of my heart that she would have let me keep the baby.

I began to view the faith my Nana had held so closely to her heart as something akin to evil.

Caroline was due around the same time as me which was great as we had each other to compare notes with, like our swollen fingers and heartburn. Another girl, Mary Anne Maguire, a small dark waif with skeletal arms and the complexion of a ghost, was due around the same time too. She never spoke, and bit her nails until they were raw. Her thin, black hair was brushed so thoroughly that her scalp was visible in places. She worshiped the nuns and followed their every word, she prayed with the conviction of a nun. Her family made no contact, ever. Her bump was small and discreet like her. We reckoned she'd never leave the place. She had neither the strength nor the courage. She had a heart-to-heart with Caroline one evening and confessed that the father of her child was, in fact, her uncle. When she discovered she was pregnant her mother had listened to her but told her never to mention it again. She drove her to the convent the following morning.

Nana finally arrived after I posted a bunch of pleading letters expressing my turmoil and grief. I was huge and approaching the end of my ninth month. She arrived laden with more gifts, cotton pyjamas, magazines and a little box of my favourite assorted biscuits. It turned out Annie had acquired some sort of virus which made her relapse. She was walking with one crutch and she and Jack could understand each other's conversation.

Nana and I walked with Sr. Nula through the beautifully manicured walled gardens, which displayed an array of home-grown vegetables and herbs; every type of colourful flower imaginable. We passed the hardworking nuns on their knees as they weeded. It looked like a haven of paradise and loveliness; a place one could only imagine having a retreat in. Then we were treated to afternoon tea in the drawing room. The spacious white room was adorned with oil paintings one of which was a Jack B. Yeats, an image of a galloping horse disappearing into an array of wild colour. The freedom was enticing. The entire room gave off an air of opulence that was no doubt afforded through cash-in-hand from families of young vulnerable girls like me. As soon as Sr. Nula left to order more tea, I grabbed Nana by the arm.

'You have got to take me home.'

'Ella. That's not possible. You know everything has been arranged.'

'Then, un-arrange it.'

'I can't do that.'

'This is all about you Nana. I want to keep my baby.'

'And then what Ella, you're only sixteen years old and I'm too old to raise a baby.'

'But I'm not. Please. This is a living hell. I want to come home.'

She smiled at me patronisingly.

'Now listen to me Ella. You have two more weeks to go before this is all over. We are doing what is best for this baby. The baby is the priority in all of this, not you or I. Your mother's not in a position to support you. Your father is not well either.'

She paused a moment and flinched, she looked at me again with that steady and guarded face and she continued with a firm and clear tone.

'I'm not going to be around forever, I'm seventy-two. You have no career in place, so you are not in a position to raise a child single-handedly. You are a bright, intelligent, human being, Ella. I'm doing this because I love you.'

'But..'

'And furthermore, young lady, you should thank God that there are refuges like this. These nuns welcomed you in your time of need.'

I distracted myself with the Jack B. Yeats painting.

'Look I'm sorry you have to go through this, but believe me, this is for the best. End of discussion.'

She looked at me, in a way I had never seen, she was afraid.

'Best for who Nana?'

'I don't know if I can take much more Ella, Jack's not great, he hasn't been great since you left.'

I was powerless, everything she said was true. With

exceptions to being bright; getting pregnant in the first place wasn't so bright. She got up and left when the tea arrived, with excuses about having appointments at home and promises of keeping in touch. She tried to hug me before she left, but she couldn't. She handed me a little brown parcel and went.

As soon as Nana left I was sent to the back of the house. I fought the tears until I made it to the dorm. Caroline opened her arms to me. Caroline joined me and we ate the entire box of biscuits she had brought. We made plans for our life after the convent. Caroline wanted to become a primary school teacher and move over to England where nobody knew her. I was going to go back to school and study to become a nurse or a psychologist; I would also move to England. We might even become neighbours, definitely lifelong friends. Later I opened my little brown parcel and found a little prayer to St. Francis and a new set of wooden rosary beads.

I went into Labour around three in the morning. I had felt twinges earlier that day and Sr. Nula had let me rest in the library and read. When the pains became unbearable, Caroline went off and got Sr. Nula and she came and wrapped me up in my dressing gown and took me down to the little room attached to the convent. The room was just like any other bedroom except for the little plastic cot that sat beside the bed, a drip on a stand and a little tin table with other bits of medical-looking paraphernalia. A large midwife arrived and introduced herself as Margaret. I lay on the bed and the pains got worse, it felt as if someone was gripping my insides with pliers every ten minutes. The only pain relief on offer was gas and air, which I sucked on for life. I reached a point where I honestly thought that I was going to die.

Sr. Nula stayed with me for the entire process.

'Did your Nana tell you about the time we got caught wearing the silk stockings to the dance? We left the house in our summer dresses and knee-high socks and sandals and changed in the bathroom when we got to the dance.

Your Great Grandmother, a beautiful, tall, skinny lady arrived earlier than expected to bring us home. Well, she took one look at our legs and marched us out of that dance with the fury of a witch. As soon as she got us home she pulled those black silk stockings off our skinny white legs, and put them on the open fire! *'No child of mine will feed the eyes of the devil'* said your Great Grandmother.'

'It was your Nana that was supposed to become a nun, not me. But then Charlie spotted her at a dance and that was that. She was always the sensible one, top of the class the whole way through.'

She paused for a moment,

'Don't be angry with her Ella. She loves you and she is very proud of you. I know from the letters and photographs she has sent over the years. It's Ella this and Ella, that. She sees herself in you.'

Another contraction came on and she held out her hand for me to hold on to and then things calmed down again.

'I hear you're a smart girl. '

'Ahhhhhh'

'What do you want to do when you finish school?'

'I don't know, I like science.'

'Oh, a scientist in the making.'

Suddenly I felt a pain that gripped my entire being.

'We are getting ready to push now Ella. Take a deep breath and push.' said the very matter-of-fact midwife. So I pushed and I pushed and I pushed. Nothing. I collapsed into the bed and wanted to fall into a deep exhausted sleep. I started to pray hard, out loud, making bargains with Jesus, like I would go to Mass on Sunday every week, if he just got me through this.

'PUSH Ella!' shouted Margaret, with a tone that chilled me to the core.

I felt a sweep of energy come over me and my body jolted into position and I pushed with every last bit of strength left in my sixteen year-old body. Out came a head and then the body of this little creature. Sister Nula kissed me with a smile. Margaret lifted the child with efficiency, checked its nose and mouth. She put a little white vest and nappy on it and wrapped it up in a little white blanket.

'Well done, Ella. It's a beautiful little boy.'

Margaret approached with a warm smile and handed me my son. I took him into my arms and my entire being melted when he opened his little mouth and his dark blue eyes. He looked up at me and fixed his stare. His little face was so beautiful, his wee fingers moving already. He was the most perfect thing I had ever seen. He had sallow skin and a head of silken dark hair. He smelt of almonds. I kissed him and held him close to my breast, oblivious to anyone else in the room. I kissed him on the head and he moved his head towards my breast which was the size of a ripe water melon.

When I looked up I realised the others had left the room. A bottle of warm milk sat by my bedside. It was just me and him.

'Hello Andrew Will Lovett'

He opened his little mouth, and made a gurgling noise. I placed him on my breast and he sucked immediately. I couldn't believe it.

'That's my boy.'

After he fed he snuggled in beside me. I now knew what unconditional love was.

Days passed with time disappearing, just sleeping and feeding my new born, conversations filled with promises and hope. I lost count of the days and reality.

I awoke early one morning to find Sr. Nula and Sr. Margaret standing over me.

My life had just begun. I was meant to have this baby and we were here to share our lives together. It was God's wish. Andrew and I would work it out. I indeed had my whole life ahead of me because now it was filled with love.

Sr. Nula approached with a baby's bottle and a little blue blanket in hand.

'Ella, he is going to a loving home, I will keep you informed. It's for the best love.' she said gently.

She stretched out her arms and took my little bundle of love away. I quietly refused to hand him over but she gently pulled him away and I watched her walk towards the door.

'I want to keep him.' I said to deaf ears because she continued walking. She walked away with my future.

'Please, I want to keep him' I roared but she kept walking away with my baby in her arms.

I got out of the bed and followed her but she turned and whispered:

'Back to bed now Ella.'

'Please.'

She walked on and I followed her to the door which swung back in my face. I stood with my hand on the door, powerless.

When I returned to my room the following morning, Nana was sitting waiting for me. No questions asked. She quietly helped me pack. Caroline had also gone into labour and another innocent, swelling girl with strawberry blonde plaits, no more than fifteen if even, waited in the colourful drawing room for my tear-drenched empty bed. I scribbled a note for Caroline and hugged the other girls who waited by the door for me on the way out. Nana thanked the nuns and handed them a cheque. I felt faint and sick. Sr. Nula threw her arms around me, and held me close as she whispered into my ear.

'I've seen lots of girls come and go, I know you'll be fine. Now promise to come back and tell us how you're getting on or, if you can't face this place, write me a card.'

When I prised myself away she waved me on with a smile. I knew nothing would ever bring me back, nothing. But I would write to Sr. Nula.

She took Nana into her arms and they hugged close.

Each bump in the car on the way home felt like a jolt of electricity.

'One day I hope you will thank me for this, Ella.'

I looked out the window knowing I would never forgive her for what just happened.

'This was all just an unfortunate mistake.'

She sounded desperate for my forgiveness.

'Can we just leave it, I don't want to talk about it anymore…in fact I don't want to discuss this with you ever again.'

We travelled for about an hour in silence and the world looked different, the landscape had become denser.

'Jack is doing better and Annie is doing great.' she said chirpily. I really didn't care.

When I got home, they all behaved as if everything was normal, Nana tried to get me to eat, Jack had bought me some new novels to read, Luke had left me a package with a card and some weed. Annie couldn't look at me. They all made me sick. I climbed straight into bed with the stolen white vest that still smelt of Andrew Will Lovett my little orange man.

JACK LOSES THE PLOT

ELLA'S STORY

I returned to school to embark on my A-Levels as if nothing had happened, with a tale that I had been absent with a virus. I still sat with Ali for lunch but I said nothing. Occasionally I would go over to Ali's for sleepovers and look on with envy. Her parents gardened at weekends together. Communicated in a responsible loving manner over meals, snuggled up on a settee together.

Ali was gorgeous in every way, strawberry blonde with legs and sumptuous breasts, lingering, green eyes. She could choose her friends. Boys drooled at the sight of her every move. When she came to our house for tea, Luke insisted on hanging out with us - even Annie had clicked with her. I would have done anything to have a mum like Ali's, someone who did your laundry, put it in order into your closet, someone who had time to drop you off to ballet and pick you up at the correct time. Someone who earmarked your best friend's birthdays in their wall calendar.

Ali pretended not to study but managed to get the grades. The most interesting thing by far though, was the fact that she recently acquired a boyfriend six years older than herself, who she met outside the cinema. James, a tall blonde carpenter, who happened to have a car.

The odd thing about Ali was that she gave a great impression of being the model angel child, and she was just that during the week; but curiously she was a devil personified at the weekends. She drank, smoked and dabbled in drugs.

A whole new world had opened up for us, socially. I was different after my experience at the convent; part of me wanted to rebel and another part of me had grown up. I wanted to make a go of it. So I studied hard during the week, and partied hard at the weekends. I lost weight, after having Andrew. Probably the stress of it all. My breasts were swollen, my waist a little tighter. New dresses hugged my rounded hips as if they were made for them. I grew my wavy auburn hair so that it came into a life all of its own. I even started wearing a little make-up. The Annie in me was coming out. I got rid of the purple walls and painted my bedroom white.

At night I spent time cleansing away the makeup; the '*I am coping very well*' face.

When summer returned, Luke had become a man. He took me more seriously; he spoke to me more like his equal. We started smoking grass together in his bedroom. He even managed to grow a few grass plants in the greenhouse amongst the tomatoes. Jack knew, but turned a blind eye, anything but confrontation.

He was more sober these days and weaker for it. He walked around with a quiet heavy shell on his back terrified anyone might remind him of who he really was. He made the effort for Annie. He often sat by her bed reading to her, fetching for her. He insisted on being the only one allowed to bathe her. He researched foods that would help speed up her recovery. He even reinstated Alan, with profuse apologies for sacking him for no logical reason in the hope that the home grown vegetables might just bring his old Annie back. We would walk her to the greenhouse and she would sit and watch Alan bring the garden back to life.

Luke would sometimes take me to his mates houses where we would get stoned for hours and say nothing. Or we would sometimes climb up into the treehouse and do the same. Luke would write letters to Government officials in regard to environmental issues and I would string beads from the new bead shop in town. Finally a little laughter returned to our home.

Nana would continue to remain the heart of the home and cook while listening to news updates. Sometimes if I was out and about at the weekend I would awake beside a friend of Luke's. Luke would phone home before we got smashed and explain that we couldn't get a taxi home because of riots in town.

The hunger strike continued, with ten men now on strike, this led to curfews occasionally. Troubles increased with the anticipation of what might happen. For some, riots were a pastime, for others it was a lock-in, making a point, belting out a tune.

Jack always had an open mind, that's what I loved about him. One never quite knew what would escape from his mouth next; he was a walking encyclopaedia regarding solar systems, natural disasters and world wonders; he was fascinated by tribal rituals and working-class habits. He was so middle-class. If he saw me chewing gum, he would go off on a rant.

'Spit that out please.... Ella, you must remember your position in society as a young lady.'

When Annie berated him for drinking too much his response was.

'My name is Jack, I'm not an alcoholic, I don't go to the meetings.'

The night I returned from the convent, he came up and sat beside my bed, he just put his arms around me and said:

'I hope we did the right thing. I suppose you will miss him.'

He was biased towards the Catholic cause and their struggle for freedom. Everyone living through the Troubles was partial to bias, it was a survival mechanism. His Catholicism was a mainstay, in part because it was important to him to be seen as an active member of the parish community.

His eternal hope was peace and a united Ireland. But as time marched on he became more disillusioned with this ideal. He became more sympathetic with the Nationalist struggle, which he felt was judicially misrepresented regarding sentencing and general arrests. He missed Annie but was enamoured by the fact he could keep her by his side. He had regained some control during her illness. At first she was taken by his attention. He went out of his way to make her feel comfortable, she was aware he drank less. He read her poetry; they watched television together, had tea and biscuits in the evening, just like any mature couple nesting. However as Annie recovered, her frustrations with Jack returned. She started getting out into the real world again and she needed breathing space. She worked hard at her physiotherapy and speech and when she informed Jack in her fiery, frustrated, now clear, speech that she needed space he recoiled like a tortoise back into his attic.

He kept up a good front for as long as he could. His continuing to wear a suit every day, with a colourful tie to match, we took as a good sign. But I saw what lay beneath the facade. I could smell the whiskey through the attic walls.

Annie had always left his suits, along with her own outfits, to the dry cleaners on the first Monday of every month. When this ritual stopped the suit became the visible decaying layers of a man who was falling apart inside. Buttons fell off, hems dropped. The jackets were the first to disappear, some lost in bars, others left on chairs, then the tie. Nana repeatedly offered to take care of his suits but he refused, he was waiting on Annie.

The man we could never shut up had to have conversations teased out of him. His contemporary office in town which boasted enviable art, which exuded an almost neurotic precision of post-modernism, had transformed into a still contemporary graveyard.

Matilda, his life-long secretary, without instruction from Jack left the office and continued work from her own home, with weekly visits to Jack's attic, where she would deliver or collect files. Matilda was an efficient spinster in her late fifties.

The saddest part was that no-one was willing to do anything to acknowledge his slow but obvious decline. Nana, Luke, and I all slipped too easily into denial. Annie was the only one who seemed brave enough to address his fall. First with Nana.

'Your son needs help.'

'He's had a very difficult time Annie, I'm surprised he's doing as well as he is … considering.'

He bit his nails and quietly drank throughout the day in a controlled and disguised manner where he never appeared to become pissed. Some days he was in great form, laughing loudly at the smallest of things, but most days he just retreated into the chaotic attic.

I did try to mention my concerns to Nana too, but our relationship had deteriorated since the convent business. She became holier-than-thou and was standing her ground. She couldn't find it in her heart to forgive me and I punished her by withdrawal. I had to cook several times a week, whilst she attended to Church duties. So I came up with a plan. Her sister.

'Why don't we ask Auntie Margaret over, she might cheer Dad up a little, she did offer to help?'

Nana looked at me over her glasses the way she used to when I had been bold.

'True, she loves Jack. It must be dreadful over there. Margaret's hard to move though.'

That evening I went up to the attic room and knocked on the door. I waited and knocked again.

'Who is it?' was the impatient bark from behind the door.

'It's me, Ella'

A moment passed and all I could hear was the shuffling of papers.

'Come in, come in.'

He greeted me with a forced smile and gestured for me to sit on his little red stool beside the desk.

The heat was stifling; he had an electric heater which sat beside his desk. The room smelt of paper and whiskey. His desk was covered in piles of hand written notes, the walls surrounded by reminders or the forgotten messages. I read *pick Ella up from school Thursday.* Forgotten cups, glasses, and mangy plates lay buried amongst the paper and books. The floor had a path of molten carpet amongst the scattered bits that lay there. The stench of mustiness and whisky overpowered my breathing capacity. I sat beside him.

'How are you?'

'I'm fine, really I'm fine,' he replied.

'Good.'

'Ella, my love, I know I've been busy with all that's going on, but I just, I just find it hard to keep on top of everything. Work has me stretched between that and the threats, and what not.. how are you getting on at school?'

'What threats Dad?'

He searched through a pile of papers on his desk, he stuck his hand straight into the pyramid of paper and magically found a little white envelope, and he handed it to me. I opened it and read *'Your days are numbered'* the words taken from news print and pasted unto paper.

'Dad, you need to contact the police?'

'Not a good idea Ella.'

'Is it serious?'

It's nothing; I've been getting them for years now.' he said, forcing another smile.

'I'm being followed you know, and they have the phones tapped. Ella, keep the curtains closed after four, they are taking photographs through the windows, they have specialised equipment, you know?'

'Who are they Dad?'

He smiled; pleased I was listening and not dismissing his crazy ideas. He was visibly shaking a tremor-like shake.

'They … Ella, are'

He pronounced his words crisply and clearly and then he whispered the next sentence:

'The Loyalists Paramilitaries, a group known as the Red Hand Commandos. They are being assisted by the police and army. They think I am working with the IRA because I defended a man who shot one of their own.

That's why I work up here; they bugged my office, my phone and my car. Now they have satellites that can take photographs from the sky. Explain the helicopters that hover over our house at night.'

'That's just surveillance Dad'

He smiled nervously and paused.

'You don't believe me do you? That's okay, I understand, really I do, it all sounds a little crazy. On top of them I have the other side on my back too; the IRA whom I have to pay monthly for protection purposes and if I don't, well then I would need to pay the other lot. It's a lose-lose situation.'

We did have helicopters hover over the house and general area at night. Most nights they hovered right above the house.

He started to fidget with his fingers, pulling at his finger nails, the bags under his eyes were dark, and his skin was so dry it was almost shedding, his shirt collar was visibly stained and he was in his bare feet, I looked away and read a note pinned to the wall which read *'six months left, put food in freezer.'*

'Dad, you look exhausted, you'll get sick.'

'Ella............ I love you so much, you have no idea. I love you too much, that's why I'm scared, you must believe me, tell me you believe me'

'I believe you Dad; I am just a little worried. I have all day off school tomorrow, and maybe we could visit the doctor, he might be able to help, you know give you something to settle your nerves.'

'No' he said emphatically. 'I'm fine, really, look I'll have an early night tonight, a goodnight's sleep is all I need. Honestly. I've said too much, I'm frightening you, poor Ella, perhaps I will tell the police about the note.'

He took the threatening note from me and pinned it up on the wall. He rubbed his eyes, and looked over at his saxophone.

'How about we go and visit Auntie Margaret tomorrow, we could talk her into coming over for a few days, it must be a living hell over there at the moment.'

'I don't know'

'They might be watching her house. She must be petrified over there with all the riots.'

He looked up at me like a child who had just been offered a sweet.

'You're right Ella, we must watch Auntie Margaret.'

Then he smiled and took out his saxophone and he played the theme from Pink Panther, because he knew I loved it and he filled my soul with the tiniest bit of hope.

VISITING A WAR ZONE

ELLA'S STORY

We got stopped five times by army and police checkpoints on our journey to the Short Strand. On one of our stops we were asked to '*get out of the vehicle*'.

This was a regular occurrence whilst driving about Belfast City, but more common in Nationalists areas. Usually an RUC man halted the car. The driver rolling down the window would be asked for a driver's licence. The questions were nearly always the same. '*Name sir, where are you going to? Where are you coming from? What is the business of your journey?*' Being asked to step outside of the vehicle was for further investigation, '*open the boot*' or when they were very suspicious you could be put up against a wall and body-searched.

It was a ritual I had come to loathe. I hated the army's filthy hands going anywhere near me. I hated that I had to let them know my business. Give them my identity. I hated them full stop. I hated anyone who pointed guns at children. But I always did exactly as I was told with good manners because fear wouldn't let me behave in any other way. If you let them know that you were frightened or irritated they would distrust you and give a more thorough search.

Dad detested them too. When he answered their questions he never looked at them, he also used a tone which was full of contempt, so consequently nearly every time we got stopped he would be asked to step out of the car.

It was always an adventure visiting Aunt Margaret, Nana's sister. She was nothing like Nana. She lived in a red brick two-up-two-down, with her daughter Bridget, who was a little 'backward'.

On our journey over Dad seemed a little more cheerful,

the sun was doing its best to peep out between showers and a huge rainbow stretched across the sky. We listened to the classics on the radio. He was sober and he even washed his hair. As we approached the Nationalist estate where she lived we could see that almost every house had hung a little black flag out their window; all the gable walls displayed political murals, painted men with balaclavas and weapons in their arms, *'brothers in arms'*. Remnants of burnt cars could be seen on the scattered waste land of some of the burnt-out houses. Young men walked past briskly, in their flares or tracksuits.

The hunger strike period seemed to be permanently dark. Grey skies and black flags. When we arrived into the estate Margaret lived in, an entirely Nationalist area, armed soldiers stood at either side of the entrance, occasionally pointing their guns in our faces as we walked towards the house.

A blackened burnt out car lay at the entrance to her line of houses, still smouldering, presumably from riots the night before. We could see young soldiers sneaking around the street corners, sliding their way down the road with their backs to the wall as they moved pointing their rifles at anything or anyone that moved. Debris from the riots the night before could be seen scattered about the streets in the form of broken bottles, rubber tubes, black tyres, shopping trolleys and bin lids; weapons received from the enemy during the rioting.

'Maybe this wasn't such a good idea Dad,'

I was worried that our car could be a target especially as it wasn't known in the area.

'Look, we will check and see how she is and go'

We got out of the car and huddled up to the door together. Despite the fact we were Catholics, we still felt out of our comfort zone. This was a different section of the zoo than the one we lived in.

Auntie Margaret opened the door before we got to it. There she stood, as predicted, with her snow-white perm, smiling eyes and floral apron, yard brush in hand. She peeked to the left then to the right of the door and beckoned us in, like a true warrior.

'I know why you are here, but you can forget it, I am going nowhere, so sit down and I'll make you a wee cup of tea, and you can be on your way, because there's riots promised for later and another curfew on the way.'

She paused to look at us both and continued before we could speak.

'How's Nana? Look at you Ella, you're all grown up and gorgeous, like your Nana was in her heyday. I suppose the men are queuing up, are they Jack? Sit down, take off your coats. Jack, you look exhausted. Would you like a wee drop?'

'Coffee.'

He smiled. She shuffled off into the kitchen and continued talking.

Jack was pulling at his fingertips uneasily. She arrived in with a tray of tea and biscuits.

'How's Bridget?' asked Jack.

'She's fine. She's with the nuns today. Nana tells me you're working hard Jack, thank God we have someone representing our own. It's been a tough few months for you. How's Annie, Jack?'

'Annie's nearly herself again. What about these riots?'

'Would you like a wee drop in that cup?

'Yes, but I'm driving.'

She retrieved the bottle from the back of the sofa and poured a large whiskey into her cup of coffee and a little drop into Jack's. She threw her eyes up to the heavens, and then blessed herself in front of the large statue of the Virgin Mary she had displayed on her mantle.

'It's bloody awful, Jack, they bang those friggin' bin lids day and night, a bloody racket. It's the women are the worst; they didn't stop until three o'clock this morning. They reckon Sands will die in the next day or so. Molly O' Connor's son was arrested yesterday, and Lilly's son is threatening to go on the strike along with a queue of others. My heart goes out to those young men and their mammies, but sure what can we do Jack, that bitch Thatcher won't budge, she should just resign. In fact she should just be taken down, God forgive me, but the world would be a better place without the likes of her, causing innocent men to die …'

We heard someone run past the front of the house, Margaret peeped out the lace curtain, and lit a cigarette; I would have killed for one.

'And how are you Ella? I hear you have a young man, what's he like?'

The whistle of the kettle blew just in time, for her four-foot-seven, round body to get up to brew another pot of tea. Dad lifted the newspaper.

A Perpetual Mother of Succour glowed in a red light on the wall. Hand-embroidered lace covers hung over the passed-down three piece suite. An old polished cabinet crammed with religious relics, a piece of St Anthony's clothing or St Margaret's bones, set in a little plastic oval pendant, all the way from Rome or Israel, kept ready for the cause at hand. She kept the place immaculate.

Her kitchen was small and basic. She had a wash area in the small backyard equipped with a washing ringer. Two bedrooms upstairs.

She continued chatting with an occasional break for breath. Her shake was similar to Jack's.

'Before you throw yourself away to any man Ella, take it from me, your independence is everything.'

Jack smiled over at me.

'She's a good girl, Margaret, top grades all the way.'

She beamed over at me with great expectation.

'I know that, don't I know that well, Jack, but what's this young man like, Nana told me he's thinking of studying medicine, is that so?'

'Are you being watched Margaret?'

Dad continued to pull at his fingertips.

'Watched?'

'He means are you safe, in amongst all this rioting.'

'I'm fine.'

She laughed nervously, and winked over at Jack,

'Now tell about this young man Ella,'

'He's history Auntie Margaret.'

She let out a belly laugh at the drone of my tone.

'Good for you, you're too young to be getting serious, you have the rest of your life to find a decent man, and believe me it may take a life-time to find a decent one.'

She sparked. I smiled like an angel.

'Young love can be overestimated, God I nearly forgot, I've something for you Ella'

She went upstairs; we could hear every step from the stairs across the old pinewood bedroom floor.

Dad lifted the newspaper and I looked around at the photos on the mantles of three of her children, all in wedding attire, or graduation gowns, all safe in America. Her husband left for war after the fourth child and never returned.

'Dad, we need to ask her to come and stay with us till the hunger strike settles. It's too dangerous for her here, Bridget can come too.'

Jack looked up from his paper, oblivious to his shake.

'She won't come.'

He then put his finger up to his lips to shush me. He walked over to the window slowly and peeped out from the side as if he were avoiding gunfire. He pulled the little white linen curtains closed.

'Dad there's no-one out there.'

Aunt Margaret gave me a box of old photographs for Nana and a box of my favourite teacakes; she wasn't one for cooking, so it was a treat to taste some actual, shop treats.

'What are you doing Jack, we can't all just sit in the dark it's midday.'

She marched over and pulled the curtains open again.

'Sorry Margaret, I got a bit of a chill.'

She looked over to him and went to her drawer of relics; she searched through it but couldn't find the right one, so she went into the locked drawer of the cabinet where she had the more treasured relics.

'There you go, a bone from St John Bosco, good for the nerves.'

She blessed him with the relic and he accepted it with graciousness.

'Keep that with you at all times and ask him for strength when needs be.'

She put her hand into her other apron pocket and pulled out a little relic for me, St. Agnes.

'Protects virginal innocence'

Dad and I looked at each other and smiled, I was impressed with Nana's discretion.

We sat for a moment comforted by the open fire only to be disturbed by some loud commotion outside; at first I thought it was gun shots. Then another bang, this time even louder.

'Not again, that's the racket I was telling you about, the bin lids, something has happened.' Dad jumped to his feet and checked out the window again.

'Margaret, will you come back with us?

She got the poker and stoked the fire, this was the only time she managed to remain quiet.

'Please Margaret, if not for your sake for ours. We are worried sick about you, especially Nana.'

'Jack love..... I'd be happier just staying put, God knows what might happen if I just got up and left; they burn the emptied houses. No, I'll stay put if you don't mind.'

'Has there been anyone hurt with the riots?'

She threw her eyes to heaven.

'Do you remember Mrs McCauley, Jack? She used to mind you when Nana worked in the bakery. Well, she ended up in the Royal Intensive Care unit with third degree burns... a petrol bomb; and that wee fellow you used to play with, Tommy Maguire, he's in a wheelchair, Sacred Heart of Jesus. He had nothing to do with anything, it's the devil's work, Jack. The devil at work.'

'I see they blew up Sean McGinns' old house.'

'Oh aye, and several houses in the next street got it, a mortar bomb attack, some got burnt out, desperate carryon, and the so-called police don't want to know anymore.'

Suddenly the banging noise got louder, it was so loud I thought it might have been a bomb.

'That's the women out again, banging the bin lids, something has happened at the H- Block..'

Jack finished his tea quickly. We could hear shouting and panic outside, cars coming to a halt.

'I wish you'd come with us, just for a few days?'

'Look I'll think about it, now go.'

Jack got up and pulled over the curtains.

'Stay away from the windows Margaret, keep the door locked at all times.'

Margaret looked up at him, a little anxious at his tone, and I knew it was time to leave. The road to home was blocked off by stolen cars that would later be burnt out. Other roads were blocked by army jeeps refusing entry. We managed to get to the main road by explaining to the army that we needed to get home to a sick relative.

The Hunger Strike struck a chord with me, probably because it reminded me of when Annie couldn't eat, not out of choice. Their demands seemed so insignificant in comparison to what was happening to people having to face a real life and death situation. I did have sympathy for the Nationalists. I even started to hush chat in the kitchen when the news bulletins came on.

I needed something to believe in to try and make sense of what was happening around me. I wasn't a Catholic per se, but I knew that the Protestant communities were carrying out atrocious attacks on Catholics and that the Loyalists were being aided and abetted by the British soldiers and the RUC, the so-called police force. I kept that relic on my person at all times. Despite its contradiction.

ELLA PARTIES

Luke and I went to see the 'Boom Town Rats' in the Ulster Hall. Luke wore a red and black Che Guevara T-shirt and half a smile. We were meeting up with Luke's friend James and James' new girlfriend.

The concert hall was packed with young people. People everywhere rolling joints , having a laugh. It was ironic really, because events like these always brought back home the concept of people actually having fun together whatever their religion. It was a real sense of freedom and people made the most of it.

Luke found his mate James; his new girlfriend just happened to be my best friend Ali, who had just spent the previous few months drooling over details about what they had been getting up to especially in the bedroom department. James was as hot as she was. He had the skin of a cherub and the eyes of an angel. After a little dramatic scene of us girls getting excited to see each other, we all started getting into the cool sounds of the backup band the 'Stiff Little Fingers'. James rolled joints; one after another and quite quickly the world became a softer place, the atmosphere filled with laughter from like-minded people.

Ali beckoned me into the bathroom; she pulled me into a cubicle and locked the door to roll a joint.

She was having a hissy fit about fancying some new guy she had met and trying to pluck up the courage to dump James. In my opinion James was a complete catch, early twenties, a handyman, a car and aspirations of becoming an entrepreneur, he looked and dressed like a member of Rupert the bear's family.

Ali had the body of a Barbie and could have had her pick. The nicest thing about her was that she was genuinely modest. She appeared to have no idea that she was gorgeous. She lit the joint and after a long-drawn out detailed account of where and when she met this new guy, she took a deep breath.

'Well what do you think ... should I dump James or what?'

But before I could open my mouth, she lifted her skirt pulled down her knickers and started to pee.

'I don't know, Ella, the problem is, he's more into me, than I'm into him, you know what I mean?'

She pulled up her knickers.

'You're beautiful, stunning, you can have whatever you want, just follow your heart.'

She paused for a minute, and then her bottom lip started to quiver.

'My parents are separating, well they have already separated. Dad lost his temper and lashed out and she threw him out. Mum's all over the place, she's popping pills and up during the night. He's met someone else, it's a right fucking mess?

I gave her a hug and handed her back the joint.

'She will be okay Ali. Just focus on the A-levels and your mum for now, and whatever you do, understand it's nothing to do with you, it's their stuff!'

'Okay.'

She smiled and she slipped her hand into her pocket and took out two little pieces of paper, she hugged me warmly, and then looked into my face.

'Open your mouth!'

I obeyed.

'In the name of the Father, the Mother and the Holy Spirit.'

She said, as she anointed me blasphemously. She placed two little pieces of paper unto her tongue and then she kissed me smack on the lips and I kissed her back, and her mouth opened as she passed a little piece of paper unto my tongue.

'Now swallow, my child.'

Time disappeared for a while. We just kept kissing and laughing. We could hear a loud cheer coming from the crowd outside as the Boom Town Rats took to the stage and it was fantastic. Everything was just fantastic, the colour schemes in the bathroom were intensely implausible, people were beautiful, and ugly. It was like a ride on a rollercoaster except on ground level. The cheer of the crowd as the gorgeous Bob and the Rats hit the stage pulled me to the dance floor with Ali like a magnet, her sexy limbs moving to the rhythm of the music with ease and confidence. I closed my eyes among the Catholics and Protestants of this torn community and danced as if I was dancing on air, in my own world, lost to all reality. When I opened my eyes, the room was alive, and awash with colour and glitter, mirrors and lights reflecting rainbows. Ali dancing like a Goddess. We danced until our men found us on the floor and did their best to entice us out of our trance. I just couldn't stop dancing I needed to dance it all out of me. James wanted his woman but she was lost in dance too so Luke and James joined us and I put my hand out for the joint in Luke's hand.

But he refused to give it to me. We danced till the music stopped.

The Rats waited for an encore, the crowds stamped their feet for more and the lights went on to reveal a washed-out crowd in need of their beds but awake with the buzz of escapism. Geldof reappeared to a huge array of cheers and the party began again, lights off, papers out.

The beauty of the stoniness was becoming less vibrant, people looked wasted and scary, some guy hitting on me approached me with hands everywhere and all I could do was push him away and laugh uncontrollably. Eventually I made my way through the hot, sweaty crowded room and found a bathroom. I managed to splash my face in a little cold water, apply my ruby red lipstick and give myself a smile of reassurance before I headed out to the dance floor again.

I found a beautiful man on the dance floor, danced with him in total rhythm, his hips moving slowly at the exact same time as mine; his arms mirroring my arms. I was in heaven, this place was heaven. He was smiling seductively at me when I felt a hand on my shoulder. It was Luke.

'Party over, it's home time, there's some trouble outside.'

The guy I was dancing with approached Luke aggressively, sticking his chest out.

'It's okay, I'm with him' I said.

I tried to pull Luke into the magic feeling of the dance but he shrugged me off.

'Come on.'

I obeyed and waved goodbye to my dance partner, who was in a similar head-state to me, he waved and blew me kisses.

'Party pooper.'

I took Luke's arm.

We went outside and suddenly the whole atmosphere changed. The night was black. Sirens filled the air with that familiar sound. We walked down the road quickly, in hope of waving down a taxi. Helicopters circled overhead, police and army everywhere. We could hear people shouting and then gunshots in the distance. Shadows disappeared around walls. We were walking through a war zone, it was the first time I had ever actually seen it like this, it was real, it looked like an actual war, like something from a film, the army had brown paint on their faces, backs up against the wall, holding their guns to their chests. I looked at one soldier and smiled, he was no more than seventeen; he looked straight back at me and pointed his gun in my face, terrified. Prepared to kill.

We walked on quietly; Luke got me safely to the crammed taxi rank. Everyone was out of it except a pale young boy of about twelve who sat with his drunken father.

'What did you take?'

'I don't know, Ali gave me something.'

'What kind of something?'

I smiled, impressed with his protective anger.

'I don't know it was small and white and it made me feel very good but I've a feeling that's all about to change. I do love you Luke, you know that don't you, I mean, I know … Oh look, he looks a bit like Bob Geldof'…

I said pointing to a hairy-looking man who was sitting opposite us.

'Sorry mate, she's had one too many.'

I tried to snuggle into him and he allowed it, but it wasn't reciprocated. Luke was clearly annoyed.

'Just keep your mouth shut and go straight to bed when you get home okay.'

He waited, looking at me.

'Okay.'

Our taxi arrived about an hour later. Luke woke me. We remained silent for most part of the journey; he was used to me being silent with him.

When we got home it appeared all was quiet, all lights were out, but when we entered the front door the porch lights went on as if for a surprise party. I was faced with Nana. She looked horrified. Luke stood in front of me but she pushed him to one side. I stood up as straight as I could, pretending to be fine or so I thought.

'Jesus, Mary and Joseph, look at the state of her,'

'She's had a couple of pints, she'll be fine,' said Luke,

'Pints! How many pints did she have to get her into this state? Look at her for Christ's sake, Luke, I expected more from you.'

I was I think standing still, saying nothing, as instructed by Luke, so why was she having such a reaction when I hadn't even opened my mouth,

'Nana, I'm fine, gimme a hug.'

'Get up to your bed at once; you're grounded young lady for a month!'

'Where's Dad?'

Suddenly he appeared with glass in hand, smiling.

'Hello little bird. Good time?'

'Yes Dad, it was brilliant.'

We hugged happily in our oblivion.

'Would you like a drink? A small one,'

'No she wouldn't! She's going to bed Jack and I would suggest you do the same. Have none of you any respect?'

Silence filled the walls. We all toddled off upstairs. When I got to my bedroom everything looked different, everything looked beautiful. The moon lit up the images reflected from the curtains on the walls. Occasionally the images moved a little, not in a threatening way, but dancing.

I opened my sash bedroom window, as I always did when I needed a smoke and I climbed out onto the slanted roof in front of it. There was just enough room to sit comfortably, and I lit a cigarette. The full moon shone onto my face.

'He's still in love with me, Mr Moon.'

The moon looked back at me and smiled. I climbed back into the room and I managed to slip on my pyjamas. I caught a glimpse of myself in the mahogany dressing table mirror. The ruby red lipstick was smudged all over my mouth and the mascara resembled the look of a panda. I lay in bed wide awake, my thoughts racing from one thing to another. I didn't wake until midday the following day.

When I came into the kitchen, Nana was sitting by the range, the rosary beads in one hand the radio in the other. I was hushed angrily as soon as she saw me approach. Annie was up and making herself a cup of tea. The radio announced, *'Twenty-seven year old Bobby Sands who had served five years of his fourteen year sentence for possessing a gun, has died in the H-Block prison today following a sixty-day hunger strike. It is expected the provisional IRA will now launch a campaign of violence and destruction in response to Sands' death. The Secretary of State for Northern Ireland, Humphrey Atkins, commented this morning. 'I regret this needless and pointless death. Too many people have died by violence in Northern Ireland. In this case it was self-inflicted.'*

I went to Annie who was pouring tea.

'Would you like a cup?'

She beamed, clearly delighted at her achievement.

'I'd love a cup' I said, catching her smile.

It felt like a death in the family. Candles and tears. Dad

had fallen asleep in the living room again, the glass half-empty nestled beside an overflowing ashtray of cigarettes with mile-high ash.

Nana got up and left for the early Mass. She was clearly annoyed with me again and left me a list of things to do, beginning with making Annie some lunch. I was still feeling the after-effects from the night before and a spell in the kitchen was probably the only thing to get me back on track. I looked into the fridge and found a chicken carcass and enough vegetables for a nice bowl of chicken broth. I set the table with flowers and white linen; I even took out the silverware.

Annie was determined to find her independence again and it was working. She was walking, albeit slower than before, and her speech was slightly slurred but fully comprehensible.

'Are we celebrating?' she asked

'Yes, you made a pot of tea today.'

'Great, looks like we will have a lot more to celebrate then.'

'Indeed.'

'What was he like?' she asked out of the blue over our chicken broth.

'Who?'

'The baby, Ella … '

'He was perfect.'

'Do you wish he was here?'

'No, and I don't want to talk about it anymore. '

'I'm sorry, really I'm sorry … I wasn't there for you'

I held that thought.

When Nana returned she sulked upstairs and left another list of chores out for me. I was starting to hate how Nana treated me these days. I hated her expectations of me, her dissatisfaction with me. Her control over me was starting to lose its grip and the more pressure she put on me the more I started to lose patience with her.

As I quietly folded Luke's and Jack's underpants and socks, I started to plot a possible escape plan. By late afternoon, she was getting ready to go to take Margaret to a special Mass for Bobby Sands.

'Get Luke and your father and my brown leather bag please, Ella.'

I knocked on Luke's door. I liked his bedroom, it looked out onto the back of the house, just opposite the vegetable patch. His walls were orange, and the wide antique floor boards were painted black. He had a large Victorian sink in the corner. It was messy but clean. The walls were adorned with posters, mounted with precision, images of pretty hippy women, Che Guevara, the Clash and Confucius. He saved for everything and bought only the best, his pride and joy being his stereo and rather oversized speakers. Luke was packing his bag for London.

'You're wanted downstairs.'

Jack was having a shower in his bedroom. I shouted through the door.

'Nana, wants you downstairs now.'

Eventually everyone gathered except for Annie. Nana stood in her fur coat.

'I've thought long and hard over the last few days, and I have decided to go over and stay with my sister Margaret for a while.'

I looked down at her full large suitcase, and the other little bags beside.

'For how long?'

'I don't know Ella, but in the meantime I hope you can hold the fort, my sister needs me, and your family need you.'

Jack looked as if someone had slapped him across the face.

'Mum, you can't, it's not safe.'

'Jack, you need to pull yourself together and I am not helping by mollycoddling you. You have a son and daughter who need you, not to mention a fragile and loving wife.'

'Mum, I won't let you go,'

Annie came in and observed our faces.

'So she told you?'

She smiled and went over to Nana and hugged her.

'Who's going to look after Annie, Mum, please can we not discuss this?'

'Jack, get it together.'

I was dumbstruck. Luke stood tall beside Nana. He helped load her bags into the awaiting taxi.

'You keep up the good work, Luke and write me.'

Luke hugged his Nana.

She looked over to me.

'Ella, we will keep in touch'.

I froze in my emotion unable to move, slapped by her coldness.

'All I ask is that you focus on your A-Levels.'

Jack walked over to her and kissed her on the forehead, 'I'll come and pick you up, in a few days.'

She smiled.

'I'll call you if I need you.'

She turned and left.

That evening I went into town and went straight to Flannery's pub and ordered myself a nice cold pint of Guinness. I sat in a corner and read the Daily Telegraph minding my own business when James arrived in. He was drowning his sorrows because Ali had left him for another man. We downed a few more pints, smoked a few joints, until darkness fell. Then he took me off to another few watering spots where we downed a few more. I wasn't quite sure where I was as the hour struck twelve but the walls were moving a little.

I woke the following morning in bed beside James. Thankfully, I was still wearing my favourite blue silk knickers and vest. We started the day with another joint and before I knew it, Sunday night approached and I needed to get home.

I waltzed in around eleven o'clock that evening. Nana's absence was plain to see. Luke had left a goodbye note with quotations from Confucius for each of us before he left for college. To Ella: *'Before you embark on a journey of revenge, dig two graves.'* Annie: *It does not matter how slowly you go as long as you don't stop.'* Jack: *What the superior man seeks is in himself, what the small man seeks is in others.'* I could understand Jack and Annie's but I hadn't a clue as to what he was or may be referring towards me. Obviously, he was pissed off with me too. Something I was clearly getting very good at. Pissing people off.

The emptiness of the house was ghost-like. However Nana and Luke's departure served as a catalyst for a renewed romance. As I made my way upstairs I heard Jack chatting with Annie. The following morning he was still with Annie and I could hear them chat and giggle.

Ali didn't turn up for school until midweek. She avoided me like the plague. I tried on several occasions to chat with her but she just kept fobbing me off. She cut me out, like I didn't exist. I didn't sit with her at lunch, in fear she would publically move to another seat. I sat on my own and read through some assignments, but none of the information was actually going in. So I left and got the bus into town. I studied during the week and worked weekends, then partied.

I spent my seventeenth birthday with James, vodka and chocolate cake. Then I went to work my shift in Flannery's. James and I would catch a late drink in Morrison's late bar, and head back to his place. His flat was on the corner of the University Road in the City Centre. James's bedroom was bare and slightly tattered. He had newspaper clippings on his wall displaying anarchy marches around the world. Punk images and idols like Johnny Rotten. He had made the bed himself but the quilt on the bed hadn't been washed since it was put on. So I brought a new one with some white cotton sheets from home and we changed the bed. The sex was nice but he was still in love with Ali who was now dating someone else.

I came home Sunday nights. Jack was making some sort of effort. He did his best to keep the house warm and he did a weekly shop on a Saturday morning, where upon he bought the same items in the same shop week-in week-out; all relatively healthy and bland. The only time he surprised us with a new item was when there was a bargain. I did most of the cooking during the week and sometimes I would make extra meals for Annie and freeze them. I got a woman to come and clean on a Friday morning as I was getting tired of being the only one keeping on top of the cleaning front. Annie managed her laundry and painting. Jack cooked at the weekends.

Annie reassured me she was fine on her own at the weekends and she appeared to understand my need for freedom. She was determined to reinstate her independence; she was able to push boundaries when I was off-side.

The Troubles never ceased, it was endless violence. More Catholics got targeted for sectarian killings. More Protestants got targeted if they were seen to be fraternising with the enemy. The entire city was stained with a hatred that seeped out over walls and pavements in painted words and images expressing their revulsion towards each other.

Jack had less clients and his paranoia grew. He lost more cases than he won, because he claimed the courts were putting his people behind bars to keep them off the streets.

Nana's visits went from once a week to once a month. She maintained a coldness with me, I never visited her.

GRANDDAD GOODIES LAST WALK

WILL'S STORY

Father asked me to join Granddad in a walk because his health was deteriorating. The Troubles were becoming more sectarian and more pointless deaths ensued. The Anglo-Irish Agreement, in 1985, gave Loyalists more cause to feel threatened. The biggest fear Loyalists held was the threat of a united Ireland where we could be guided by the hypocrisy of the Catholic Church or governed by a corrupt Irish system. The Anglo-Irish agreement allowed the Irish Government to have a consultative role in the internal government of Northern Ireland. That concept threatened everything we held dear, our schools, our Churches, our policing and healthcare.

More than sixty civilians, police and soldiers, died in violence directly attributable to the Hunger Strike. Ten men died of starvation, because they wanted to be recognised as Prisoners-of-War rather than ordinary criminals. I didn't get it, criminals are criminals. Many prison officers died by way of murder or suicide.

Riots were expected today as the Nationalists were protesting over Loyalists walking in Nationalist areas. There were whispers of peace talks. Loyalists were engaging in talks with the Reverend Roy Magee and the Anglican Archbishop Robin Eames. John Hume, the leader of the Alliance, and Gerry Adams, leader of Sinn Féin and rumoured head of the IRA, were also engaged in peace talks. On the more negative front, the Loyalists paramilitaries had obtained arms and explosives from South Africa, which led to the killing of Catholics.

My father didn't ask Sam to join Granddad and I, because he had finally managed to start letting go of him. He no doubt still prayed endlessly for him.

Sam basically did whatever Spider told him to do these

days; he would have walked over hot coals for him. He'd lost the little amount of respect he had for our parents. They tried everything in way of professional and spiritual guidance, offering to fund courses, but he was an obstinate young man determined to make his own choices. He remained loyal to the Orange Lodge, and occasionally we made contact through walks. This was, in fact, the only way I could gauge where he was at. Spider and his mates also remained loyal to the Lodge along with its other seventy-five thousand members, it being the largest Protestant organisation in Northern Ireland.

Granddad and I drove to the Lodge and took a bus from there with the other walkers to the beginning of our route.

Granddad knew everyone in the Lodge personally, he was once asked to go forward as a Master; humbly he declined. He was a popular man amongst his community. He was involved in the parish in a big way. He did the collections and he was chairman on the parish committee.

Today the sky was painted a dark and miserable grey, heavy rain started to pour before we ventured out.

We walked, alongside the other local groups and the various visitors that had been invited. Some North Americans joined us wearing their tribal Indian wear. I walked alongside my Grandfather. We played our flutes together. The walk was coming to the final destination where we would stop and listen to some speeches before departing. The grey sky boasted a huge rainbow on the last leg of the walk. I was happy and relaxed that there was no trouble; then the Catholics appeared out of nowhere. They were stood on a high wall, just a few young boys; throwing stones and a couple of petrol bombs that amounted to nothing. Some walkers ran towards the wall, but there was no way of getting up on it and they got pelted the closer they went.

'Let's go home son.'

I was relieved, nodded a yes and we started walking towards the bus with a crowd of other walkers keen to leave. As I walked I questioned why I was here. My new life in Stranmillis was a safe haven of mixed people trying to live together. Maybe the Catholics had a point in not wanting us to walk past their homes, maybe we were provoking them. But when I looked at my Granddad all polished-up, I remembered exactly why I was here. I was here to keep up the tradition of good Protestant people. We walked towards our burning bus, and clouds of black smoke. Thankfully, we could hear police sirens in the distance. We stopped walking like a swarm of bees hovering. Then we got besieged with stones, I watched a young boy of about eight, his head buried into his father's stomach as bricks narrowly missed him.

I got pushed to the ground by a stranger who saved me from a hit. I looked up for Granddad and I could see the outline of his figure lying on the ground. I got up and ran over to him; he lay still on the ground. His rounded well-fed stomach protruding, his pants wet from fear, he looked up into the sky, still alive, cold and weak, I prayed until the ambulance came and took us away. That night in the presence of my mother, father and my grandmother, he passed away peacefully as we prayed around his bed.

There were no visible wounds. The post-mortem declared death by myocardial infarction otherwise known as heart attack.

JACK ATTENDS A PARENT TEACHER MEETING

ELLA'S STORY

I did my best to hide the fact that the parent-teacher meeting was coming up. Nana always knew when they came, because she had, to date, attended all the meetings on my parents' behalf. I managed to keep on top of my workload, albeit with less ease than in the past. I also knew that I could still do well with a little effort put in. Mummies and Daddies arrived at the convent with their heads held high in expectation of glowing reports of their daughters. We sixth-formers were assigned to making tea and biscuits to hand out to the parents.

I was carrying a tray into the large assembly hall to the awaiting parents when I saw Jack stagger in through the door, no tie, shirt slightly open revealing some chest hair, unshaven. He waved at me delightedly.

'Ella, over here.' he shouted above the mannered whispers. I knew instantly he had taken drink, because I could always tell. I knew that smile like a wart I couldn't get rid of. I waved quickly to shut him up, smiling through gritted teeth, wanting to dig a forty-foot hole and kick him into it. He mortifyingly stood obliviously in the middle of the school hall with a grin slapped across his face. I decided my best option was to approach him and I made my way towards him, but unfortunately Sr. Agnes, the headmistress, came in our line of walk.

'Why it's the lovely Sr. Agnes.'

He hugged her.

'Don't you look radiant this evening? I hope there are no unwanted surprises for me in store; we all know that Ella has a mind of her own.' he said a tone above the rest of the crowd.

'Oh, Mr Lovett, Ella's father. It's Sr. Fidelma you need

to speak with, Ella be a good girl and send your father over to prefab four. Right away please.'

'Yes Sister.'

'I hope you're not fobbing me off Agnes, I know she's bold but she's a good girl really,'

'Right away, Ella'

I took his arm and led him out of the hall. I managed to walk him to the car park.

'Dad, go home now. Please. You shouldn't even be driving.'

'Ella, I'm fine honestly, a little respect please, I'm here to discuss your school work. What's wrong with you?'

'You've been drinking.'

'No I haven't, and so what if I had a drink, I'm entitled?'

'You have a problem.'

'No, it's you that has the problem Ella.'

'Whatever, now please leave.'

'I will do no such thing, are you trying to hide something from me?'

'No. '

'Don't be like that. All the effort I have went to for you. Do you know what I think?'

'Dad, please.'

'I think you are a little spoilt. Do you know how much you have upset Nana? You do realise that you're the reason she left us all?'

'No Dad, it's you who let Nana down.'

'She's back at the house right this minute you know, she remembered this parent's meeting, and made her way over to go to it until I stopped her, you need to show her a little more respect Ella'.

He then swiped his arm away from me and took off in the direction of Sister Fidelma's classroom. I followed behind knowing that it was pointless trying to stop him. Fortunately Sr. Fidelma was in her early seventies and deaf in her left ear. As soon as he was finished I walked him to the car and we left.

'What did she say?'

'You could work harder'.

When I got home Nana was sitting reading the paper by the unlit range. She looked as if she had never left. The house had been cleaned and I could smell vegetable soup coming from the stove. For a moment my heart skipped at the thought she might have returned.

'Did you know he was going to the school?'

'Hello Ella, nice to see you too! How have you been?'

'Did you ask him to go up?'

'What have I done now?'

'You let him go to the school in that state'.

'Someone had to go'.

'You are determined to destroy my life.'

She lowered her bifocals and looked up at me and smiled.

'Ella darling, you are doing that, all by yourself. Now you just need someone else to blame'.

She returned to her paper. I walked over closer to her. She never flinched and she was a master at avoiding confrontation.

'And what about you Nana? Never made any mistakes have you? No, it's everyone else. You who are so perfect .Great chef, organiser, you name it she can do it … Great at cutting people out of your life when you don't get your way, I wonder what does that say about you'.

'I'm sorry you feel that way, Ella. I did what I thought was best.'

'No you're not. You have no idea what you did to me'.

She took the bifocals off and stood up facing me.

'You got yourself pregnant Ella, I didn't get you pregnant. You were only a child for Christ's sake. Did you want to bring a poor defenceless baby into this house, with an alcoholic grandfather and a sick and worn-out grandmother … did you? I did what I thought was best for that child. And yes, I'm sorry if you think what I did for you was wrong. I admit I had hoped you'd make something of yourself, I had hoped you wouldn't have

216

been so bloody foolish. Maybe I was wrong, but tell me what should I have done?'

I started to cry. She went over and stirred the soup.

I put my arms around her frail and warm body only to realise that I was a full head above her.

She pulled herself away gently, packed the newspaper into her little brown leather bag. She lifted her ancient little fur coat and hid inside it.

'Stay, Nana, please. I'll make some supper'.

'I'm too old for this Ella.'

Her eyes had welled up.

'Okay, but come over on Sunday, I'll do a nice roast'.'

She agreed, then left and I felt the kick of hopelessness as soon as she shut the door. She was right, I needed to take responsibility. Sorry wasn't such a big word.

WILL'S STUDENT LIFE IN STRANMILLIS

Queen's University opened a new world to me. I studied Politics and Social Sciences. I lived in number 23 Colenso Parade, a beautifully restored Georgian redbrick house. I lived with Rosa and Marie, two other students from the University. The house was situated opposite the Botanic gardens, a mixed middle-class area. The street unto the front of the house was lined with oak and cherry blossom and my bedroom overlooked the Botanic Rose Gardens. I loved that room.

It was a simple white ornate room with two bay windows and a white marble fireplace. The ceiling was hand-crafted with plaster moulds. I put up white muslin drapes and awoke to a subdued room bathed in sunlight every morning. I had piles of books, yet to be shelved, on the floor; that was all I treasured, apart from my various coloured karate belts, my collection of vintage cars and my flute. I relished the space and the nakedness. '*Very Protestant looking*', my mother had said when she first visited. I got a job with the local newsagents at the weekends and Mum and Dad helped me out with money from savings they had saved for me going to college. I liked my housemates, albeit a challenge in that they didn't get on great together and I was often their go-between.

Rosa was a quiet, well-spoken, hard-working, rural girl who was studying Biochemistry. She got on the bus for Ballymena every Friday afternoon after class and headed home to '*Mammy and Daddy*' as she called them. Marie was quite the opposite, a bubbly brunette who lived off pizza, jam sandwiches and nuts. Marie was from a broken marriage. She studied English literature and partied when she was, and wasn't, studying. The parties could happen at any time, with sometimes only an hour's notice, sometimes big, sometimes small. She had a Scottish boyfriend who had the manners of a goat and the appearance of a man who lived alone in the wild. But it worked. Sometimes Marie's party-like atmosphere was just what Rosa and I needed to bring us out of our shells. Rosa, whom I reckoned was a virgin, didn't date and didn't party. I would go up and drag her out of her safe, comfy bedroom to join us and reluctantly she would sit on the sofa and observe people until some young aspiring gentleman might approach whereupon she would blush and then run.

I hadn't been with a woman since Ella. I didn't want to be with someone. I was open to the idea that if the right person came along that I would know what to do. I still thought about her every day.

I had started to distance myself a little from the Sam drama, despite my parents' dependence on me finding him on a regular basis. He would disappear for days, sometimes weeks on end. When I found him he was usually doped up and obliviously happy. So why should I care? I was worn-out being his caretaker. I resented that he had made Mum feel so exhausted and helpless and I was frustrated that there was nothing I could do. Sam did his own thing and I couldn't change that. I knew Mum and Dad were aware that Spider was now known to be a prominent member of the UVF.

They were also aware that Sam was using drugs of some sort; I hoped and believed it was just smoking hash but had my suspicions.

I was getting to the point where I needed to detach from Sam for my own sanity, I knew that there was little I could do, he was stubborn and the more I tried to bring him back to some sort of reality the more he wanted to break free from all ties connected to his family. He had phoned Mum to inform her he was living in a commune in Portrush, a seaside village an hour away from Belfast. She wanted to go and investigate because it had been some months now since she had last seen him. I knew that we would just drive around Portrush, a small but busy little town, until we were irate with frustration. I was afraid we might find him strung-out and unwilling to come home. I tried to reassure Mum that he was probably better off in a commune than hanging out with Spider.

I explained to Mum I had assignments coming up and that the following weekend I would consider going up on my own.

The truth was I had met Andrea, at one of Marie's parties. She was studying archaeology. She reminded me a little of Ella except we had a little more in common. She was Protestant and approved of the Orange Lodge, this I knew because a discussion arose in regard to the current bad press the Lodge was receiving and she defended it saying *'that it was a small minority of Orangemen who were out to damage the good name of the organisation.'* I managed to ask her out on a date and I took her to the Queen's Film Festival where we sat and watched 'Betty Blue'. We had an adult conversation afterwards about the film and then we had a bite to eat, a kiss outside the restaurant and the kiss was quite nice. The dates continued and we did the same thing every time: cinema, a bite to eat, a nice kiss. About two months later I brought her home for coffee and had prepared my bed just in case I decided to go wild. We talked for a couple of hours and then I took her upstairs. We undressed, and climbed into the cold sheets and kissed more. We had sex. Andrea sensed that the earth hadn't moved and was gone before I awoke. I was a little confused.

ELLA AND JAMES

Nana arrived over on the Sunday for an early dinner. I did my best to tidy the house before her arrival. The last cleaner had disappeared for no apparent reason. Nana told me about living with Aunt Margaret: riots, bombs, shootings and hijacks, it was difficult to fathom her current reality because we lived in a different reality in East Belfast. But I could sense she was familiar with her territory.

We managed to find some common ground. She complimented me on the Beef Wellington. We didn't mention James. She quizzed me in detail about my A-Levels and we parted with the agreement she would return for dinner next Sunday.

After she left it was like someone switched the lights out. Jack went to the attic and then there was silence. Annie came back and forth from Donegal. Neither of them did much around the house, drains needed cleaned, the washing machine was on the blink again. The house slowly fell into disarray, it smelt like a damp holiday house, paint started to crack, cupboards grew mouldy, dust settled into the old carpets while Jack blew whatever energy he had into the saxophone and I was just too tired to keep the house alive.

I arrived at James' flat at eleven o'clock on a Saturday night. He was stoned and in giddy form with his two friends, Peter and Fritz. James was once described by his financial consultant older sister as *'an upper class fuck up'*. He took comfort in her words because she was everything he despised. He wore colourful silk shirts and grew his hair down past his shoulders. He was into magic and mystery and kept a box of tricks at the end of his bed. His father was also a financial consultant and his mother was a GP. James could have got on to any course he wanted to, he was as clever as a cat but he hated authority. He got four straight A's for his A- levels. When he was twelve his mother took him to see a professional psychologist. They assessed him and informed her he was in fact a gifted child, he was bored at school. He was a bookworm and he had a particular interest in poetry.

He smiled when he saw me approach through the open door that Saturday evening laden with bags. It took him a while to register what the bags meant, but without a word he opened his bedroom door to let the bags in. He kissed me gently.

'Welcome Home.'

We then went and joined the others. Peter, his best friend, who was about ten-foot-three and weighed about seven stone, laughed a lot and always walked about with a stoop. He was polite and intelligent and he rolled joints consistently. The other guy, Fritz, a tiny five-foot-four guy with a round belly and eyes as shifty as a meerkat, was on another planet altogether, he talked endlessly about aliens and conspiracies. His pet conspiracy was NASA Headquarters. They apparently held alien hostages in Alaska somewhere. Oddly enough though it was just what I needed. I continued to visit home every Sunday, as did Nana. I cooked a dinner and returned to James on the Monday after school. Dad would ask me to come home every week but without drama. I convinced him I was happy and he convinced himself I was too. Annie gave up asking me to return home, she seemed to blossom more and more as the weeks passed, her paintings were taking on a new life, they contained a magic of sorts, and she and Jack seemed to be more contented in each other's company.

Most days I made it to school, no questions asked. However Sr. Agnes was observing me; and she was genuinely concerned and offered to contact social services if needed. I reassured her everything was fine.

Some evenings we would mingle with Belfast's unwashed lost souls looking for a getaway in our flat; we would sit and look at each other in the little blue and white Sixties wallpapered room, huddled around our gas heater entertained by Minx and Mist the goldfish.

James had friends who lived in a commune in the middle of nowhere just outside Portrush. They grew grass and vegetables. One Friday morning we had run out of hash and everyone seemed to be out of supply so we packed a small bag and drove to the commune. It was a small derelict farmhouse with surrounding outhouses. Caravans peeped out behind trees. A colourful tepee stood tall in the front garden. There were about twelve adults and six kids running around. James was familiar with most of them; in particular a pretty young girl called Patricia, their body language exuded a sexual chemistry. James would have fitted in well. We happened to arrive the day before one of their birthdays. People arrived in droves, bonfires were lit, the hooch was produced, and the party began. It wasn't long before James disappeared off with Patricia and I started to mingle through the small crowd.

Surprisingly, amongst them was Sam, Will's brother. He looked so different in this environment, his hair was long blonde and wispy, his cotton shirt hung loose, he seemed happy.

He came and sat beside me in front of the open fire, and we watched the sun disappear, Someone played a flute accompanied by a boron in the back ground, he told me about the commune and how it started with a couple looking for an alternative way to live. Everyone helped out with the garden and general upkeep. We passed joints, sipped wine and relaxed in each other's company, it was a relief to know someone. Curiously he brought Will into the conversation. I had buried Will away somewhere.

'Will's at university now, studying Social Something or other, still Mr Perfect ' he said with a hint of resentment.

'He's not so perfect.' I said with a crack of emotion.

Sam poured me more wine, intrigued, he was warm and handsome; he enlightened me as to how Will had called to the house a while back and had spoken with Nana. He told me he had to get away from Belfast because it was too dangerous. His mate Spider had joined up and was putting pressure on him to join up too. He had been living in the commune for over a year, he was happy there. He had got into gardening and was learning how to sew. I encouraged him into contacting his mother. He listened and promised he would call. We continued rolling joints, chatting about music and the silly neighbours we shared and when the sun started coming up he got me a blanket. I shared some secrets I shouldn't have with him.

James found me at about seven in the morning, asleep by the fire's embers, I didn't care that he had disappeared, I was too tired.

It was heart-warming to be amongst contented people. They refused to sell us grass as it was against their principles. So they just gave us a large bag to go home with. The following day we reluctantly left the commune to return to our cold urban flat.

The flat had once been part of a beautifully ornate home to the better-off, and was later converted into flats. The toilet had a chain for the flush which kept getting stuck whenever you flushed it and the fridge would sometimes freeze all the food. The oven didn't work but the hob did. It was kind of romantic. I made it into school on the Monday morning looking a little rough. Just before my last class, I sneaked off to the back of the prefab for a smoke, I closed my eyes and felt the sunlight rest on my eyelids, and I drifted away, only to be awoke by an abrupt Sr. Agnes.

'Get up of the floor, young lady, I will see you in my office in five minutes.'

She sat in her office, and looked across at me with a determined look on her face.

'How are you Ella?'

'I'm fine'

'Really?'

'Yes'

This was followed by a pause, and she went to her filing cabinet and got some papers. I noticed some pictures of her family framed on top of the cabinet, some were of children.

She sat opposite me again, and her face softened.

'I don't know what's going on with your home life Ella, other than your mother has been very sick and your father is a little troubled, if you need to talk I'm here. I have copied past exam papers for you to complete, you can work in the Library after school if you like and I can arrange a lift home for you after that. God has gifted you with brains Ella, you must receive his gift with thanks and use them.'

I don't know how or why Sister Agnes knew how to work me but I followed her instructions and worked in the private convent library for two hours each day after school, in a beautiful old room surrounded by books and old pine desks. I liked the little wooden desks with lids that lifted and a drawer underneath. The ceiling was vaulted, I loved vaulted ceilings.

Time just went on and I passed my A-levels, miraculously. Jack and Annie did everything they could to try and talk me into applying for a course in some university but I had no interest. They even got Luke to try and persuade me. I continued to work in Flannery's. A year later I made James a chocolate birthday cake spiced with hash and covered in chocolate sauce and Smarties. James didn't like birthdays. Fritz called early with a buzz in his eye. He had brought some promised birthday goodies, a mix of tablets, and a small package of white powder. He was dressed like a pimp.

It wasn't long before they were swimming in ecstasy, incoherent, literally out of their minds. I eased off on the drug and alcohol intake since the night of the ruby lipstick. I didn't like or want that out-of-control feeling; James took anything going. He found it difficult to lose control, any amount of drugs, and he maintained a relatively together stance, he reckoned his inability to lose it was because both his parents were total control freaks. One joint was enough to send me close to orbit.

The doorbell started to ring just after the pubs had

closed. By one-thirty the door was just left ajar and people were streaming in. I'd made a point of inviting Ali and she arrived and threw her arms around me like a long-lost friend. Ali and I chatted about everything; she was in love with the current boyfriend. She was in her first year of nursing and loved it. She was able to tell me how everyone in class was.

'Why didn't you apply to college?'

'I'm a loser Ali, I'm sorry about James, I didn't mean to ...'

'Don't be silly Ella, I've moved on, and you're not a loser, don't you have brains to burn, what more do you want?'

'He's still in love with you, and my brains are already burnt'.

'I'm glad you called me.'

The following afternoon I awoke to the hum of Bob Marley and the Wailers. James lay in a heap beside me. I got up. The living room was still full of stoned people rolling joints and mumbling. I didn't want them here. I made a cup of tea and went into them.

'Listen, the party is over,'

They all looked at each other and nodded. One by one they quietly departed. The flat was trashed, cans everywhere, ash everywhere. I drank tea and tidied for a while then went back to bed. When I got up later James and Fritz and several other strangers were sitting amongst more debris doing it all over again. Bob Marley, wailing again.

I got washed and dressed for work and left a little confused and hung-over from yet another late night. When I returned to the flat they were all still there.

'James, we need to tidy up.'

He laughed and the others joined in. I went into the bedroom, tidied it up and got into bed with a book.

I awoke early in the morning to a rattling noise like a tin can being trailed on a string. It was James, he was lying in a pool of vomit and shaking and as he was having a fit, froth was coming out of his mouth. When I got over to him I found a needle hanging from his arm. I removed the needle and called an ambulance. He eventually stopped shaking and lost consciousness. Two policemen and an ambulance arrived very quickly; they took him to the hospital immediately. A female police officer stayed with me and comforted me, making tea and chatting. Her name was Hannah. I will always remember that. She was warm and comforting. After she left I phoned Annie, I was frightened.

'Come home Ella …please'.

'I can't, it's not my home anymore'.

'... Ella it's better now.'

After I got off the phone I looked around at the mess and squalor I was living in, this wasn't my home either. I got some black bin bags and started to tidy. The place was filthy and smelly. I was scrubbing a burnt mark on the little pine table James had made for me. Some idiot had stubbed a cigarette out on it. When I looked up Nana was standing in front of me. She had let herself in. Quiet as a ghost she approached. She looked around.

'Ella, this is no place for a girl like you.'

She took the cloth from my hand and gave me a warm hug.

'I'll wait outside in the car love, I'll bring you home.'

'I need to be here for James, for when he gets back, he's in hospital.'

'Finish up what you have to do here and then leave or you'll end up in the same place as James. I know it's not easy at home Ella, but we will just have to pull together and make it home again.'

'Will you come home too?'

She looked at me and smiled.

'For you. Yes. If that's what you want.'

'Ok, tomorrow. Give me until tomorrow '

'And I will join you at the weekend.'

I hugged her, as warmly as I could. She left just as quietly as she had arrived.

James survived. He was released from hospital a couple of days later after they pumped out his stomach and within hours he was on the chase for more drugs. He sat rolling up butts in desperation. I cleaned and cleaned until there was nothing more to clean and I cooked him chicken broth.

'You need to stop James, you need to go home and sort yourself out.'

'This is my home. '

'What about your sister?'

'What about her?'

'She will look after you, James.'

'Look Ella, I slipped up, it's no big deal, and I'll stay off the hard stuff.'

Peter arrived, with a bag of fruit and some chocolate.

'Jesus man, you're alive, I told you to stay away from that shit.'

'Have you got a smoke? I'm gasping.'

'Shouldn't you be taking it easy for a while, until you're back on your feet?'

'Please man, I've just spent the last forty-eight hours lying beside a man who had bowel troubles, not to mention the fucking police interrogations.'

Peter smiled and took out the makings of a joint.

Later that night James watched me pack my bags with the same expression on his face as when I'd arrived to move in, but I could see his fear underneath.

I went home the following morning. The entire house smelt of whiskey, socks and cigarettes. The fridge was empty except for a pint of milk, two cans of Guinness and a packet of blue moulded cheese. Annie was in Donegal. She was due home at the weekend. Dad was standing in the kitchen in his suit, drinking a pint of milk with a raw egg floating in it. He was heading out to a court case.

'I was thinking of coming home.'

'That's fantastic Ella.'

He came over and held me in his arms; I could hear his heart thumping in his chest.

'I have missed you terribly.'

'Nana is going to come home for a while too.'

'Right, we'd better get organised then.'

He smiled, disappeared, came back and handed me a wad of cash. I spent the entire day cleaning and rearranging my old home. Whilst I stocked the cupboards I retrieved memories. The garden was looking great, apple trees laden with apples. New cabbages and onions peeped out.

Nana returned home the following afternoon to the waft of freshly baked short bread. I impressed myself. Annie returned gobsmacked at the transformation of her home. She was ecstatic. It didn't take too long before everything settled into a place called home again. Annie in the garden. Nana in the kitchen with me, except I was the chief cook now. And Jack was still Jack but he started making an effort to be back home early, usually laden with flowers and a bottle of decent wine we all shared over a nice dinner. He unethically discussed his confidential cases with us and was genuinely interested in our opinions. I even started to research several university courses with Annie's encouragement.

I made a conscious choice not to get too attached to men for a while. I liked men, and they appeared to like me. I settled with the knowledge that love was way overestimated. I started to decipher the difference between love and lust.

I kept my job, which give me a little financial freedom. I met Martin, a forty something laid-back tall and lanky man with a thick head of black hair, and tattoos down both arms. He was often at Flannery's but he rarely drank. One evening he offered me a lift home on his Harley Davidson. We had an on/off relationship with no strings attached. He came on a bit hot and heavy with the love thing at the beginning but my clear guidelines calmed him down and he took us for what we were. Martin was attractive in a fatherly kind of way. He was kind and intelligent, lived with his mum, signed on once a week and had an interest in music and graphics, often a profitable side-line, he played the guitar, was generous in bed, and that was it really. As time passed we saw less of each other because he was looking for commitment. I dated some other men but no-one worthy of mention.

Time just trod by, with a meaninglessness that was liberating. Luke came home looking more like a man, he told me all about Petra, a puppeteer who had studied clowning in Paris.

I started yoga classes and Jack eased off on the drink. I began to see a little glimmer of light at the end of the tunnel. I gave up smoking and went on a health food spree. It was boredom that forced me to start studying psychology at Queen's University. Surprisingly it became my all, I actually fell in love with what I was doing and I hit the grades I was aiming for. The lecturers were impressed. I occasionally drank wine and had the occasional fling. I even attended a counsellor at college. I was determined to make someone of myself.

I had contemplated moving to England but because of the IRA attacks in London I didn't see the point, at least I knew the Belfast territory. I was also tempted to get a place of my own but because of Nana I felt obliged to stay.

PEACE AT LAST

WILL

In April 1994 the Provisional IRA announced a cease fire. The whole of Northern Ireland breathed a sigh of relief. Peace finally. It was like someone had cleared the black clouds off the Province. Trust began to develop amongst both sides with an unspoken mutual understanding. A healing began.

I was now a qualified social worker who specialised in child protection. I was appalled at the lack of government resources for children in need; especially for kids in working class areas that had taken a direct hit from the Troubles.

Sam returned to Belfast. He was burnt out, too many people, too much smoke he claimed. The commune had been good for him. He returned to the Lodge and signed up for a degree in mathematics at Queen's, but it didn't take Spider long to cast his web, and pull him in again. His power over Sam drove me crazy simply because there was no logic to it.

Sam's commitment to the Lodge meant more to him than it did to me. He needed approval. It was a rite of passage. I felt relieved that Sam was part of this family because without him our chain was broken.

The Sunday after our recent walk Dad had made a little speech at Church about the values of family unity and understanding. Often he would reflect on our home life and create a meaningful sermon from it.

'*Man should have sincere love for his heavenly Father: a humble and steadfast faith in Jesus Christ, the saviour of mankind, believing in him as the only mediator between God and man. He should cultivate truth and justice, brotherly kindness and charity, devotion and piety, like that of a true loyal Orangeman, like that of a Father.*'

One would have to admire Spider's dedication to his cause. He organised the gathering of Catholic icons to be burned on top of the sixty-foot high bonfires, mostly images of the pope or nationalist politicians and the like. As soon as someone new joined the Lodge he would move in and groom them to become one of his pack, just as he had with Sam. I hated Spider. He was strategic in that he occasionally attended Church, behaved well during meetings and parades; he waited until the elders left meetings before he started rolling joints and encouraging antagonistic actions against innocent Catholics. He lived by his own set of rules.

Within the rules set out to become an Orangeman it states that we:

'Oppose the fatal errors and doctrines of the Church of Rome and scrupulously avoid countenancing any act or ceremony of Roman worship; he should by all lawful means, resist the ascendancy of that Church, its encroachments and the extension of its power, ever abstaining from all uncharitable words, actions or sentiments towards any Roman Catholic.'

It was clear in regard to our opposition of Catholicism but it was equally clear that we respect others regardless of their religion. In my opinion, the Orange Lodge was losing its platform to honest hard-working Protestant Christians but rather becoming a platform for a political agenda that increasingly attracted negative media.

Sometimes I fantasised about leaving the Lodge and finding Ella and running off with her but in reality I knew being with Ella and maintaining my position within the Lodge was only a dream. I knew I would have put her life at risk if I had made our connection public. There was also the reality of my family's absolute fear and rejection of such a mix. I fantasised then about converting Ella into becoming a Protestant who supported my family tradition but the phrase 'Orange bastards' just wouldn't leave me.

Protestants reluctantly welcomed the Good Friday agreement. Anything for peace. No-one really knew what lay ahead regarding the agreement because there were no definite guidelines as to what to expect. Fears of losing our identity and becoming an integrated Catholic Protestant community living in a united Ireland were rife. But people on both sides of the community were willing to put aside their bias and hurt because they needed peace. The very smell of it was intoxicating. It was peculiar that Northern Ireland housed so many religious people considering the sectarian divide. It is estimated that currently eighty percent of Northern Ireland claimed to be part of a Church membership, a contrast to its neighbour England which only holds thirteen percent of church-goers.

However as the small print of the Good Friday agreement became clearer the hurt resurfaced and the hatred returned.

Despite existing fears within the Protestant congregation, my father was driving the message of peace in his weekly sermons. He helped found an inter-denominational group of two hundred clergy that presented the pro-agreement parties at Stormont with a statement entitled 'Faith in a brighter future.' He read, from his heart, that Sunday.

'We appreciate the integrity and courage with which you have travelled so far. We encourage you all to take the next steps together.'

Sam dropped out of college within a few months despite all our efforts to keep him on track. His excuse being that he didn't like the course work. He called to me in Stranmillis explaining he left home because of a personality clash between him and Father. Spider helped him with his move.

The Lodge had taken many media attacks, petrol bomb attacks and various members who created trouble had encouraged hate campaigns across the globe, but the Brown children shook the organisation to its core.

A petrol bomb had been thrown into the bedroom of two sleeping girls. Just when we had begun to embrace the hope of peace and put the violence behind us. I sat with stones in my heart as I listened to the news item delivered on the radio.

'Two young sisters have been murdered in a loyalist arson attack in Ballymena, Northern Ireland. The Brown children were Catholics living on the predominantly Protestant Glen Side estate, but they were accepted by the community and attended a Protestant school.

Chief Constable of the RUC Richard Flanagan said: We believe we're investigating the sectarian murder of two children."

The attack comes after a week of protests by Orangemen demanding access to the mainly Nationalist Garvaghy Road as part of their annual march at Drumcree Church.

Police dispersed a demonstration and barricades on the main road outside the Glen Side estate last night. The Orange Order's Co Armagh Chaplain Rev William Marcus expressed his sorrow to his Loyalist congregation: "No road is worth a life let alone the lives of two little girls."

Nationalist residents of the Lower Ormeau Road in Belfast have already announced that they will not block Orange parades as a mark of respect and the RUC have scaled down their forces.'

Media reports about the two Brown children raised questions about the Christianity of the Orange institution to discriminating proportions. The perpetrators were known to be marching earlier that day.

The Drumcree Road in question was predominantly Catholic. The main objection by Catholic residents was the notion that the walkers were provoking local families who had been victims of the Troubles. An internal dispute amongst the Lodges argued terrorists didn't belong within the Orange community because they didn't adhere to the stringent Christian ethos that was the heart and core of

Orangeism.

Orangemen were torn and divided because the majority didn't want to provoke the Catholic residents but they had no way of completing their walk without access to this road other than take an alternative route altogether. This would break years of a tradition and add miles on to their intended route. The Grand Master held a meeting and agreed to a face-to-face discussion with the Catholic residents regarding re-routing the walk.

The Catholics requested a re-route. The deaths of the Brown children destroyed any ounce of credibility that the Order held.

Sam was disgusted by the deaths and he joined father and me at the funerals. It was reassuring to see the human side of him rise above the nonsense he was immersed in. Before we went to the Church he called me upstairs to his old bedroom, everything was as it was, his soldier collection in order atop of his set of drawers. His map of the world hung framed on the wall.

'I probably should have told you this before now, but a few years ago I met Ella, she was pretty drunk and with this asshole called James who didn't give a shit about her.'

'Why are you telling me this Sam?'

'Because she told me something I think you should know.'

'What?'

'She had a baby'

'What ...?

'She said the father was a fine Orangeman.'

'Are you sure about this? '

'Look Will, she had had a lot to drink and when I ask her outright was the baby yours she smiled and said, "now that would be telling".'

'Where is she now?'

'I have no idea.'

'That's great.'

I sat in my father's Church beside my mother and brother which was actually a sanctuary for me, full of nostalgia and memories of my mother watching Father's every word with a sense of belonging. He was happiest when up in his pulpit.

'It is with deep regret and a heavy heart that I feel I need to address my utter condemning of the murder of the two innocent children this week. These children lost their lives to sectarianism at the hands of Protestant people whom are not of Christian mind. The attack provoked because of objections to Orangemen walking up a hill in a predominantly Catholic area. These little girls have no doubt found a new home in heaven, with their maker, but sadly have left a trail of broken hearts. Let us pray.

Sam left immediately after the service.

JACK TRIES TO COVER HIS TRACKS

Peace was in the air and everyone in Belfast felt it. There were fewer soldiers and police vehicles on the road. It was contagious, everyone a little raw, celebrating quietly.

Jack was currently happy because he was making Annie happy. Often he would spend the entire night with her and she would come downstairs with a smug smile on her face. His work was picking up and it was evident that he was well-respected within his field because he was now in a position of selecting cases. The house smelt of the roses he showered upon us all. I was actively looking for a flat again, but I felt obliged to stay with Nana because she was getting older. I started a placement at the Royal Hospital.

Annie was about to open her first exhibition since her accident. It was a big show in the Arts Council and a big deal. The paintings were different, abstract figurative, but they had more life, spirit and colour in them, you could feel her freedom. She had been preoccupied with perfection in the past, which caused stagnancy, now her precision was brought to life. Luke flew over for the weekend and we all attended the opening which was officially opened by the curator of the Tate Modern in London. We ate in the new posh restaurant, Rosscoffs, and it felt like we were a family, a functional family.

The following morning Jack had poured himself a cup of tea and sat with me reading over The Times paper. Nana switched on the radio for the usual morning update.

At least 28 people, including an 18-month-old infant, have been killed in the worst paramilitary bombing since the start of the Northern Ireland conflict 30 years ago.

Political leaders have been joined by the Queen in expressing their sympathy for the bereaved and those injured in the explosion in the market town of Omagh.

The blast left about 220 people injured or maimed. Both Protestants and Catholics were hurt and killed.

RUC Chief Constable Ronnie Flanagan said: "These are people who have murdered here today because they want to murder."

The peace process had caused an opening of the heart making us all the more vulnerable. We all descended into the television room and switched on the television to watch the horrors unfold on the news. Later that evening Jack sat in the attic on his own playing the sax, his melancholic notes travelled around the house. It turned out twenty-nine innocent people had been killed, eight critically injured, others seriously injured, seven dead children and unborn twins.

It was torturous listening to every grim detail. I kept turning the radio off but Dad kept switching it back on.

That Friday Annie packed a bag for Donegal; she dropped Nana over to Margaret for the weekend.

I made Jack and myself some lunch and we sat down together to eat. He read the Guardian and I scanned the Telegraph for flat rentals, a habit I had become accustomed to with no real enthusiasm because I felt obliged to stay with Nana as I felt it would be unfair of me to leave her with my parents. We heard a noise outside, nothing alarming but since the window incident we were always on alert.

The kitchen adjoined the backyard, which had a coal-shed with a green tin roof attached to it and often a cat or a gathering of birds would run along the roof. Nana often threw bread crumbs up for the birds. The noise sounded like a stone hitting the roof, it startled both of us. We looked at each other then Dad got up to have a look.

'It's that bloody cat from next door again'

I started eating my lunch. Dad put his finger up to his lips to silence me. He quickly went out and locked the back door, then ran into the hall to lock the front door; he sat down again.

'Ssh listen. We need to go upstairs quietly to the attic and lock ourselves in, they are outside' he whispered with an agitation. My options were limited; I knew that I had to go with this, even though I knew it was ridiculous. It was most likely just a cat that had just crossed the roof.

'What do you mean Dad? Should we call the police?'

He looked back at me with fear, his warm brown eyes as frightened as an animal in a snare, he touched my arm softly.

'Go upstairs until I check the situation out.'

When he arrived on the landing I thought he might be calmer, but he seemed even more intense. We made our way up to the attic.

'Dad, there's no one out there.'

He looked back at me with a scary intensity

'Ella they could kill us, they sent me photographs of you, don't you understand how serious this is?'

All of a sudden we heard a loud banging, a vibratory sort of banging, like drums. Dad put his finger up to his lips to silence me. Now I was frightened.

'Keep away from windows and doors; in fact, get under the table,'

I obeyed. He phoned the police. The banging got louder and louder.

'I'm going to take a look Dad.'

'No Ella, it's too dangerous.'

I climbed up onto the little red chair in the attic room and opened the skylight; at first I couldn't see anything other than the blue sky. I lifted myself up so that I could see below and to my utter amazement I watched a band of Orangemen, walking around our house. I recognised that bastard Spider; he had a huge drum and was leading his private little army of Orangemen around our home. I came down from the window filled with anger.

'Who is it?'

'It's the Orangemen, there's about twenty of them, they're marching around our house.'

Dad took his gun out of his drawer and placed it on the desk beside us.

'We'll just wait for the police.'

We listened to the drums and laughter of these Orangemen invade our home shouting *'Fenians out'* between the beats. I decided that the only thing to do was to go out and face them.

'I'm going down to talk to them Dad'

'Over... my.... dead.... body...........'

He said with a little too much conviction.

By the time the police arrived Jack had consumed a half bottle of whisky and not an Orange bastard in sight.

The Orangeman incident was the last straw for Jack, a justified reason to hide in the attic for safety, an excuse for an early morning Bloody Mary. The scribbled notes and codes that lived in the attic started to creep outside of the attic. They could be found anywhere, in the tea caddy or in books.

The notes were usually welcome and philosophical. Like the note I found placed under my pillow one morning: *'Live and have your blooming in the noise of the whirlwind'* or the note Nana found in the bathroom stuffed inside the loo roll tube: *'No apple tree tries to grow pears.'*

Either Nana hadn't heard the melancholic saxophone playing at three in the morning, which sometimes turned into a rather loud Beethoven concerto, or she just never mentioned it.

'Why didn't you tell me things had got worse?' Luke had asked on the phone one night. 'I didn't think he was too bad the last time I was over, has it got worse?'

'I don't know Luke; I can't decipher what's normal anymore.'

The thing was, Jack waited for Friday night to arrive before he really let loose because Nana usually went over to Margaret's and Annie to Donegal, it was just him and me most weekends. For the remainder of the week he was relatively civil.

One Sunday morning I climbed out of my warm bed into my freezing cold bedroom and when I looked out of my window I saw the snow gently fall on the apple tree in the back garden, a little red robin landed on a branch; '*a sign of hope*' Nana would say.

Nana was due home around twelve and Annie was due back from Donegal at some stage that day.

I made my way upstairs to Jack's bedroom with a strong cup of coffee. It was always untidy, and a little dark; he never slept in Annie's room when she was away. I knocked his door as was custom and waited for his reply. I heard nothing and knocked again, still nothing, the cup was burning my fingers so I opened the door. His clothes lay draped over an old carved wooden chair and the saxophone lay propped up against the wall. Stacks of paper files lay side by side, spilling over each other with the agony of people's lives.

He was lying on his stomach.

He just lay there quite still.

'Dad?'

I approached his bed, and I saw an empty jar of pills sitting on the bedside locker beside him some spilled out on top. An empty bottle of whisky and a half empty glass sat beside the emptied jar of pills. I poked him and he didn't stir. I turned him over and he appeared unconscious. I put my head unto his chest and I picked up a heartbeat.

'Dad waken up, it's me.'

But he didn't. I ran downstairs and quickly phoned an ambulance, they arrived about thirty minutes later and I showed them the tablets, they asked me some questions and I signed a form. I don't know why I didn't go back upstairs until they came; I suppose I was too afraid. They made their way upstairs and as they were on the second landing a fully clothed Jack greeted them with a curious smile as to why they might be here. He efficiently packed them off with apologies and excuses regarding my neurotic and inappropriate behaviour. As soon as they left, he poured himself a large vodka.

'I couldn't waken you! I saw the spilled pills beside your bed. You scared me Dad.'

'Ella darling, you have nothing to be scared about, I am

241

a grown man and I can take care of myself, you just overreacted.'

'That's the problem Dad; it seems you can't take care of yourself. You're lost, you can't function in the real world anymore, that's why you spend your life locked upstairs in an attic full of alcohol and tablets'.

'You're over-reacting again.'

He downed his glass and poured himself another one.

'You need help Dad, you need professional help.'

His eyes drilled me with contempt and I could smell the anger. I had said enough.

'I think you're the one that needs help Ella.... of the professional kind. I'm the only one around here putting the bread on the table. You are in your thirties now and you are still living at home!'

I walked out of the room. He disappeared upstairs for a short while, came down looking like a lawyer and sped off in his car. Later he arrived back, drunk with a swelling above his right eye. He parked the car in what was left of the rose bushes again. Nana, Annie and I were sitting in the kitchen, listening to the radio, when he literally fell through the door, managing to keep his arm outstretched with a bottle of whiskey wrapped up in a paper bag in hand. He got up and wiped away any dust from his coat. He grabbed a chicken leg from the counter, and turned and smiled at us all.

'My lovely ladies, you're back. It is nothing … to love … but something … to be loved … and everything to love and be loved back ...'.

I thought about what he had said and maybe he was right, maybe I was the one who needed help, at least he could smile and philosophise. I couldn't. I just got depressed.

I stayed in bed the following days pretending I had a 'flu. I didn't want to face the world. I gorged on cigarettes, pizza and milk. I kept the curtains closed.

Day four; Nana came into my room. I crept under the blankets.

'It's time to get up Ella, Come on we have work to do, life to live.'

I ignored her.

'I'm not leaving this room until you are up.'

I peeped out of the bed, to face Nana wearing her fox fur hat and scarf.

'Well Mr Fox, shall we get her up?'

I thought for a moment she would stay put but she approached me, waving that fox's head, and my reaction was just as it was when I was six, I jumped out of that bed as fast as that fox would have chased a chicken. I realised I needed her. She made me realise that she was still my rock.

'There's a nice gooseberry pie with vanilla cream waiting downstairs for you.'

'I'll be down in a minute.'

I got dressed and put on some makeup when I heard a gentle knock on the door. It was Jack, I knew the knock.

He stood in front of me, all six foot of him.

'I'm sorry.'

MEETING MR. GOODIE

WILL'S STORY

I called to Ella's house again. This time her father answered the door.

'Hi, I'm a neighbour, Will Goodie, I'm looking for Ella?'

'Look Mr Goodie, I know who you are and I would appreciate it if you could stay away, Ella is getting her life back together.'

'I'm sorry, but it's important I speak with her.'

'It's simple Mr Goodie, I have friends who could deal with people like you, now stay away or I will call them. I know where you live'

'Where is the child?'

'There is no child, now get off my fucking property'

I walked down the driveway, then turned and walked back as Mr Lovett remained standing at the doorway with a glass in his hand, he tried to close the door on my face but I stopped him with my foot and faced him.

'With the utmost respect Mr Lovett, I care a great deal about your daughter and I have a right to know if there is a child'

'Do you love her?'

'Yes…. I believe I do'.

'You have more balls than I thought you had.'

I handed him my number and left.

We hadn't seen Sam since my father's service for the Brown Children. The police were still investigating the murders and there was a rumour Sam was apparently a suspect because he had attended that walk with Spider. I knew in my guts that Sam had nothing to do with the murder of those children. I had spoken to Spider at a meeting in the Lodge, quizzing him regarding Sam's disappearance; he had been defensive and warned me to stay out of his business. He didn't give a damn about Sam.

Mum and Dad were distraught with worry. We prayed for Sam every day. We put out posters, went on to radio shows, all to no avail. I started to wonder if he might be dead. Living in Belfast and having connections with Loyalist paramilitaries made this fear all the more real.

The police had hundreds of missing people on their lists from both sides of the community. Sam was just another statistic at the bottom of the pile. I made regular visits to the police who promised that they were doing everything they could. I was reassured that they believed that Sam was not connected directly to the murders but that they were concerned he may be withholding information and was in hiding because of possible threats by the people who were more directly involved. They were happy with me keeping in touch and every now and then we would come up with new possibilities.

My commitment to the Lodge was withering and I found it difficult being anywhere within human reach of Spider, who was now a dominant spokesperson. He maintained he had no idea as to where Sam might be. I believed him because he was also adamant that I inform him immediately of Sam's return.

Dad had made it his vocation to speak out about sectarian violence. He even started inviting Roman Catholics into his Church to share in prayers of peace. He wasn't deterred by the threatening letters he received.

Dad was often asked to speak after a walk and had always received great applause. However these days he received more murmurings than applause. He didn't realise however how frightened Mum had become. She insisted on locking doors internally, and putting extra locks on exterior doors. Dad joked about his hate mail, the more he got the more determined he became. One letter however became too much for Mum, she phoned me at work and asked me to call over, she wanted to show it to the police but Dad insisted it be discarded like all the others.

Mum was drained of colour and life, when I arrived over at lunch time, her rose complexion replaced by makeup and powder she normally only wore for Sunday service. She handed me the white envelope when I arrived. It was an amateur attempt, an A4 size sheet of paper with the cut-out words 'SHUT UP OR DIE'.

'Where is he?'

'He's taken to watching afternoon television.'

'It's not serious Mum; it's probably kids, have you contacted the police?'

'No, he's forbidden me.'

My father was watching the news. He was oblivious to me being in the room.

'Dad. I've seen the note. It's best we go to the police.'

'Have you seen or heard from him?'

'No.'

'I can drive you down to the station and go in with you if you like.'

'It's probably just kids again Will. If I am to be a lesson for others, then so be it.'

He grabbed the remote control and put up the sound of Felix the Cat.

The doorbell rang, and before I could answer there was a heavy rap. I opened the door to two uniformed police officers.

'Could we speak with the head of the household, please sir?'

'Is this in regard to my brother Sam?'

'I'm afraid so'.

Mum and Dad appeared behind me at the same time. The knock informed them. Sam was being held in the interrogation quarters at the police station for the suspected murder of the Brown children. Someone had given evidence against him. He had been set up.

WILL GETS BEATEN UP

Forty-eight hours later, Sam visited home with a friend called Alan. He seemed like a genuinely nice sort of guy, he was evidently gay, not that our parents noticed. Physically, Sam looked fine, despite his interrogation in prison. He was alive and I was overwhelmed by seeing him. He had been hiding out in a bedsit with his friend; they had met in the commune. He reassured Dad that he had nothing to do with the Brown's deaths. He couldn't tell Dad where he was staying for safety reasons; suffice to say he was still in the country. He had spoken with the police who had kept him in custody for withholding information. However if he could help them with their inquiries, any pending charges could be dropped. I pleaded with him to come and stay with me that night. It was like talking with the old Sam. He sent Alan off with a warm hug and came back with me. We had a real heart-to-heart, he was happy I liked Alan.

'He studied fashion at St. Martins, and we are both heading to London to start afresh. I'll get a job.'

'What about the police, and Spider?'

'The police have my passport. I know you hate him, Will but he's been a mate.'

'It's good to see you looking happy for once Sam, let's just forget about Spider.'

'Okay.'

'Promise to keep in touch.'

He smiled and hugged me. I got up early for work and when I got back he was gone.

I didn't hear from him over the next few days, and then Alan called to say he hadn't seen him either and he was worried. I went up to the notoriously rough housing executive pad that housed Spider and his cronies. The entrance to the estate was bedecked with a multitude of Union Jacks hanging out of windows. The gable wall had a large colourful mural which read 'Freedom Fighters Unite' under an image of King Billy. The next gable wall read 'Irish Out' in huge black and white letters. Red, white and blue flags and edging of pavements decorated the rest of the estate. I had once been a part of this culture but now I wasn't. I was Irish, albeit Protestant Irish, and Northern Irish to be precise. I was now proud to be Northern Irish and felt proud of the city I grew up in that was currently striving for a journey towards peace.

It wasn't too difficult to find Spider's house, empty cans and bottles outside the front door which appeared to be slightly ajar. It was three o'clock on a Friday afternoon and I could hear them partying inside. I knocked on the front door and despite everything in my entire being saying *'leg it'*, I stood and waited. There was no reply. I was afraid of these people. They were probably out of their heads on drugs and completely unpredictable. I knocked again in the hope of finding the whereabouts of my brother. No one answered. So I went over to the front window which was draped in a filthy nylon net curtain full of holes. I looked around the housing estate at the neatly erected Union Jacks, all with the same plea of acceptance and defiance. An old woman hunched over a little, with a cigarette hanging out of her mouth shuffled past me with a look of several lifetimes written across her face.

'You want to stay away from that lot, dirty druggies the lot of them.'

I turned to leave. The front door flung open and Spider stood in front of me dressed in a blue vest and electric blue track suit bottoms with a white stripe going up them. He was in his bare feet which were filthy. His arms and shoulders were covered in amateur tattoos and the inside arms covered in what looked like needle marks. His head was shaven to his skin, which only brought out the appearance of the wasted vacant look in his eyes.

'Yeah?'

'Is he here.... Sam, is Sam here?'

I asked as nicely as I could. The truth was that my instant impulse when I saw him was to pull him outside and grab him by the throat and kill him.

'No.'

'Do you know where he is?'

'No … Right ...now fuck off.'

He took a swig from his can and looked at me with the slightest smile. I knew he knew more.

'For fuck's sake, if I fuckin see him, I'll tell him big brother's looking for him.'

He closed the door in my face. The hatred was mutual. I didn't know where else to look so I knocked the door again, a little more loudly this time. It opened immediately,

'What the fuck!'

'He said nothing in regard to that house fire.'

Spider's face changed to one of intimidation. His eyes squinted and his colour paled. He grabbed me and trailed me into the house and kicked the door closed. Within minutes the tiny hall way was filled with similar skinny looking young men with the evidence of years of Troubles and dysfunction written all over them. All bearing the trademark shaved heads and tattoos. Spider pinned me up against the wall by the throat. I could see a little mountain of white powder sitting on the table, alongside a collection of credit cards.

'Are you suggesting something, taig lover?'

His spit wet my face.

'Lads, big fucking brother here wants to know if we were involved with the house fire that killed those fucking Fenian kids.'

I couldn't get the words out because of the tightness of the grip around my neck.

'Let's fuckin give him one.' said Simon, smiling.

'He's long overdue.' Spider yelled with glee.

I was dragged out of the hallway through a small unfurnished living room into the backyard. I was thrown to the ground and kicked until I can't remember. Blows to the head, kicks in the groin, they continued kicking after I lost consciousness.

I don't remember being in pain, the last thing I remembered was looking up and seeing what I thought was Sam looking down on me. Several hours later I awoke at the bottom of the road to the estate, in the pouring rain. I was being lifted unto a stretcher and put into an ambulance. I was in severe pain all over, I felt totally paralysed and my clothes were covered in blood. A nice young nurse was standing over me attaching a drip to my hand. She looked into my eyes with a little torch and smiled.

'You've been through the wars, but I think you're going to be okay. How's your head, is it sore?'

I managed to nod a yes and felt the nurse injecting me. I fell into a deep sleep.

The following day I awoke to my mother standing over me, her sadness spilling out of every pore of her being.

'I'm so sorry Will. I didn't mean for this to happen.'

'Where is he?'

'I'm sorry, don't move love, you have several broken ribs.'

She stroked my head gently and bent down to kiss me on my forehead and I felt her tears trickle down the side of my cheek.

'I'm okay, Mum. Don't be sorry, it's not your fault.'

I forced a smile. The nurse came in and helped me sit up a little. Sam had been taken in for more questioning. He then went straight home and told Mum that he was being set up, that Spider and his mates had said they saw him throw a petrol bomb into the house. Dad knew nothing. Mum did her best to pretend she wasn't worried and I did my best to act as if I wasn't in pain.

Later that evening Sam came to visit me in hospital. I had had another injection just before he arrived which helped the pain of the six cracked ribs, internal bruising to the head and chest and a cracked collar bone. I asked for a mirror after mum had gone. I resembled something from a Frankenstein movie. Sam didn't look so good either.

'I'm sorry. I'm really fuckin sorry.'

I looked at him.

'You were there.'

He looked at me as quick as a bird searching for the right words.

'I was out of it; they spiked me with a cocktail of drugs. They wanted to know if I had said anything to the police. I rang the ambulance,'

'Bastards.'

'They're going to kill me if they find out I told the police the truth.'

'I'm the one in hospital, hello. Look you can stay in my place.'

'They know where you live. The police phoned me this morning, they know I'm innocent, I told them that it was an accident.'

'Was it Spider who threw the petrol bomb?'

'He didn't know those kids were in bed, Will.'

'It was Spider and of course he knew those kids were in bed, it was because they were Catholics. Look he's already tried to incriminate you. Why are you protecting that bastard?'

'I need to let him think I told the police nothing.'

'Stay away Sam, you and Alan go and hide until this dies down.'

'I need to put things straight; I can tell him I told the police it was an accident.'

'Why has that guy got such a hold on you Sam?'

I looked up at him, and I felt a pang of sympathy. He was broken. His shoulders were falling in around him; he was being swallowed in his own ocean of fear.

'He didn't mean, to kill anyone, that's not him.'

'Spider doesn't give a shit about you.'

'He not that bad, Will'

'And the cold-blooded and dangerous side?'

'Only if you're on the wrong side of him, he's saved my ass, on several occasions.'

I looked at him blankly. I was beyond getting angry with him. I knew on some level he couldn't help himself.

'Are you on drugs?'

'No.'

Then he looked to either side of himself like a little bird ready for take-off.

'Look Sam, I'm your brother, I'm trying to help you but I can't, if you don't let me'.

'There's nothing you can do Will. I know I've fucked up. I'm sorry, I've been a shit brother, and you didn't deserve this.'

He got up and started to hover around nervously. He was becoming human again, the light was coming through.

'Sit down Sam, we can work through this, I know you're not a bad person, I know you Sam.'

He started chewing his knuckle.

'Look. If you need to get him off your back then phone him for Christ's sake. Convince him that you told the police nothing, and that you are laying low for a while.'

'Yeah, okay.'

'Sam I want to help you because I'm your brother, Spider's not. Spider's not a brother.'

He looked at me almost bewildered.

'Do you love him?'

He hadn't expected that, I threw it in like a wild-card, but his silent response and his piercing eyes said it all.

A nurse dropped something made out of tin creating a loud bang that echoed through the ward and I could see him physically jumping out of his skin. He was scared.

'We need to talk about this Sam.'

And away he flew.

WILL MEETS ELLA IN HOSPITAL

As I watched Sam leave, I studied his thin, long, skeletal body move through the sky-lit hospital corridor. His fine blonde hair moved in a ray of light, which for some reason filled me with a little hope, especially after finally talking with him like a brother again.

As he disappeared into the light I saw what looked like Ella, walking towards me. I presumed it was the medication. She stopped for a second as Sam passed, he was oblivious to her. She too, was reflecting the light, except all of her seemed to shine. She stopped abruptly by my bedside and it seemed to take her a moment to recognise me.

'Well, well. Will Goodie, is that you under all those bruises? Is my loyal Orange boy not feeling too good?'

She checked my charts with aplomb. I was gobsmacked.

'Ella?'

'Was that Sam who just walked past?'

'Yes, yes it was him. What are you doing here?'

'I'm the in-tern psychologist, and I'm here to see if you're suffering from any post-traumatic stress. Do you want to tell me what happened?'

'Am I a father?'

She looked at me and froze. Then she sat down beside me.

'Who told you?'

'I had the honour of being told by my brother.'

She looked me in the eye and nodded a yes.

'Are you fit enough for me to wheel you to the quiet room?'

'Yes'

At first she couldn't speak. Then she started to cry. An hour passed, like a flash of lightening and in all that time all I retrieved was that his name was Andrew and that the nuns somewhere, not sure where, give him away to she didn't know who.

'Is there any point in trying to contact him?'

'No, he's happy where he is'

I held her hand a moment.

'I'm sorry you had to through that on your own.'

I realised it was pointless trying to do anything regarding our situation. Then she jotted back into being a psychologist and I had to talk to her. So we talked for another hour, I was emotionally exhausted.

She managed to extract the entire story of Sam's decline and the pain that he had put our family through. She was good at her job.

'And what's your role in all of this Will?'

'What do you mean?'

'Well, you have spent the last hour talking about your brother. How are you?'

I was afraid I had already told her too much. I paused.

'A psychologist, it suits you.'

'What about you? Are you working? '

'I work in Child Protection. I'm a social worker, I still organise the peace trips, like the one ...'

A young enthusiastic House doctor arrived with the briskness of a train arriving.

'I'll leave now, Will'.

'Do you have to?'

A moment passed and she was still there.

'Sit up, and open your shirt' asked the doctor.

I did my best to sit up and Ella helped me take off my shirt. He took out his stethoscope from around his neck and pressed it into my chest.

'Now take a deep breath, and then another.'

I took a deep breath but my heart was jumping out of my body with the intent of a wild horse escaping.

'Try and relax a little, Mr Goodie.'

'Sorry.'

'I just need to listen to your heart, now, another deep breath please?'

By now my heart was galloping down the corridor. Ella

took my hand but that just made matters worse. I took another deep breath and I managed to calm down a little.

'When can I go home, Doctor?'

'At the moment we need to focus on getting you better. You have cracked a few ribs and you have quite severe internal bruising, you will need a lot of rest and TLC. Where will you go when you get out, have you someone to look after you?'

'No. I live with a couple of girls, flatmates.

'We won't let you out until the swelling has reduced. I'll see you tomorrow.'

And off he sped.

Ella was still sitting beside me and I felt safe with her there, it was odd.

'Why the hurry to leave?' she asked curiously.

'Sam.'

'Can't Sam wait?'

'No, he's in danger.'

As I spoke, she buttoned up my shirt again.

'I'll pop into you after lunch if you like, I have an hour off.'

'I would very much like that.'

'All part of the job.'

After lunch, Ella wheeled me down the darkened old pale green stone corridors of the Royal Victoria Hospital that smelt of bleach and warm school dinners. We arrived into the newly-built physiotherapy room. She didn't look a day older from the last day I had seen her, in fact she was even more beautiful than I had imagined. More woman. We grew comfortably silent between our exchanges, and she offered to stay and help me through my physiotherapy. We worked together, stretching and pulling my limbs and life back together. She then offered to wheel me down to the public canteen; it was such a breath of fresh air.

'Are you still an Orangeman?'

'No. You were right, they are just provoking Orange Bastards!'

She laughed out loud. I decided there and then that I

255

would give up the Lodge. I had to if I was to have her.

'Why did you leave?'

'I don't know what I believe in anymore. I don't believe in any of it Ella, not if it brings so much strife.'

'I believe that you are a good man, Mr Will Goodie.'

And the wild horse returned, galloping and tramping into my insides until I couldn't breathe, literally.

She calmly got up and came around and placed her hands on the front and back of my chest, until I regained control of my breath again, it was at that moment I knew. I KNEW.

She wheeled me back to my ward and I was too embarrassed to speak any more, she explained I had a panic attack which was common after a trauma, but I knew different.

'When will I see you again?'

She smiled.

'I don't know, I can try and arrange to pop over tomorrow, that's if you would like ...'

I took her hand.

'I would like.'

She left with a huge smile on her face.

'Did you marry? '

She stopped walking and turned around.

'No.'

The reply was clear, which made me smile for the rest of the day. She took over my thoughts. I relaxed a little and so began the beginning of my healing process.

After she'd left, I phoned my mother to try and put some of the hope her way, regarding Sam. She was relieved to hear he had visited me in hospital.

'Pray for him Will; pray that the Lord will keep him safe, love.'

And so I prayed for him and my family, including Ella, and I had a sudden feeling of hope.

Ella visited briefly in the late afternoon to give me a real coffee. They were going to keep me in for a few days to settle the cracked ribs and ensure the wounds were kept clean.

'You're lucky to be alive.'

As the day passed I realised how lucky I was, to be alive.

The following morning the minutes seemed like hours until my next arranged meeting with Ella, and I was upset to discover Ella had taken the day off. I was whisked away to the physiotherapy unit by a matron with little to no manners and put through an arduous, brisk routine which resulted in overall body pain. I had no time for a panic attack. I was back in my room before I could blink and found my mother waiting on the little gray plastic chair beside my bed. She looked frightened.

'Mum, is everything alright?'

The tears started to flow,

'Yes. Sorry love, everything is fine. Are you okay?'

I had never seen her cry before so I didn't do anything because I didn't know what to do.

'I'm fine.'

More tears.

'They have arrested Sam again.' she said, almost choking on her words.

'The children that got caught in the house fire, after the walk, the last little boy died this day last year.'

She swallowed and took a breath. I looked at her hurt and confused expression.

'Why have they have arrested Sam again, Will?

ELLA ON DUTY

I walked towards a young man covered in bandages and it took me a few moments before I realised it was Will. As I approached him, I passed his brother Sam, whom I hadn't seen since the commune. I stopped to say hello but he was in another world. I thought it might be mistaken identity but when I looked over at Will, who was staring at me, I knew it was him from his very outline. It's odd how you get to know a person's outline and never forget it. Our brief but significant history, unbeknown to him, was buried deep within me and I preferred to keep it that way, but here he was all beaten up.

What I didn't realise was that during that meeting Will would stir up unwanted and buried emotions. Mentally, I had convinced myself that that chapter in my life was well and truly over. Over and never to be revisited. My gut reaction however, was deep shock and sadness that it was him, because he was hurt and vulnerable.

He still had a mop of dark brown hair and big soft brown eyes. We discussed Andrew. He was very understanding.

I had hoped to see him the following day but my car didn't start. I could have taken a bus but I was scared. I'd face him in the morning.

FINDING SAM

1999

I signed myself out of hospital, and went straight to the police station. There I was informed by Police Officer Constable Jennings that they were still questioning Sam and he wouldn't be in a position to let me see him. He was being held under arrest and they could keep him for up to seventy-two hours. They had two witnesses; I tried to make them see reason explaining that it was Spider and his mates that they needed to charge. I gave them as much information as I could in regard to names and addresses and my own beating. I explained that I had spoken with Sam before he was arrested and that he feared for his life especially after seeing what they had done to me. I could tell that they were not convinced. And so I left for home. Dad was sitting outside with a cup of tea and his prayer book; he was praying quietly to himself, it was obvious by his peaceful demeanour that he was oblivious to what was going on. I saw Mum through the kitchen window behind him as I tried to tiptoe past so as not to disturb him. I wasn't in the mood for one of his inquisitions, she put her finger up to her mouth to shush me, a trait she had always used with Sam and I as kids to be quiet. I gave her the thumbs up, thinking I had made it past him unnoticed.

'Will, sit down here beside me. We need a chat.'

He pointed to the black cast iron chair across from him. He stared at my bust-up face for several seconds.

'I hope they get the thugs who did that to you. I have been praying for you both. You and Sam. Have you seen him?'

I stalled for a moment, unsure of how much he knew.

'Your mother thinks I'm oblivious to everything, it's best kept that way, she's enough to worry about.'

'Sam visited me in hospital and we had a good chat'.

'That's good ... He's currently in custody. He's not a bad boy Will, I know that, he has just lost his path, God's path, he's in darkness and we need to help him find the light again.'

We paused long on that thought. I didn't interrupt him; he didn't like to be interrupted. He liked one to listen to his every word. Strangers listened to him every day, relied on his word, and no-one ever questioned him, no-one except Sam. Sam's curiosity consistently questioned him, in innocence really. But Father took it personally and often punished him because of his lack of understanding. I remember one occasion when we came home from Church, after Father had given a sermon about the importance of Church attendance.

'Why do we bother having to go to a Church to speak with God when God is everywhere, can't we just speak to him in our bedroom, Dad?'

He was grounded that day. It was a mark of respect and respect was essential in Father's book. He looked at me with his now frail, pale, dog-eared face.

'Will, I'm not sure how I can help him find his path again. You see, he appears to see me as a threat. Your mother and I have talked to him until we are blue in the face. I can't understand it; he appears to have no faith at all, in God, or me, ironic really. Perhaps it's my fault I didn't spend enough time with him. Foolishly, I believed he may one day have followed in my footsteps.'

I looked out into the once well-manicured garden that was beginning to show signs of neglect, old and new weeds peeped out. I didn't respond to him, because perhaps it was his fault, he was a broken man and I couldn't fix it. We sat in silence. I looked over at this struggling old man and I felt sympathy.

'Don't blame yourself Dad'.

'I was too strict with him, I know that now, he was a difficult child for me, always questioning me, always, answering back, you were such an easy child Will. He must have been aware of that.'

Suddenly Mother came running out into the garden.

'Will! He just marched in, '

Spider pushed her to one side; he walked over to Father and me. He pointed his newly-tattooed fingers at my father as he spoke. The letters on the knuckles of the right hand spelt l.o.v.e. the other hand h.a.t.e. He wore tight jeans like drainpipes and his DIY skinhead almost made him look deformed. He was pitiful.

'You tell that bent fucking brother of yours to stay well away from me, and if he touts, he's a dead man.'

He spat the words out, the saliva visibly spraying as he spoke. I got up and faced him calmly, because at this stage for some strange reason I wasn't afraid anymore.

'You have nothing to worry about Spider, Sam won't say anything.... I'll make sure of it.'

He looked me in the eye and smiled.

'You stupid fuck.'

'Leave him.' ordered my Father. I wanted to kill him. As in I literally wanted to kill him. I wanted his blood to spill. But I took a deep breath, and let my shoulders drop. Like they had taught me in physio, to relax.

Mum was as white as the whitewashed wall she stood against, clutching her teacloth, as if it was some sort of protection. He spat at her feet as he passed and she jumped like a pile of ash. I ran up to him and grabbed him by the red shirt collar at back of his neck, I had to. I felt no pain as I did this despite my broken ribs. I pulled him straight to the ground, the years of karate started to kick in, it was just me and him, he had no hope, I managed to pin him to the ground in seconds. I was elated. I pinned his arms down with my knees and put my hands around his scrawny throat, and I squeezed tight, he begged me to stop. He tried to scream.

'Stop! Please Will!' he whined but I tightened my grip until he couldn't get any more words out, I had him.

Father approached me nervously. I held him steady, tighter.

'Will, leave him. Get up. He's not worth it.'

I looked up at my sad shaking mother.

'Take Mum inside, Dad!'

Dad tried to pull me off. I held one hand up to reassure him I was in control and I loosened my grip.

'Please Will, I'll ring the police son, I'll ring them now.'

'NO.' both Spider and I yelled collectively.

'Spider is just about to leave, aren't you Spider? He's sorry for coming here isn't that right Spider?'

'Fuck you, Will Goodie'

I tightened my grip again and I knew his arm was ready to snap, I knew by his squealing.

He sounded like a pig on his way to the slaughter.

'Okay I'm leaving …now let go!'

'Never return to my home, do you understand me?'

'Yes.'

'Yes what?'

'Yes I understand …Will!'

I released his throat but firmly kept hold of one arm to guide him in the direction of the front door. We walked across the lawn and towards where my parents stood. He turned towards me and spat in my face. I winced and he broke free. Before I knew it he pulled out a gun and pointed it at me and cocked it.

'Keep your fucking hands off me'.

He pointed the gun at my father, whilst looking at me. Mother let out a yelp and he moved the gun around to her and laughed.

'Shut to fuck up, all of you, and listen to me, tell Sam to say nothing. Nothing! Period! It's simple, stick to what I tell you and I will stay away from that moron.'

He looked frightened but I knew what he was capable of.

'Okay,' I said.

A siren could be heard, which panicked him. Spider lowered the gun slightly still pointing it at us and ran like the rat he was to make his exit.

My mother looked twenty years older. Dad went and

held her, he was surprisingly calm.

'Go ring the police, Will, tell them what's just happened.'

So I went inside lifted the phone and pretended to ring the police, claiming that I would go down to the station to make a statement. I spoke to a dead line because I knew that I was putting Sam at further risk if I said anything more to the police. I sat on the little oak chair beside the phone, powerless, as I started remembering the attack that had put me in hospital. I could see Spider's face, smiling with a stoned stupid satisfaction, before he sank his boots into my ribs. My core instinct was to protect my baby brother, because I knew he was putty in their hands, but if I didn't phone he was putty in their hands anyway.

I lifted the phone again and I rang Ella, I asked to speak with her father. Mr Lovett came around immediately and escorted me to the police station. He spoke to Sam and had Sam released within a few hours. He was able, through people he knew, to get contacts and a witness to prove Sam's innocence. He also got an anonymous caller, a man called Simon, to give evidence against Spider.

The following day Spider was killed in a chip shop, on the Shankhill Road. The bomb was targeted for a meeting of a new Loyalist group. They were to meet above the chip shop that evening. Eight innocent people were killed. One of those eight was my brother, Sam. He died instantly.

THE GRAVEYARD: PART TWO

It was funny, how Ella reacted to Sam jumping on the graves, she was superstitious, I suppose that was the Catholic in her. I put my flute down and tucked into our picnic. As I tucked into my egg and onion sandwich, I watched Sam jump around with his chocolate coated caramel square. He stopped to read the initials on the grave.

'Look Dad, he has the same name as I do, 'S.a.m.u.e.l.'

Then he read *'Sadly missed and in our hearts forever, our treasured son, Samuel Goodie who died tragically'*. He paused for a moment and then he read *'William Goodie a loving husband and Father 1934-2005'* RIP.

'Did I know Samuel, Dad?' he asked innocently.

'No, Sam, he was my brother.' I said, with stones in my heart.

'Like my new baby brother.'

'Yes'

I put my arms around Ella. She was wearing her light cotton shirt that let me see the roundness in her breasts. Feeling her warmth I pulled her in close to me, I needed her. Sam pushed his head between our heads

'What are we going to call my new brother?'

I looked to Ella, smiling.

'Perhaps we could call him Andrew.'

Ella's head sank with the mention of his name. Sam paused for a moment, considering the name, not too impressed.

'How about William, like Granddad?' he said. Ella smiled.

'If it's a boy or maybe a girl I was thinking of calling it Sunny'.

She said and we all smiled.

SUNNY IS BORN

Ella and I had decided that if the peace in Northern Ireland stayed intact then we would consider moving back from London. On our return from our last visit she caught me in a lull, as was common upon my return trips from back home.

'What's the matter?' she asked.

'Nothing, really.'

'Really?'

'It's just I miss home. It's odd, it's not just Mum, I miss the place, the trees, the humour, the edge.'

She came over and sat her pregnancy on my knee, I looked down at her belly, kissed her and smiled.

'I miss it too, especially my family, so why don't we put a plan together?'

The following day some of the London fog had lifted and a blue haze stretched like a crisp sheet across the sky. Sam had insisted on leaving the shed door open, so that the newly-hatched starlings could swoop in and out at their pleasure. We didn't have much in the shed, other than my old Lodge uniform which was packed up inside a wooden box, like a coffin. It was Ella who insisted on keeping it.

Mary King, the Irish midwife, arrived that morning. She routinely checked the blood pressure, ankles and wrists and then we all huddled around the white cotton draped bed and listened to the sound of new life that nestled in Ella's tummy. She decided to lift Ella's skirt and confirmed her suspicions that things were already well in motion. I wasn't overly enthusiastic about the idea of a home birth, but I knew that once Ella made a decision about something, I hadn't a hope in hell. Ella was insisting on going out to a local cafe for lunch, despite having mild contractions. Mary permitted it but was to be called as soon as contractions were coming every six to eight minutes.

Ella ate little bits of brochette and continued to dish out

orders between the mouthfuls food.

'We need to make up the cot and put the baby bath into the bathroom.'

Sunny was born in our bedroom, on the Victorian hand crafted queen bed we had purchased in the Saturday auction. I played some chilled-out flute tunes that I had composed myself during the labour. I played one entitled *'Dance of the starling'* until I was told to shut up. I put down the flute and sent Sam downstairs to watch the new Spiderman movie. Several pushes later and a little head of dark silken hair peeped into the world. Ella was ecstatic, Mary handed the baby into Ella's arms as soon as it was delivered, still attached to the cord, she held our new baby into her chest. I then cut the cord.

'Hello Sunny.'

She put our new-born baby girl to her breast and she latched on. Nana Lovett arrived with Annie the following day to assist. For a woman in her eighties, she was inspiring. She took over with the orders and the house was soon in shipshape. There was a constant supply of vegetable broths, breads, and desserts. Sam and Annie went back and forward to the little Indian grocers on the corner, fetching all necessary ingredients. After their chores were completed, Annie took Sam off to the museums and art galleries. In the evenings Annie sat in the corner of our bedroom and nursed Sunny and Ella to sleep with lullabies.

They packed light and quietly collected their things before flying home. Ella got up early to bake a cake to see them off. We sat around our box kitchen contented.

'I'm very proud of you Ella.'

'Thanks Nana, thanks for everything.'

'I was never as strong as you. I never became what I wanted to become, I was the top of my class in school you know and the nuns encouraged me, but it wasn't the done thing then, ladies working. Then I got married, and sure in my day once you got married … '

'What would you have studied?'

'I always fancied myself as a journalist ...'

'You never know, it's never too late ...'

'I'll keep that in mind. Now do we have a plan in motion in regard to getting you over to visit your old Nana soon with this new baby; Jack will need to meet his new granddaughter ... He's stopped drinking, Ella.'

'Again?'

'He attends meetings twice a week.'

'Well then, yes we do have a plan in motion. We are planning on moving back. He's finally decided to make a decent woman out of me.'

'Tell the truth, Ella.' said a smiling Will. 'Nana, she has at long last agreed to marry me.'

'Well my man, it's about bloody time too.'

The words jumped with joy across the room like a rubber ball.

A KNOCK ON THE DOOR

I loved my new job back in the Royal where Will and I had rekindled our love. It was a bit of a juggle at first working and being a Mum. Will had plans of setting up his own cross-community youth reach centre. Annie minded Sunny while we worked - her idea. Sam was enrolled for the Educate Together primary school which was multi-denominational; this helped with on-going discussions of which religion we would raise our kids. I was happy to covert to Protestantism and it was important to Will to give them a moral upbringing. We settled with the Church of Ireland.

We got married in Will's Dad's Church; Nana swallowed the news like a brick but was appeased when we invited her parish priest to assist in the ceremony. I wore a plain cream silk dress, so did Sunny. Will and Sam wore blue suits with white brushed linen shirts. I arrived into the Church on Jack's arm to Will playing '*Dance of the starlings*'.

Catholics sat on one side of the quaint little church, Protestants on the other. When it came to giving each other the sign of peace everyone made a concerted effort to cross over and greet each other with hearty handshakes. Caroline flew over from Italy; she married an Italian and was pregnant with her fourth child. Ali arrived with her Scottish girlfriend of ten years looking as fabulous as ever. Sr. Nula appeared laden with gifts and her and Nana were inseparable.

About a year after we married, I had just dropped Sam to school and I was reading the last chapter of my book in my shiny new chrome kitchen at the marble island we had sat around earlier that morning. The kitchen looked out unto Will's newly planted garden of lilies, salads and herbs in pots. I watched the swallows on the telephone wires ahead preparing for their flight to Africa, so I had been informed by Sam. The house was still.

My peace was disrupted by murmurs of Sunny waking out of her afternoon sleep and the doorbell ringing at the same time. I was waiting on the electrician to come and fix the connection for the freezer in the shed.

I answered the door and a tall handsome young man stood in front of me. He had an inquisitive look about him.

'Hi, are you Ella Lovett?'

He asked as if I was about to bite.

'Yes, that's me.'

He proceeded to study me with urgency, he looked away for a moment and as he did I saw the familiarity, the square face, the turned-up nose, the brown locks, the image of the young boy who had come to my rescue.

The word 'Andrew' fell out of my mouth.

'Yeah, I'm Andrew. I'll leave if you want'

'No. No don't leave.'

From nowhere my arms rose to smother my son and he received me, albeit a little awkwardly. My emotions erupted and tears sprang out.

'Sorry. Come in Andrew, please.'

But he just stood there looking at me. Nervous. I noticed he was carrying a little flute case.

'You play the flute?'

'Yeah, look, I know this is probably a shock and I probably should have written.'

He handed me a small note with his address printed on it.

'That's my parent's house. If you want to get in touch, you can find me there, my mum is cool with it. I have to go; I'm late for band practice.

'Okay. I don't know what to say'

'I have a good family, I have a brother too. And you?'

'I have two small children, Sam and Sunny.'

'Oh ... ?'

'Look I'm sorry….It was for the best.'

'I know. I need to go.'

'I'll call you'

'Okay'

My heart kicked me as I watched him walk away until he disappeared. I closed the door and put the note safely into my pocket. Unconsciously I went upstairs and took out the wooden box that that travelled around with us. I opened it and I took out the uniform and the little white vest I had carefully wrapped up inside it. I washed, starched, and polished every piece of that uniform until it shone on its hanger, fit for another walk.

Acknowledgements

Thank you to New Generation Publishing for their excellence; to Colm Hogan for his kindness; to Vanessa O'Loughlin from writing.ie/kazoo publishing for her generosity; to Brian Kennaway for his inspiring book, 'The Orange Order: A Tradition Betrayed', and to Eoghan Harris for planting the seed to this idea; to all my family, especially my parents, who did their best to lovingly raise me without bias; to Annemarie and Gabe, Stephen and Cara, Ethna and Denise for their support; to Patricia Ford for her early input, Patsy Murphy for her teaching and for believing in me. To Maire and Gerry Galvin for their encouragement and to Carole who quietly nudged me into action. Very special thanks goes to Marin D'eath for her editing and proofing, and whom without her sharp mind this book would not have happened; to Rachel and Siobhan my dearest friend, whose continuous support and no nonsense approach thankfully brings out the protestant in me; to my in-laws for their encouragement; to our beautiful four boys, Peter, Líthgen, Caomhlú and Dáibhí; and lastly to my loving husband Michael who is responsible for getting this book to the finish line.

Cover design by Julia Roddy and Joshua St John.

Cover photograph by Colm Hogan.

About the author

Julia lectures in screen writing in Galway where she lives with her husband and children. Her short story Émigré was short listed and published and won runner up prize earlier this year in the Words on the Street Anthology. This is her first novel.

CPSIA information can be obtained at www.ICGtesting.com
Printed in the USA
LVOW11s1736300816

502494LV00007B/475/P